SCORNED PRINCESS

CROOKED PARADISE #1

EVA CHANCE
& HARLOW KING

Scorned Princess

Book 1 in the Crooked Paradise series

First Digital Edition, 2021

Copyright © 2021 Eva Chance & Harlow King

Cover design: Jodielocks Designs

Ebook ISBN: 978-1-990338-02-1

Paperback ISBN: 978-1-990338-03-8

Mercy

Just one more day until I'm free.

I held onto that thought as I looked around the restaurant. The light of the brass chandeliers glanced off the long table that stretched down the middle of the room, covered in a white tablecloth and set out with fine china and silverware. Soft jazz spilled from the speakers through the chatter of the arriving guests.

This was a classy place, about as nice as you could expect to get in the Bend. Colt had picked it, since his family was hosting the rehearsal dinner. I liked it, which felt like a good omen.

"There you are, Mercy." My aunt Renee adjusted the pendant on my neck before flashing a grin at me. "You look beautiful, honey."

That was all that was supposed to matter in our kind of life—if you were a woman. But as much as I hated that fact, I couldn't exactly have shown up in one of my typical tees and beat-up jeans. I smoothed my hands over the silky turquoise dress that fell to just past my knees and smiled back at her. She meant well. "Thanks. Turns out I don't clean up so bad, huh?"

She scoffed. "Anyone could have seen that. Your husband-to-be should consider himself very lucky."

I glanced toward Colt automatically, but my gaze caught on another man first. The one who made my stomach tighten.

My father was easily the tallest man in the room— and the most intimidating one. Tyrell Katz held the kind of ruthless magnetism that made even the toughest men shake in their boots. That was how he ruled over the Claws, one of the most powerful gangs in the Bend, without challengers.

That was how he'd ruled over my life for the last twenty-one years. But tomorrow, I wouldn't be *his* anymore. I couldn't wait to be out of his iron-clad grasp.

And I would be out, thanks to the man poised next to him right now.

Colt Bryant stood only a little shorter than my father, laughing politely at some probably off-color joke dear old Dad had told. I let myself smile again, watching him. He filled out his dark suit to impressive effect, and the chandeliers' light brought out the gold in his pale hair.

What I really liked about him, though, was that he acted like he gave a damn about more than how I looked in a dress. Over the year of our engagement, we hadn't gotten into the deepest of conversations. We both knew this was primarily a business arrangement, after all, and the truce between his gang and the Claws had still been shaky. But he listened when I talked and had intelligent things to say back instead of spending the whole time ogling my boobs, unlike the other two assholes Dad had brought around before him. Thank God Dad hadn't liked their terms.

Colt could make me laugh. He'd spent more time considering my comfort during the dates we'd gone on than Dad had in my entire life. So I'd call this a win. Tomorrow's wedding would solidify the truce between the Claws and the Steel Knights, and I'd stop being Dad's bargaining chip and become Colt's partner.

Maybe it wasn't a perfect kind of freedom, but it was the best I could hope for given Dad's insistence on using me to expand his reach through the Bend—and, he imagined, to bring about the male heir he'd always wished I was.

Colt caught my eyes across the room. He excused himself and strode over to me. "Hey, you okay?"

I nodded, shoving aside all thought of my father. Just the fact that Colt had come over to check on me proved he was the better man. He'd been leading the Steel Knights since he was just nineteen, after his father had died several years back. He knew what it was like being underestimated and having to prove yourself to doubters.

Soon he'd see I was just as capable as the guys who helped run things for him—that I could be a *real* partner in every way. We could call the shots together.

And who knew? Maybe someday this battered heart of mine would even feel love again. If it was going to happen with anyone, I had to think it'd be him.

"No wedding jitters, then?" Colt asked in a teasing tone.

"Not yet," I shot back. "Just stay on your best behavior."

He laughed and clinked his wine glass to mine. Honestly, I wished we could skip all of this family nonsense and get married straight away. The celebratory buzzing felt like it was for everyone but me.

Or maybe that was just me being cynical. Grandma was walking over to me with tears in her eyes. She dabbed at them with a tissue. "You'll be the most beautiful bride when you walk down the aisle tomorrow."

I wagged a finger at her. "Hey, hey, no crying until the ceremony. There are rules about these things, you know."

"The first rule is no telling your grandma what to do," she informed me with a light swat.

I laughed and hugged her, and she hugged me back tightly. Grandma had always been there for me in the periods when Dad switched from training me like the son he'd wanted to pretending I didn't exist at all—or punishing me for being a daughter instead. She hadn't stood up to him over how he treated me, because everyone knew telling Tyrell Katz he was wrong never went well, but she'd done her best to make up for it.

My two uncles, Dad's right-hand men, ambled over. Their swagger seemed a tad subdued—possibly they felt a little naked without their usual weaponry. In recognition of our newfound alliance, both sides had agreed to attend the dinner unarmed, other than the bodyguards posted at the door for protection.

There was still plenty of testosterone to go around. Aunt Renee's husband, Uncle Steven, bumped his elbow against Colt's. "You've gone all out for us here. It's a nice place. Say, I've heard you've got quite the MMA tournament running these days. Now that we're relatives, maybe you can score us ringside seats."

Aunt Renee rolled her eyes, but Colt chuckled. "Sure. We've got a new fighter who's become a real talking point—a woman who's been taking on the men, and she's good enough to topple them. You should see her."

One of the servers called out over the chatter that dinner was about to be served. As I walked toward my seat by the foot of the table across from Colt at the head, Dad caught my arm. He leaned to speak gruffly by my ear. "Let's see more of that smile. Remember this is a *happy* occasion."

I gritted my teeth behind the grin I plastered on. "I know." I'd been a lot happier *before* he'd spoken to me. My hatred unfurled like tendrils in my chest.

Just one more day.

I wasn't getting away from him just yet. He sat down next to me, and I let my fingers curl around my fork. Imagining stabbing him with it also made me happier.

You could do a lot of damage with a fork. I knew from personal experience when one of the lower-level Claws lackeys had tried to get handsy with me.

Everyone had taken their seats except the servers,

who were standing back as if waiting for permission to fetch the food, and Colt, who'd stayed on his feet at the head of the table. His cousins and a few other close associates from his gang had turned toward him. He raised his glass, and everyone quieted down. Even the music stopped.

"Thank you for coming, everyone," my fiancé said. "I'd like to make a toast. Here's to the beginning of a new era for the Steel Knights!"

Something twitched in my stomach. Why would he mention the Steel Knights and not the Claws too?

That was all the warning I got before the servers around the table whipped guns from beneath their aprons.

Colt's men jumped up from the table, drawing their own concealed weapons, and the room exploded with ear-splitting booms of gunfire. Uncle Steven caught two to the chest in mid-yell. Aunt Renee's scream was cut off by a bullet to her neck. As I sprang out of my chair, her blood splattered all over my dress. I looked down at it with shaking hands.

Colt's eyes were pure ice as he pulled out a pistol of his own and aimed it at my father. His first shot caught Dad in the shoulder.

Dad lurched and more shots rang out around us. My heart racing, I dropped down beneath the level of the table. My knees jarred against the tiled floor.

"You traitor!" Dad shouted, heaving to his feet.

"It's only business, Tyrell," Colt replied, crisp and even.

With another bang, Dad fell to the floor, his eyes

staring. Blood streamed from a circular wound in the middle of his forehead.

He was dead. They were *all* dead.

I stared numbly at the bodies scattered around the table, limp and blood-splattered. Oh, God, *Grandma* was lying there just a few feet away from me, one last gurgle working its way out of her throat. The front of her dress was drenched with red.

No, no—this couldn't be happening—

"Make sure you get *everyone*," Colt said in the same awful voice, and my own blood turned cold. He meant me too.

Grief and horror constricted my chest, but my heart was still pounding, my fingers still clutching the damn fork. A searing haze closed in on my mind.

I'd been so close to claiming my freedom. So goddamned close. Just one more day...

I was *not* going to fucking die here.

My head jerked around. The two bodyguards had left the door to join in the carnage. At the same moment as I marked their positions, one of them caught sight of me.

I flung myself toward one of the smaller restaurant tables, ricocheting this way and that as years of tumbling and parkour practice guided my body, trying to keep some kind of furniture between me and the various attackers while my pulse thundered on in my head.

There must have been a couple of people on the Claws side still living, because a few more shots rang out behind me, followed by a thump. I dove right under another table and sprang out the other side, hurtling toward the door—

Another *bang* rattled my eardrums, and a blazing pain cut across my upper arm. *No.*

Swallowing a gasp, I threw myself onward. One of the servers charged at me, and I whirled to the side just long enough to stab the fork as deep as I could into his gun hand. Then I burst past the door into the night.

Pain kept throbbing in my arm. Shouts carried after me. I dashed along the sidewalk, stumbling and then kicking off my stupid heels. My bare feet pushed me faster, but footsteps stomped out of the restaurant behind me.

At the end of the block, a guy was standing next to his car, one hand resting on the open door. He tossed his keys into the air with the other as he chatted with friends at a patio table lit by café windows.

I summoned a fresh burst of speed. The guy and his friends all whipped around at the sound of my feet, but I was close enough. I snatched the keys and dove past the open car door.

The guy yelped, but I'd already yanked the door shut. Jamming the lock in place, I tossed myself into the driver's seat, pushed the key into the ignition, and slammed my bare foot down on the gas pedal.

The car tore down the street, tires screeching as I avoided a parked truck just ahead. I sped around one corner and then another, weaving back and forth, nothing in my head except getting the fuck away from the guns and the blood.

Well, the guns, anyway. There was plenty of blood

here, spilling down my arm from where the bullet had gouged it. My head started to spin.

Where the hell did I go now? What the hell had just *happened*? Colt and his men—they'd just killed my whole family—he'd tried to kill *me*—

Had this been his plan all along? Some kind of long game to wipe out the leadership of the Claws? He'd been playing me—and Dad—for the entire year of our engagement?

My stomach churned, but only some of the nausea was thanks to the pain burning through my arm. I'd trusted Colt. Not completely, but enough to be willing, even happy, to tie my life to his. He'd acted as if he cared about me. I'd pictured a whole future with him.

And now it was gone in a hail of gunfire.

I'd had no love for my father, and I couldn't say I'd liked most of the rest of my family either, but I hadn't wanted them *slaughtered*. And Grandma... A lump swelled in my throat, my vision blurring with tears.

As I blinked them away, anger crept up through the grief. It expanded through my chest, searing almost as hot as the gunshot wound.

How *dare* he? How dare that snake turn this night into a massacre, steal my entire family from me—shitty as most of them were—and for what? If I got my hands on Colt...

My knuckles ached from gripping the steering wheel. My arm throbbed, more blood streaking down it. I blinked harder and refocused on my surroundings as well as I could through my growing wooziness. I'd been driving without paying attention for who knew how long.

I'd ended up in Paradise City, the jewel of Paradise Bend County. Skyscrapers towered on either side of me. And up ahead loomed the big hill at the north end of town with its massive white mansions, aglow now with the gleam of their security lights...

When I was a kid, Dad had driven me up there sometimes to point out the biggest mansion, smack in the middle. "That's where the people who rule all of Paradise Bend live, Mercy. The Nobles. Play our cards right, and one day we might be half as posh as they are." Then he'd laugh.

I'd never been sure what the joke was.

A plan formed in my pain-addled mind. I turned at the next intersection and cruised past polished storefronts followed by increasingly overblown houses.

People who figured they were somebody lived in Paradise City. The rest of us got stuck with the Bend, the sprawl of grungy suburbs and smaller towns that bled into one another in a loose arc around the city—so close and yet so far from Paradise. But I'd bet there were just as many assholes here as there. At least we knew what we were.

As I aimed the car up the steep slope that led to the peak of the hill, a wave of dizziness swept over me. I clenched my jaw against it and rammed my foot farther down on the gas. The engine grumbled, but we made it to the top.

My father had battered enough sense into me that I parked three houses down from the Nobles' grand mansion rather than right out front, because at this point the car was basically a moving crime scene along with being stolen. My thigh stuck to the seat for a second before I peeled myself out; the whole side of my lovely dress was soaked with my blood. I staggered a little on the asphalt.

There wouldn't have been anywhere to park in front of the Nobles' house anyway. Sedans and sports cars cluttered the broad driveway and both sides of the street almost as far as my car. Tuning out the pain in my arm and the trickle of blood over my skin, I gathered myself as well as I could and strode across the expansive lawn to the front door, which stood half open.

These were the people who ruled all of Paradise Bend. If anyone could crush Colt into the smithereens he deserved, it was the Nobles.

The faint bass of a rock song thumped through the doorway, hitting me at full force the moment I stepped into the foyer. People milled around—men and women bobbing with the music, waving glasses around, mashing their faces together and sometimes their hips too. A few older guys stood stern-faced watching the crowd.

I avoided them, melding into the mass of bodies. None of the partiers seemed to notice my seeping wound or the blood saturating my dress. Too caught up in their posh, powerful lives, huh?

These idiots couldn't help me. I needed the actual Nobles. Dad had pointed the father and heir out to me once a few years back when we'd crossed paths with them at a distance. Fancy suits, fiery auburn hair, faces like carved marble. *Rich pricks*, I'd thought at the time, but I'd also committed their names to memory. You never knew when a stray tidbit Dad or any of the other Claws dropped might come in handy.

I dragged those names out of my whirling head. Ezra. Ezra Noble. He was the big boss. And the son—

I stepped through another doorway, and my gaze latched onto a head of tousled auburn hair. Speak of the devil. My lips curled into a wobbly smile.

Wylder. That was him. He was bent over a pool table right now, lining up a shot. No suit jacket tonight, just a navy-blue button-up with the sleeves rolled up over his muscular forearms, brawny shoulders flexing in a way that would make a lesser woman want to run her hands all over them. I had more important things to take care of tonight.

As I wove through the spectators to the table, the guy landed his shot and straightened up into a cocky pose. The man next to him, a handsome hulk with cropped black hair, shot him a grin. A skinny blonde in a dress that covered more of her arms than her boobs shimmied where she'd decided to dance stripper-style on the edge of the table. The guys didn't seem to be paying much attention to her, but she glowered at me.

I ignored her too and marched straight up to Wylder. Or maybe it was more a sway. The floor was getting tipsy on me.

"Wylder Noble," I demanded, prodding him in the arm with a determined finger.

The guy turned, his eyebrows rising. Fuck, he was stunning up close. Blazing green eyes, sculpted jaw, nose just a tad crooked so he was perfectly imperfect. That kind of face should be illegal.

"You want something?" he said coolly, and another surge of dizziness rose up over me, fogging the edges of my vision. Wylder's gaze dropped to my dress, and a flash of something beyond calculated boredom crossed his expression. Probably peeved I was bleeding all over his swanky floor.

"I need to talk to you," I announced. "*Now*."

Which might have gotten me farther if the world hadn't closed in on me completely then. My legs gave, and everything went black.

2

Mercy

THE VAGUE FEELING OF BEING CARRIED IN SOMEBODY'S arms crept over me. Groaning, I instinctively curled into a hard chest, seeking its warmth. The arms tightened around me as I was carried up a flight of stairs. A door banged open, and a few moments later, I was laid down on a bed while a voice barked orders to someone nearby.

I tried to open my eyes, but they felt heavy. I faded out again.

When I really came to, somebody was prodding the side of my arm. Whatever they were trying to do, it stung like holy hell. Adrenaline jolted through me, and I kicked out blindly. Someone—a man—cried out in pain.

"Holy shit." Strong hands descended on me, pinning me down. I screamed and thrashed, my mind flashing with the images of the bloody slaughter. My father,

Grandma, my entire family, sprawled and savaged on the restaurant floor.

"Stop," a voice commanded with an unshakeable air of authority. My body stilled as if keyed to his wish. Blinking hard, I slowly brought the world around me into focus.

Bright green eyes stared down at me. A gorgeous man who was familiar in ways my hazy mind couldn't quite identify yet was poised right over me, his knees bracketing my hips. The weight of his body pinned me to the bed.

The sense of being trapped made me squirm again. The guy's grip on my wrists tightened, his eyes darkening. Something unfurled deep in my stomach, and all of a sudden I wasn't completely sure I did want him off of me.

"Wylder," a voice warned behind him, shattering the bizarre impulse.

Right. Wylder Noble. My would-be savior—at least, I'd thought he could be. So far he was mostly being a criminally handsome menace.

I heaved at him as well as I could, but he didn't budge. "Kitten's got claws," he said and then chuckled darkly. "The irony."

"Get off me," I snarled.

"Wylder," came the voice again.

This time he listened and finally his weight lifted off me. On the other side of the bed, a man was cradling his arm, looking at me like I was a psycho. He must have been the one I'd kicked. Wylder jerked his head toward him.

The brawny guy with the dark buzzcut who'd been with Wylder at the pool table stepped into view. "Frank was just trying to stitch you up. From that gouge on your arm and the way you bled all over the living room carpet, it looks like you didn't quite manage to dodge a bullet."

The faint thump of dance music carried from beyond the door. Apparently I hadn't been out too long —and it took an awful lot to shake up one of the Nobles' parties.

"That's one way of putting it," I said a little faintly.

Come on, Mercy, get a grip. But my arm was throbbing again, and my thoughts kept jumbling with images of the massacre.

Wylder motioned to the man at the end of the bed. "Can you finish the job?" A few smears of blood marked his bare forearm where he must have held me. He picked up a rag someone had left on the end table and gave it a brisk wipe. I'd probably gotten some on his shirt too, although it was hard to tell against the dark fabric.

"Yes, Mr. Noble," Frank said, still eyeing me uncertainly.

"Not even properly shot and you passed out," the brawny guy remarked. "Not your usual scene?"

I didn't speak. If my father hadn't been dreaming of grandsons, *he* would have put a bullet through my head years ago.

Frank eased closer. "I have to finish cleaning the wound, and then you're going to need stitches."

"Fine, fine," I muttered. "Just be quick."

The guys' stares burned into me as their doctor—or whatever he was—dabbed more antiseptic around the raw flesh. I clenched my jaw and refused to let out a sound, no matter how it burned. They thought I was enough of a wimp already.

My lips might have twitched a few times from holding back the pain while Frank closed the wound with a needle and thread, but the antiseptic seemed to have numbed the spot a bit. When he'd taped a bandage over the injury, he offered me a bottle of blue liquid.

I eyed it suspiciously. Any woman in the Bend learns at a very young age not to accept drinks from strangers. "What is that?"

"It's an energy drink. It's the best option I've got on hand for your blood loss."

I didn't take it. Wylder stepped forward and swiped the bottle from Frank's hand, twisting the lid open. "Drink up."

I stared at him stonily.

"Drink, or I'm going to throw you out of my house. I don't care why you turned up here bleeding half to death."

Well, if he'd had nefarious intentions, he probably wouldn't have waited to see me stitched up first. And I was a lot more likely to get into a bad situation while my head kept whirling.

I snatched the bottle from him and chugged the blue liquid down. The sour taste of it made me wince, but I managed to finish it.

Frank stood up, clearly in a hurry to get out of there.

"That's the best I can do. As long as you keep it clean, it shouldn't get infected or need further treatment."

After he was gone, the brawny guy started to laugh. "You scared the doctor away."

A cool voice spoke up from behind him. "To be fair, Frank does scare pretty easily."

Another guy came into view at Wylder's other side. His hair was dyed a bold, sapphire blue and jaggedly cut as if he'd done it himself. He considered me with narrowed eyes so sharply intent I had to resist the urge to squirm.

"I wasn't trying to scare anyone," I said, taking in the room more thoroughly now that I could focus better. I was sitting on a queen-sized bed in a small room with no other furniture except the ebony bedside table and a matching chair in the corner. It had the blank impersonal vibe of a hotel room. No one had bothered to shut the gauzy curtains on the window, which showed total blackness outside.

Wylder glanced at the brawny guy. "Did anyone see us bring her in here, Kaige?"

"Oh, maybe a few," the other guy—*Kaige*—answered. He winked at me with a flex of his massive biceps. Tattoos of vines climbed up his muscular forearms, disappearing beneath the sleeves of his V-neck tee. "But they were too out of it to remember tomorrow. Most of the drinks have been laced with the good stuff."

Ah. No wonder nobody had paid attention to me. Drunk and high without a care in the world. No doubt the Nobles had enough cops under their thumb to ensure they didn't get so much as a noise complaint.

Wylder returned his attention to me. I met his gaze head on, even though it felt like his striking green eyes could see right down to my deepest, darkest secrets. He cocked his head. "All right, spill. Why did Princess Katz of the Claws show up at my door looking like this?"

My mouth fell open in surprise. "You know who I am?"

He chuckled. "It's kind of my job to keep tabs on all the gangs that operate in and around Paradise Bend, Princess."

I made a face at him. "Don't call me that."

"Don't like the nickname? I could call you Kitty Cat instead, because you've sure got some claws."

I ignored him. I wasn't about to take his bait again.

The pain in my arm grounded me. My body felt stiff, and I shook my feet to bring some flow of blood to them. At my movement, my dress rode up to my thigh, and all three pairs of eyes turned to my bare flesh like it was a flaming beacon. My spine tingled with apprehension—and maybe the tiniest bit of heat—under their collective attention.

I was in a room with three guys who belonged to the most dangerous outfit in all of Paradise Bend. Time to get on with the plan that had propelled me here, even if that plan was seeming foolhardier by the second.

I swallowed, clenching my fists at my sides. The basic idea hadn't been bad. If anyone could take Colt and the Steel Knights down for what they'd done, it was these guys, gorgeous assholes or not.

"You look like you're about to stab me in the eye," Wylder said, giving me an amused look.

"I'd be interested to see her try," the blue-haired guy said in the same coolly detached voice as before.

Wylder snorted and elbowed him. "Of course you would, Gideon. We can hold the battle royale later. Come on, Princess. Cat got your tongue?"

I dragged in a breath. "I was engaged to Cole Bryant —the leader of the Steel Knights." The words made bile rise up my throat. For a second I couldn't go on. The screams echoed in my head alongside the blare of the merciless shots of the guns. The memory of the bodies dropping in quick succession flashed behind my eyes. My grandmother lying dead in a pool of her own blood...

The bedroom door burst open. "I heard that you—"

The new arrival stopped mid-sentence when he caught sight of me on the bed, and my world tilted sideways.

I was hallucinating, right? No way could Rowan Finlay, my first love—and my last, after the way *he'd* betrayed me—be standing just a few feet away from me in Wylder Noble's house.

It *was* him, though, even if he wasn't the skinny boy with an adorable dimple I'd met in junior high. He'd cropped his once floppy ash-blond hair short and spiky, and he was wearing a suit as if he'd just stepped out of a meeting. He had grown into his height, his shoulders broadened. But seeing him shocked me back five years to the last time I'd seen him as if no time had passed at all.

We stared at each other as if challenging the other

to look away first. Could he see the fury and pain in my eyes?

Our unspoken exchange could hardly go unnoticed. Wylder frowned at me. "Do you have a problem with the company I keep?"

I blinked. Rowan looked uncomfortable for a moment before smoothing his face to be expressionless. Of course, I meant nothing to him. He had made that crystal-clear all those years ago.

Shaking my head, I pushed any lingering hurt and confusion out of my mind. The past should stay in the past. It—*he*—didn't matter anymore. "No," I said flatly.

I inhaled slowly. Once. Twice. I needed to remain calm and coherent. "Cole Bryant killed my entire family tonight."

All four pairs of eyes widened. Rowan took a step toward me and then seemed to check himself.

"The Claws are all dead?" Kaige asked, gaping openly.

I nodded. "Everyone who had any kind of authority —my dad, my uncles, their top men. I'm the only survivor. It was supposed to be our rehearsal dinner." A laugh with no humor at all in it sputtered out of me. "I was supposed to walk down the aisle tomorrow to marry Colt. But it turned out to be a trick to lure us in without weapons."

The first time I'd met Colt, his easy smile and kind eyes had seemed like a breath of fresh air. He'd spoken to me respectfully and with warmth that I hadn't received in a long time. And all of it had been a lie.

How long had he been playing me? I'd been so

blinded by the hope of the life he'd allowed me to dream of that I hadn't seen the truth right in front of me.

"Why the fuck would you walk into enemy territory without weapons?" Wylder demanded.

"Both sides agreed, as a matter of honor. Our marriage was supposed to solidify an alliance. We thought we weren't enemies anymore."

He scoffed. "Honor means shit when you end up dead."

I bunched the bedsheet in my palms in an effort to not punch him right where he stood. He spoke so carelessly, not giving a flying fuck that my entire family had been murdered tonight.

"It's a dog-eat-dog world," Wylder went on. "Or should I say Knights-eat-Claws. This is a game of survival, and if your father couldn't protect what was his, then he deserves to be dead."

None of the other guys argued on my behalf. But why would they? I was some blood-drenched stranger who'd showed up at their door. This wasn't a fairy-tale, and they were definitely not any kind of Prince Charmings, despite their terribly handsome facades.

But I couldn't lose hope. I was Mercy Katz, and for all his flaws and torments, my father had honed me into something stronger than he'd ever imagined. I could do better than this.

"Colt went back on his word," I said firmly. "He betrayed us. And for that he needs to pay."

Wylder raised his eyebrows. "And how do you figure I come into that?"

"He took down one of the most powerful gangs in the Bend. What if he gets ideas for more? You Nobles are supposed to have all of Paradise Bend at your beck and call, aren't you? How's it going to look if you let some upstart get away with shit like that and walk free?"

"I'm not getting involved in some lovers' spat," Wylder said, but I had the sense I'd gotten more of his attention.

I fixed him with a glare. "We weren't in love. It was a business transaction, and more for my father's benefit than mine—although yes, I was happy enough with what I thought I'd get out of it. Clearly Colt wasn't. What if he still isn't happy? He could be coming for Paradise City next."

"And if he does, he'll regret it. So far it sounds like all he's done is removed a weak link. If you think I'm going to jump at the command of some small-time gang princess who came begging for help, you're sorely mistaken, Kitty Cat."

I held back a snarl at the nickname. "I didn't come here to beg. I came to call on you to prove that the Nobles really do rule—that this kind of backstabbing won't get a pass under your watch."

Wylder shrugged. "I'm still not convinced the Claws didn't get what they had coming to them. Look at you, barely making it two steps into my house before fainting from a bullet wound."

"Bullet wound?" Rowan spoke for the first time and then snapped his mouth shut.

Wylder ignored him. "You're weak. It's going to take

more than batting your pretty lashes at me to prove your case."

"I. Am. Not. Weak," I said, biting out each word. "I'll be right there with you every step of the way—I want to watch him ground into the dirt. I can hold my own."

A speculative gleam lit in Wylder's eyes. "And what if I said I'd need you to prove that first. Follow my orders, show what you're made of. Are you ready for that, Princess?"

Follow this prick's orders? Every nerve in me resisted the idea—especially when I remembered how my body had briefly responded to his own pressed against it.

But this was my opening—the only one I was likely to get. I had to take it. There was nothing he could throw at me that was worse than what I'd already been through.

I lifted my chin and held his gaze. "Whatever it takes if it means Colt Bryant burns."

3

Rowan

OF ALL THE PLACES I COULD HAVE COME FACE TO FACE
with this ghost of my past, I'd never have expected it to
be one of the Nobles' spare bedrooms.

Mercy Katz's gaze cut to me again, her words
ringing in the air, the pale blue eyes that had once gazed
into mine shining with love now filled with pure venom.
Of course she hated me. All she knew was that I'd
broken my promise, abandoned her... I'd never meant to
look back.

It shouldn't have affected me now. I wasn't the boy
she'd known anymore. I'd quickly climbed the hierarchy
within the Nobles and stood at the right hand of
Wylder Noble despite joining only a few years ago.
There were many people other than her who hated me.

But none of the others had ever bothered me like
this.

Her dress had ridden dangerously close to her upper

thigh where she sat on Wylder's bed. It clung to her body, damp and darkened with... blood? Wylder had mentioned a bullet wound, and someone had bandaged her arm.

The outline of her underwear showed against the thin fabric. My cock twitched in spite of everything. Tendrils of her hair had come loose from a carefully made chignon that spilled down her neck. But most dangerously tempting of all was the fire burning inside her. She commanded attention.

From the way both Wylder and Kaige were watching her, I didn't think I was the only one who'd noticed. My jaw clenched.

"We should talk about this," I said to Wylder. There was no fucking way I was letting her into my life again. If I'd ruined hers, then my relationship with her had ruined mine just as much. I wanted her nowhere near me ever again.

Wylder glanced at me. "I haven't agreed to help her yet. I just want to see what the kitty's made of. If you've got ideas on that score, I'm all ears."

He jerked his head for the rest of us to follow him and strode out of the room without a backward glance.

I gave Mercy one last look before I turned on my heel and followed. Fury flashed in her eyes at the brisk dismissal. For a second, the thought of the loss she'd just endured, the horrors she must have witnessed, gnawed at me.

But I had no choice. I had to protect what was mine, including the life I'd so carefully built in the years since I'd parted ways with her. I couldn't let it all go to hell all over again.

Music from the party trickled upstairs, the noisy, nonsensical beat of it grating on my nerves. It was past midnight already, but the festivities weren't showing any sign of dying down.

Wylder came to a stop on the landing, looking down over the partygoers in the main foyer. Writhing bodies danced to the music. A few of them were singing along to it in off-key voices that made me want to take my gun out.

Was I upset at them or Mercy?

"She isn't good news," I said. "Forget testing her—just get her out of here."

Beside me, Kaige shrugged with the flirty smile that always came out when he was about to put a move on some chick. My hackles rose before he even spoke. "I don't know. She seems like she could be a lot of fun."

Gideon leaned against the banister with his hip, his analytical gaze as penetrating as always. "We do have to consider the territorial implications. Colt Bryant took down the entire Claws. That's going to have an impact."

"Is that necessarily a bad thing?" Kaige said. "Haven't we been getting news of them stirring up trouble?"

"The Claws were the most powerful force in the Bend, and Colt massacred them in one night. He's cold and precise," Gideon replied levelly. I'd never witnessed the guy raise his voice, but he always managed to get his point across nevertheless. "That makes him a potential threat, one we have to consider."

Wylder turned to me. "How do you know the girl?"

The question caught me off-guard even though I should have seen it coming. There were rarely things that Wylder didn't catch. He had a crazy knack for making people spill, which was why his father used him for most of the interrogations.

I cleared my throat. I knew lying wasn't an option. He would catch my bullshit right away. "She and I dated for a while back in high school. Before I moved to the city. I was surprised to see her—and vice versa—that's all."

He nodded, but I could tell he wasn't exactly satisfied with my vague answer. "I'm not saying I trust her, and it sounds like you know her better than we do. But Gideon's right. She raised some fair points about the Bryant prick getting out of hand. And *she* knows him better than any of us do."

I sucked in a breath, but Wylder's eyes were still trained on me, as if he were waiting for some reaction. He obviously suspected something else was going on between Mercy and me, but I wasn't going to give him any more information. That was completely unrelated to the gang, and I kept my private life out of this business.

Before I could protest, a flash of limbs and pale skin threw herself at Wylder. He scowled down at the girl who was now practically hanging off him.

"Wylder, I was looking for you all over the place." Gia's voice was slurred from all the alcohol she must have consumed. The skimpy outfit that she was wearing threatened to fall off any second, and the mounds of her breasts were all but exposed.

All the sight did was make me think of Mercy in that bloody dress.

Wylder shook her hands off him and stepped away. "Gia, I think it's better that you sleep it off. You're drunk."

Gia pouted in response and then turned her attention to Kaige, running her finger along his jaw. "What about you? You want some of this?" She thrust her hip out at him.

Kaige rolled his eyes, but he took her by the waist and leaned in. "No," he said, loud enough for us to hear.

Gia's lower lip wobbled. "I just want to be good to you," she slurred and then scampered away, stumbling in her high heels.

"Is it just me, or is she more annoying when she's drunk?" Kaige asked.

Gideon sighed. "Don't even pretend that you don't like the attention."

Kaige grinned in answer.

"I think it's time we pull the plug on this party." Wylder put his hands on the balustrade and raised his voice. "Everybody gets out in five minutes, or I'm going to start shooting."

The music stopped abruptly. Everybody stared up at us in horror, Wylder's words cutting through the haze of alcohol and drugs in their system. There wasn't a person in the room who didn't know they were looking at the second most powerful figure in the Nobles.

He raised a brow and motioned to the outline of the gun at his hip. "Do I need to repeat myself?"

People started rushing out of the foyer immediately, their urgency to get away almost comical. Wylder shook his head at them and returned his attention to us, swiping his hands together. "Always an effective way to break up a party fast."

As the last of the partiers hustled out, we walked down the stairs, examining the aftermath. Throwing a party was one thing, cleaning up afterwards was a whole lot of trouble.

I stepped on what looked like a used condom and winced in disgust. Kaige toed the pizza crusts and the crumpled paper cups out of his way. "People are such fucking pigs."

"Thank God for the cleaning staff." Wylder paused, and a smirk that set off warning bells in my head curled his lips. "Although I say we tell them to leave one room untouched for the time being."

What was he up to? I studied him and couldn't stop the question from tumbling out. "What about Mercy?"

"What about her?"

I knew I was pushing it, but I had to give it one more shot. "Even if Colt is a problem, we don't need her to tackle him. We're the Nobles. You just cleared a hundred people out of the building by pointing at your gun. Why keep her around?"

Wylder shrugged. "I don't believe in throwing away a useful tool that's fallen into our laps. Colt Bryant could become a problem for us in the future. And Mercy Katz has the inside scoop on him. Maybe she'll even prove herself somewhat useful in other ways. It's been a long time since high school, Rowan."

I bit back any retort I might have made to that. I'd worked my way into Wylder's inner circle by doing whatever he needed me to do, being whatever he needed me to be, and I was still a relative newbie here. He'd been counting on the other guys way longer. If I made a single misstep, I wasn't totally sure he wouldn't be casting *me* out of the house at gunpoint.

Kaige snorted. "Do you think she'll have any idea who her fiancé really is? He murdered her family in cold blood and then tried to kill her. He obviously wasn't the most upfront dude ever."

"No," Wylder said. "But they had been engaged for a year. They'll have talked. She'll have seen things. I don't get the impression she's the type to wander around with her head in the clouds."

"At the very least, she'll have some idea of his schedules and habits," Gideon said in his familiar analytical tone.

Kaige frowned. "There's something I don't get though. Why would he go to all this trouble for a whole fucking year? He couldn't have found an excuse to get enough key Claws members together sooner?"

"Maybe it took him that long to build enough trust?" I suggested.

Gideon nodded. "Tyrell Katz wasn't an idiot. It would have taken a lot for him to agree to go in without weapons."

"Well, his loss is our gain." Wylder's smirk came back. "If there's anything the kitty cat hasn't told us yet, we'll get to the bottom of it. And if she's a rat as well as a Katz, *she'll* be the one we're crushing."

"We shouldn't go easy on her," I said quickly. "Whatever our history, I won't." If Wylder wouldn't kick her out right away, then I'd just have to make sure she decided leaving of her own free will was better than staying.

It might even be better for her. Her dad was dead— Tyrell Katz was gone from this world. Part of the reason I'd started on this path was with the vague idea that someday, *I* might be in a position to end that villain's life, and now it was already done. It felt weirdly anticlimactic, like it wasn't quite real.

This bastard from the Steel Knights had screwed Mercy over too, and I couldn't condone what he'd done to her entire family or tried to do to her, but at least she didn't have to live in fear of Tyrell anymore. She could go anywhere, do anything... The last thing she should have wanted was to get dragged down into even more violence.

Why the hell had she had to come here when she'd had so many other options?

As I grappled with the clash of concern and anger inside me, Wylder's gaze slid to Kaige. "Anyway, having her around might distract attention from *you* while Anthea's still working her investigation."

Kaige's shoulders stiffened, but he couldn't argue with that.

Wylder motioned toward the staircase. "Get to bed, all of you. I want you sharp in the morning when we get to work on this new development."

I didn't like the sound of that at all, but I dipped my head in agreement and set off for my bedroom.

As soon as the door was closed behind me, the frustration that'd been building inside me overflowed. I slammed my fist against the doorframe. "Goddamn it."

I walked to the bed and ripped the mattress off it, throwing it against the wall. It wasn't enough. I pummeled it a few times, but the motions only made me feel more ineffectual. In the end, I sank to the floor, my hands still fisted.

For years, I hadn't let myself think of her. And now Mercy Katz had shown up at my door, stirring up all kinds of trouble.

And the worst part was, something in me still wanted to save her.

Mercy

Dark figures chased me in my nightmares, getting closer and closer. It didn't matter how fast I ran, they caught up to me, swirling around me, choking me, cutting off my breath until the shadows materialized into the grinning face of Colt Bryant. He was drenched in blood.

I woke up damp with sweat. At some point in the night, somebody had turned off the air-conditioning, and the room was stifling hot. I wiped the beads of perspiration that rolled down my neck to my cleavage as I struggled to catch up to reality.

It was just a bad dream.

But I hadn't outrun my nightmare. I had just woken up to another one. I closed my eyes and saw the lifeless faces of my grandma and Aunt Renee lying beside her. They were dead. Every person who'd had much of any impact on my life growing up was dead.

Desolation crept up inside me followed by a surge of rage so powerful I had to bite back a scream. No, I wasn't going to freak out or break down. I'd tamp down all my emotions, just like Dad's drills had forced me to.

"One step at a time," I muttered to myself. I wasn't going to take down Colt in a day. I would have to work up to it.

My head throbbed with what felt like the beginning of a headache. I swung my legs over the side of the bed, and my bare feet hit the pooled fabric of last night's dress where I'd left it on the floor. The blood had crusted over, the silk utterly ruined. I grimaced at it, a shudder running through me.

At least I wasn't wearing it anymore. While I'd been sitting here wondering what to make of that conversation with Wylder and his men, a woman who must have been part of the household staff had bustled in with a clean T-shirt and sweats for me to change into —and clean sheets for the bed I'd gotten a fair bit of blood on too. She hadn't even tutted over the stain that'd seeped into the mattress, but then, in this household blood was probably a common sight.

That'd seemed like a clear enough invitation to spend the night. Now the sun was beaming through the thin curtains. I rolled my shoulders, testing my wounded arm. A shallow ache ran through my bicep, but I'd felt worse. Seemed like the doctor guy had known what he was doing.

My eyes fell to the gold engagement ring with its glittering diamond on my finger. A fresh surge of rage rushed through me, sudden and desperate. I yanked at the ring, but it stuck on my knuckle. Gritting my teeth, I pulled harder. It felt as if my skin was melting under the cursed thing. I finally ripped it off and hurled it at the wall next to the door.

The door that was now opening. My engagement ring clattered to the floor and rolled in front of a pair of steel toe boots.

I raised my eyes, my gaze skimming beefy thighs outlined against tight jeans, hips with a perfect V, and then the heavily muscled chest above. The guy Wylder had called Kaige was watching me with an amused smile. "Woah, easy there."

My temper flickered, but I wasn't likely to get Wylder's help by pissing off his inner circle before I'd even started proving myself. "I wasn't aiming at you."

He bent down and picked up the ring. "Considering what that asshole did, I get the sentiment, but you might not want to throw this away just yet. From the looks of it, you could get a few K for it easily. Might as well make the bastard pay for his sins, right?"

He could've easily pocketed it himself, but he walked over to me, turned my hand up, and rested the ring in the middle of my palm. Heat spread from his fingers into mine. His gaze slid down my body like a caress, lingering briefly on my chest.

I'd have been more annoyed if I hadn't just been checking *him* out a minute ago. And if the approval in his eyes hadn't sent a tingle of sharper heat through me.

"Like what you see?" I found myself saying.

His smile widened. "You know what, I do."

Okay, that was enough of that. I jerked my hand

away from his, my fingers closing around the ring, and stood up, stepping away from him in the same motion.

Kaige held up both of his hands as if in surrender, but I knew better than to trust him. Wylder hadn't agreed to help me yet. They were probably still debating on my usefulness. Nobody was my friend here.

"I'm just supposed to collect you for breakfast," he said with a twinkle in his deep brown eyes. "Do you need me to show you to the facilities first?"

My bladder said yes. I crossed my arms and raised my chin. "Lead the way."

Kaige led me down the hall at a casual stroll. Of the four guys I'd met last night, he seemed the most easygoing, but he was awfully intimidating without even trying. I wasn't a shrimp at five foot six, but this guy had nearly a foot on me—both in height and probably more than that in width with all that muscle. Pretty easy to guess what his job in the crew was. No attacker was likely to get at Wylder through him.

He swept his arm toward the bathroom with a jaunty little bow, and I held back a glare as I strode past him. Inside—with the door *firmly* closed—I looked at myself in the mirror and grimaced. My eyes were bloodshot, and my hair had turned into a bird's nest. I wasn't going to generate a lot of respect like this.

I splashed water on my face and under my arms, and combed my fingers through my hair, wishing I had an elastic to pull it back into one of my typical ponytails. The pins that had held it in its updo for the rehearsal dinner had all fallen out. After a couple more tugs at it,

I ventured back into the hall where my new shadow was waiting.

"Twice as gorgeous without the bedhead," Kaige said with a wink.

I glowered at him, but my stomach chose to gurgle at the exact same time. Gee, thanks. "You mentioned something about breakfast?" I said pointedly.

My lack of responsiveness to his charms didn't appear to bother Kaige one bit. He offered me one of his brawny arms. "I'll give you the tour along the way."

I declined to be led along like a lady in one of the historical melodramas Grandma had loved, as tempted as I might have been to find out just how solid those muscles were, but I fell into step beside him.

Everything about this place screamed money, from the gilded windows that looked out into the sprawling lawn to the slew of framed paintings scattered along the hallway. Kaige waved toward the doors we passed. "Guest bedrooms here, Wylder's part of the house farther down. Including my bedroom, if you ever want to drop in on me."

"Noted," I said dryly.

We emerged into a larger section of hall overlooking a winding staircase and the huge foyer I'd stumbled into last night. On the way down, Kaige pointed at the set of huge oak doors. "The main entrance. Kitchen's this way. Plus various sitting rooms and living rooms and I-don't-know-if-they-even-have-a-name rooms. You need to get something done, there's probably a room for it here."

As we entered the kitchen, an expansive space full of shining stainless steel and marble countertops, the smell of frying sausage and eggs hit my nose. My mouth watered, and my stomach outright roared.

"You took your time," Wylder remarked from where he was standing just inside the room, his head cocked to the side. He was dressed in black jeans and a black shirt that I couldn't help noticing fit him snugly, showing off his well-defined chest.

Kaige aimed his grin at the other guy, apparently unperturbed that he might have pissed off the Noble heir. "Hey, I like to make sure a lady's treated right."

I wandered farther into the room, ignoring them and any amusement I might have had at the idea of me being a *lady* while I chased the delicious food smells. Gideon and Rowan were leaning against an island in the middle of the kitchen. Whatever conversation they'd been having trailed off as they both glanced at me, Gideon coolly and Rowan hesitantly. Rowan's gaze stopped on the bandage over my gunshot wound, but he didn't comment on it.

Beyond them at the stove, a woman I hadn't met yet was flipping something in a pan. Her red hair, a more vibrant version of Wylder's and his father's auburn, cascaded to halfway down her back. She was petite, maybe half a foot shorter than me, but when she turned, I guessed from her face that she was around her late twenties. With her blue paisley dress and pearl hair pins holding the ruddy waves back from her temples, she didn't look like she belonged here at all.

She slapped a piece of French toast and some bacon on a plate and motioned me over to the island. "I assume you're hungry."

I was starving, but I didn't admit that. Warily, I stepped forward and took a seat as far as I could get from Rowan. This felt like some kind of a trick.

The woman poured orange juice into a glass and pushed it toward me. I was parched too. I'd never gotten to eat much of anything and hadn't drunk anything but a few sips of wine last night before...

Gunfire and blood splatter flashed through my mind. I shoved those memories aside and grabbed the glass to take a swift chug, as if I could wash last night away completely with the tartly sweet liquid.

"I feel introductions are in order." Wylder took a seat next to me at the island, so close the scent of him, like leather and brandy, filled my nose. I resisted the urge to inhale deeply as he gestured toward the woman at the stove. "Meet Anthea Noble, my aunt, babysitter, and proxy mother. She's kind of the all-in-one package."

Anthea rolled her eyes. "Mother? I'm only, what, five years older than you?"

"Six," Wylder said, causing her to shake her head.

I relaxed a little. She was family, not a business associate. That made more sense. Although the two factors did often end up pretty mixed up in our line of work.

Wylder gestured to me. "And Anthea, here we have the only living representative of the Claws' leadership in our kitchen. Say hi to Mercy Katz."

Anthea's gaze roved over me with cool efficiency, and I got the impression she'd known about my arrival long before I'd actually stepped in here.

"Anthea's here to keep our asses in line while

Wylder's dad is away," Kaige said. As if to make a point, he wiggled his butt. I had to bite my cheek to stifle a laugh.

How had this guy ended up with the rest of this bunch? Or Rowan, for that matter? Back when I'd known him, he'd been on a fast-track course to get into an Ivy League college.

But then, obviously I hadn't known him anywhere near as well as I'd thought.

Gideon was easier to figure. He might not have packed anywhere near as much muscle as Kaige on that slender frame, but he had the detached gaze of a stone-cold killer. "Some people are harder to manage than the others," he remarked with a pointed look at Kaige.

I took a bite of my French toast—slathered with the perfect amount of syrup—and had to muffle a moan. Embarrassment turned my ears red hot.

Wylder chuckled. "I don't blame you. Anthea is a great cook. That's one of her specialties—along with concocting the perfect poison, of course."

I almost choked on my mouthful. Wylder thumped his hand against my back. I took a big gulp of the juice to push the bread down my throat.

Anthea smiled at me but without much humor. "You don't have to worry about deadly poisons this morning. If we wanted to kill you, you'd be dead already and not know any better."

I guess she had a point, but I remained on guard as I took another bite. The guys shifted around the island. They were watching my every move, and after a while my skin started to prickle with their attention. It didn't help that even if they were assholes, they were undeniably attractive assholes—ravish-me-in-the-dark attractive.

"So, tell me about Colt," Wylder said, studying me as intently as the others.

I drained the last of my juice before answering. "What do you want to know about him?"

He shrugged. "Let's start with the basics. What do you know about his business?"

"It's typical Bend stuff, mostly. Moving drugs and stolen goods, collecting from the local businesses—you know the score. And he runs regular MMA fights, collects bets on them. Those have gotten pretty popular since he started them up."

Gideon nodded, tapping the screen of a tablet he'd pulled out while I was talking. "I've heard about those."

Wylder picked up a fork and twirled it between his fingers. I couldn't help thinking of the one I'd stabbed into one of Colt's men. "And that's what appeals to the Katz princess in a husband?"

I glared at him. "I told you, it was a business arrangement. My father's more than mine."

"What made your father so eager to give away his only daughter to a rival gang?"

A strange heaviness was spreading through my head, like the grogginess just before a cold sets in. I rubbed the back of my neck. "They'd had a few clashes. Disputes over territory, interrupting deals. The kind of thing that's inevitable. It didn't have to be Colt. Dad would have been happy to expand his influence with any of the gangs in the Bend he could have connected me to."

I shut my mouth before even more words could tumble out. I didn't need to tell the guy my entire life story, for fuck's sake. What was wrong with me?

Wylder tapped the fork against the countertop. "That's all you were worth to Tyrell Katz? A bargaining chip?"

"And a broodmare," I muttered without thinking, and nearly bit my tongue. I sure as hell hadn't meant to say *that*.

Something was wrong. I tried to push myself off of the stool, but my balance wobbled. I couldn't even stand up straight.

My gaze shot to Anthea. "You—you *did* poison me." I snatched at the knife I'd used to cut my toast, but Wylder grabbed it first and sent it spinning across the counter to his aunt. Then he put his hand on my shoulder and sat me down on my seat. My body obeyed, just like my mouth had answered his questions automatically. My stomach listed.

Anthea set her elbows on the counter and propped her chin on her folded hands. "I said I didn't want to *kill* you. This is just a little concoction to loosen your tongue and make it harder for you to lie. Most of the symptoms will recede in a bit, and you'll barely feel anything at all."

She was right. The heaviness in my head was easing already. My stomach was settling. But my thoughts drifted with a floating sensation, as if my mind had been cut off from the rest of my body.

These pricks. Like I would have lied to them anyway. I was the one who'd come to *them*—had they forgotten that?

Of course, maybe they saw that as suspicious.

Wylder glanced over at Gideon. "Where were we?"

Gideon flicked at his tablet's screen. "The reasons for the engagement."

"Right." The Noble heir turned his bright green gaze back on me. "So your father wanted any alliance he could get within the Bend to strengthen his power base, and... grandkids?"

"An heir," I bit out, irritated with myself but unable to hold back the words. "I didn't count, seeing as I don't have a dick."

Kaige made a sound as if he'd choked back a snort. Wylder moved smoothly onward. "And you went along with this because...?"

"Because it was a chance to have some kind of life he wasn't totally controlling. Colt seemed like he'd be open to a real partnership, even if it was more business than love to begin with. You don't know—" I managed to cut myself short before I got into the messed-up sob story of my life under Tyrell Katz.

But of course Wylder wouldn't let it rest there. "I don't know what?"

I forced myself to look at him head on, directing the words as well as I could while they spilled out. I could talk without telling him *everything*. "He wasn't shy about his dissatisfaction with my dickless state. It was not a happy home. Zero sunshine, zilch roses. Do you really need the gory details?"

"I think I get the picture," he said casually, as if we were talking about a day at the park and not twenty-one years of horror. Well, fuck him.

Except no, I really shouldn't do that. Or want to. Oh, God, how long was this brain-melting "concoction" going to last?

Gideon looked up from his tablet again, all professional cool. "Walk us through what happened last night. You said it was your rehearsal dinner?"

"Yes. Colt made all the arrangements. It was supposed to be his contribution since my father was paying for most of the wedding." I dragged in a breath. "He picked the venue. I'm assuming now that the supposed staff were actually members of the Steel Knights. To avoid any old tensions bubbling over, both sides agreed not to bring weapons, other than a few bodyguards posted around the space who were meant to be a joint hire."

Wylder sighed, and I remembered his disdain for that idea last night. I barreled on.

"As soon as we sat down at the table, the servers, the bodyguards, and Colt and his men pulled guns on everyone on the Katz side and just opened fire. I saw most of them dead with my own eyes—my dad, my aunts and uncles, my grandmother..." I paused, swallowing hard. "Colt ordered them to take me down too, but I managed to get to the door and grab a car outside."

"That lines up with the official reports, as much as has been reported," Gideon said.

I peered at him. "You've got access to the police

files?" Maybe I shouldn't be surprised. A sudden spurt of hope rose in my chest. "Was anyone at all from my—"

He shook his head before I could even finish the question. "Twelve dead. Your father, your grandmother, two aunts and uncles, and miscellaneous figures I believe were close associates of your father's."

I sank back down on the stool. "Yeah." He'd brought them along to show off the union he'd arranged. Lucky them.

Wylder drummed his fingers, eyeing me again. "Now we get to the important questions. Starting with, why did you come to me?"

"I didn't have anywhere else to go," I blurted out, the stupid drug from the drink still keeping my tongue loose. Damn it. I sucked in a breath and tried to make the best of it. "Colt wanted to kill me. He'd have checked my house. And I didn't want to just go into hiding. I want him taken down for what he did. I want him to *suffer*."

The last word came out more emphatically than I'd intended. The guys all stared at me for a moment. Then a smirk stretched across Wylder's handsome face.

"Bloodthirsty. I can appreciate that. But why *me,* Kitty Cat?"

Did he really need to ask? "Everyone knows the Nobles run things in Paradise Bend. All the gangs in the county operate only as your family permits. Who better to crush that asshole?"

"Ah, so all you see when you look at me is a ticket to vengeance, huh?"

"And a prick who's too hot for his own good," I

muttered, and almost chomped on my tongue when I realized what I'd said.

Wylder threw back his head with a laugh, twice as hot now that he was amused. I definitely wasn't watching the perfect curve of his throat and wondering if he tasted as good as he smelled.

Kaige rolled his eyes, while Rowan looked at me with a tense expression. If I didn't know any better, I'd think that he was trying to hide his annoyance, which didn't make any sense. He was the one who'd essentially dumped me.

Gideon broke in, his voice as flat as ever. "Why do you think Colt turned on the Claws? Did he ever seem unhappy with the arrangement?"

Deciding the best course of action was to pretend I'd never let the slightest compliment toward Wylder slip from my mouth, I focused on his friend instead. "No. If I'd had any idea, I'd never have walked into that restaurant in the first place. We'd been engaged for a year. I thought... I thought we were at least something like friends at that point."

Wylder and Anthea frowned. Gideon fixed me with a stare. His pale gray eyes were impossible to look away from once they'd homed in on their target. Something about him both unnerved me and made me deeply curious about what made that mind tick. Out of the four guys, he was the hardest to read.

"And how do you feel about him now?" he asked.

Hadn't I already laid that out? "I think he's a rat bastard who deserves to drown in a pool of blood," I said. "Preferably while also choking on his own testicles.

If you want to get even more creative than that, I won't argue."

Kaige let out a low whistle that sounded impressed, but Gideon held my gaze. "Is that *all* you want?"

"Yes," I said. "Other than for this conversation to be over so we can get on with hunting him down already."

Without realizing it, I'd started shredding a paper napkin that'd been left on the island. Kaige leaned over and tipped his head toward my hands. "What happened to your fingertips? Did you try to remove your fingerprints like some kind of super spy?" He only sounded half joking.

I dropped the napkin, my fingers curling toward my palms. I didn't have to look at them to know what he'd noticed: the pads at the ends were mottled with tiny crisscrossing scars that'd cooled over time from angry red to faded white.

"Looks like the kitty cat almost got declawed," Wylder remarked, his tone playful but his gaze searching.

The light-headed sensation was dwindling. I found I could control what I said a little better than before. "I scraped them up pretty bad during a job for my father. He didn't go easy on me."

Rowan shifted in his seat, and my pulse hiccupped. He knew the truth—I'd told him in a moment of weakness and never regretted it until this moment. I looked up and caught his eyes. He met my gaze but didn't open his mouth to speak.

Why not? His loyalty was obviously with the Nobles now. He hadn't given a shit about my feelings before.

But maybe he just didn't see how it was relevant, so he wasn't going to distract from the real issues by bringing it up.

I glanced around the island at my audience. "Listen, I'm here for only one thing—getting justice for me and my family. I know you're the only people who can help me deliver it. I've given you all the answers you asked for. What else do you need from me?"

To my surprise, Gideon closed his tablet. "I think we're done here. Wylder?"

Wylder observed me for a few beats before he said, "Yeah, I think we are."

I knew he didn't quite trust me yet but I was getting closer. Relief rushed through me. I'd passed his first test.

Anthea cleared her throat. "I'll just remind you that the serum only makes lying *harder*, not impossible."

There was no emotion at all in Wylder's voice when he replied. "And if she has been lying to us, I'm sure she knows I won't hesitate to put a bullet through her head." A smile curved his lips. "But for now it's time to put the princess to work."

5

Mercy

IGNORING MY IMMEDIATE CRINGE AT THE "PRINCESS" nickname, I turned to Wylder. "Put me to work how?"

He beckoned me with a curl of his index finger. "Come with me."

I followed him out of the kitchen and down the hall. Partway along it, he halted in his tracks and swiveled toward me. In that moment, his eyes looked as fiery as his auburn hair.

"Just so you know, Gideon is like my brother and Kaige will willingly carve out his chest to prove his loyalty. I don't expect anything different from Rowan."

I stared at him. "Why are you telling me that?"

He shrugged. "Just making sure you don't get any ideas. You may look like sin incarnate, but you're never going to sway my men."

As if to prove his point, his gaze slowly traveled down my body. It felt as if he'd touched me instead, lighting up flames all across my skin. He looked at me as if I was standing bare in front of him instead of wearing sweatpants and a loose tee that showed only the slightest hint of cleavage. My pussy clenched.

I found my voice. "I've already taken your test."

Wylder laughed. "Only the first part. You said you'd do whatever it takes to earn my help."

"So what's next?"

"I volunteered you for cleaning duty." He took a few more steps and pointed through a doorway.

As I reached him, I recognized the room where I'd found him last night—the one with the pool table off to one side. All traces of the party had been wiped clean from the rest of the house, but this large space was still littered with trash. A sickly smell like stale alcohol and... vomit? turned my stomach.

Wylder rested his hand on the small of my back. Despite the stink and my wariness of him, my nerve-endings lit up where he touched me. So much that I almost didn't process the words when he leaned close to my ear and murmured, "Well, get to it."

I blinked at him. "Pardon?"

"You heard me." He stepped back, waving to the room. "Clean the whole thing. I want it spick and span."

Was he kidding me? "I'm not your *maid*."

"Oh, no? Wasn't that you begging me for my help last night? Are you backing down so easily, Princess?"

"I'm not backing down. I'm just saying this has nothing to do with how strong I am or whatever it is you want me to prove."

Wylder moved toward me again with an air of

menace, but I stood my ground. I realized the error in my judgment when he stepped right up to my face, close enough that he could have kissed me with just a little tilt forward.

"You are going to clean this room for me," he said, emphasizing every word. "Because I told you to, and while you're here, what I say goes. If you can't learn that lesson, you can forget about getting anything from me."

My eyes dropped to his mouth and the quick flick of his tongue as he spoke, and another flare of unwanted heat washed over me. Wylder smirked as if he knew exactly what I was thinking about. "No questions, Kitty Cat?" he said in a low, husky voice that made my stomach tighten. Suddenly, the nickname didn't sound half bad.

I snapped myself back to reality. What was wrong with me?

I *had* said I'd do anything. If this was what he wanted, I sure as hell wasn't throwing in the towel over a messy room. "Fine. Get out of my way, and I'll get to it."

I ventured farther into the room, my gut lurching as the smell thickened. Empty chip bags, half-eaten pizza slices, and bones leftover from sticky chicken wings lay in total disarray. Apparently Wylder's guests hadn't been familiar with the concept of garbage cans. There *was* a pool of vomit dried into the carpet in one corner, and... had someone taken a *shit* on one of the chairs? What kind of drugs had been in the drinks last night, exactly?

And now it was up to me to get rid of all this crap to the Noble heir's satisfaction.

Wylder propped himself in the doorway, his bright eyes tracking my every move. "What are you doing?" I asked, annoyed both at him and at me for being affected at all by his presence. "Don't you have more important ways to spend your time?"

"I don't know. I think supervising you for a bit should be both important and incredibly entertaining." He folded his arms in front of his chest. "Go on. There are cleaning supplies in the closet at the end of the hall."

Girding myself, I stepped past him and marched to the closet. From the shelves inside, I grabbed a box of garbage bags, a pair of rubber gloves, a package of bristly sponges, and a heavy bottle of cleaning fluid. I lugged it all to the pool table room and then went back for a bucket that I hauled to the kitchen to fill with water.

Wylder watched the proceedings with no shift in his faintly amused expression. I resisted the urge to claw his eyes out like the cat he kept saying I was and tugged up my shirt collar to cover my nose. It wasn't enough protection from the stench to prevent me from wanting to gag every five seconds.

It also left a band of skin around my waist bare. "Love it," Wylder called out teasingly. "Getting a bit of a strip show too."

I'd have stuck my tongue out at him, but he wouldn't have seen it anyway through the shirt. Tuning him out, I concentrated on my work as well as I could, humming a soft tune to distract myself.

Bit by bit, I worked through the disgusting mess. I

let my mind detach, paying no attention to what I was putting my gloved hands on, just getting through this chore. Everything I could easily pick up went into a garbage bag until three were stuffed full.

Beneath a pizza box that'd been wedged under a chair, I found one treasure amid all the trash: two tightly rolled fifties with a faint dusting of white powder. Fucking rich assholes who could afford to snort coke with a bigger bill than some people in the Bend ever had in their wallets—and to forget those bills on the floor. But hey, their loss was my gain.

When I looked up, Wylder was gone. I guessed watching me wiggle my ass in the air while grabbing junk off the floor hadn't been so exciting after all. I definitely wasn't disappointed to have lost his company. I wiped the powder off the fifties and tucked them into my pocket.

Then it was time to get down to scrubbing.

For a little while, my nose had gotten numbed to the horrendous stink. As soon as I started working the worst of the offenses out of the carpet and the furniture, the smell rose up twice as strong. Only now it was combined with the pungent tang of the cleaning fluid.

My stomach lurched, and I nearly lost my breakfast to add a second pool of vomit to the room's décor. Gritting my teeth, I pushed through the nausea. Why not imagine that with every rub of the sponge, I was throttling Colt's neck? Bashing his arrogant face in. He'd deserve nothing less.

Less than twenty-four hours ago, I'd still thought I

was going to marry him. The idea seemed so foreign now I almost laughed.

In the most horrible of ways, he'd given me what I'd wanted, hadn't he? I didn't have to answer to Dad anymore, that was for sure. But—God, as much as I'd hated my father sometimes, as many times as I'd pictured pulling a gun or a knife on him myself just to make the torment stop, I hadn't enjoyed seeing him go down.

Colt had killed him without provocation while under a treaty of peace most people even in the Bend would have considered sacred. There was no justification for that, let alone what he'd done to every other Claws member in that building. What he'd tried to do to me.

It wasn't even just killing them. Who would have been left to mourn any of them if he'd succeeded in taking me down too? Even with me still alive, it wasn't as if I could organize a dozen wakes, say a full farewell to any of them. If no one else, Grandma should have gotten a proper send-off.

But Colt's people would be searching for me, I was sure of it. He wouldn't take the chance that I'd come back for revenge. I was a loose end, and men like him didn't get where they were without learning to stamp out every one of those they came across.

I thought back to our last couple of dates—the lunch we'd grabbed at that new café he'd recommended, the chick flick I'd dragged him to less because I was eager to see it than because I wanted to see how well *he'd* endure it. Colt had laughed with me, held my hand, looked at me as if he couldn't wait to discover more of me on our wedding night.

And it had all been a lie. Even if he hadn't been planning the massacre all along, he must have known by then, right?

How could I have been so *stupid?*

I wrenched my hands against the rug in a particularly brutal motion, and the last of the vomit stain disappeared. Sitting back on my heels, I let out my breath and surveyed the room.

There were still a few splatters of what looked like cola to deal with and a scattering of crumbs I'd take the vacuum over later, but I was getting there. And Wylder had thought this request would be enough to send me running.

Rolling my eyes, I got to work on the next stain. I'd zoned out so deeply that the voice that broke through my thoughts practically gave me a heart attack.

"Who the hell are *you?*"

I startled and lost my grip on the sponge. Three beefy middle-aged guys with polos tucked into their jeans were standing by the door. Tattoos edged up their necks from beneath the folded collars. Nobles men, and pretty high up in the pecking order from their slightly posh clothes.

The man who'd spoken, a bald guy with another tattoo decorating his scalp, stepped toward me with a scowl. "I asked you a question, girl."

One of the other men snickered. "Just look at her, Axel. She must be one of the groupies." His open leer sent a wave of disgust through me. Suddenly I missed Wylder.

I kept my gaze steady. The trick with every gangster I'd ever met *other* than my father had been to show no fear, not even any concern. If you outdid them in boldness, they stopped seeing you as prey and decided it was easier not to see you at all. "Wylder told me to clean up this room. I'm just about finished."

The first man—Axel—narrowed his eyes at me as if he had expected me to simper. But now that my initial shock had faded, I considered the layout of the room and how easily I could dodge around these jerks to the door if they came at me. It never hurt to be prepared.

The guys turned away from me, muttering to themselves. "Why the fuck did Wylder even let an untried chick in here?" the leering dude said in a voice not quite hushed enough. "It hasn't even been two weeks since the Titan bit the dust."

The Titan? Was that one of the Nobles' people— he'd died? Here? I frowned. If it'd been bad enough for these guys to be disturbed about the death two weeks later, it mustn't have been a typical loss while on the job.

"Who knows what goes through the kid's head," Axel said. "He's a loose cannon."

The third guy shot me a dark look and grumbled to the others. "Not as much as that hulking thug of his we all know did Titus in. First he brushes that off, then he's hauling more trash in here?"

I scrubbed the carpet very emphatically, torn between wanting to remind them loud and clear that I could hear them and knowing I was probably much better off if they thought I wasn't listening at all. Just some ditz at Wylder's beck and call. A "groupie." I restrained a shudder.

That hulking thug of his. Did they mean Kaige? I couldn't see anyone describing Gideon or Rowan as hulking or a thug. They thought Kaige—flirty, laid-back Kaige—had killed some dude named the Titan or Titus?

Axel let out a huff. "I hear you. Hopefully Ezra will too when he gets back. By now, the kid should be more careful about who he lets into his quarters."

They walked away, and I realized I'd been scrubbing a spot that was already clean for the last minute. I paused, catching my breath.

Either those assholes were wrong... or Kaige was the kind of guy who'd murder one of his own colleagues. I'd better keep that in mind—and be a little more careful how I dealt with Mr. Flirtatious going forward.

6

Mercy

By the time I was done, my shoulders were aching, my bandaged wound burning, and the weariness seemed to have sunk into my bones. It wasn't as if I'd gotten the best of sleep last night. As I straightened up and stretched, my back protested. I collapsed on the sofa that I'd just finished wiping off.

I looked down at my borrowed T-shirt. I'd gotten water splashed on it, bits of debris were sticking to it, and I was pretty sure the stink from the room had sunk right through it all the way to my skin. I needed a shower, stat.

I gave the room one last look before I left. The carpet was unmarked, if a bit damp, and all the furniture clean, the garbage bags set to the side since I didn't know where they went. I couldn't see any reason for Wylder to complain. No, I enjoyed imagining the smirk falling off his face when he realized I'd handled it all without faltering once.

As I climbed up the stairs, Gideon stalked right past me, his eyes glued to his tablet screen. I was abruptly aware of just how tightly—and kind of see-through-ly—my shirt was clinging to my chest. I folded my arms over the most questionable spots, and the movement drew his gaze.

He glanced at my arms over my chest and then at my face, with a distant air as if he wasn't totally sure who I was. Without speaking, he walked on. Alrighty then. It wasn't as if I needed his attention.

The bathroom Kaige had shown me before contained a narrow but perfectly serviceable shower stall. I soaked under the steaming hot water for several minutes, rubbing the expensive-smelling soap someone had left in a cabinet all over me, until I was sure I'd gotten the last traces of grime off.

My bandage ended up soaked—oops. I peeled it off carefully and examined the stitched-up flesh underneath. The line of the gunshot wound glared starkly red against my pale skin, but a scab was already forming along it. I dug through the drawers until I found a half-empty tube of antiseptic and a roll of gauze, smeared most of the rest of the tube over the wound, and then wrapped a few layers of gauze around my arm. That'd have to do.

I grimaced, tugging my still-grimy shirt back over my head, but when I returned to the guest bedroom Wylder had set me up in, a fresh tee and sweats lay on the bed. I looked around, but there wasn't anybody here.

The only people who might have noticed the state of my clothes were those leering jerks who'd been talking smack about Wylder and Kaige... and Gideon. Had he sent someone to make sure I had something halfway decent to wear? The thought that he'd have bothered was flattering and uncomfortable at the same time. I didn't like accepting favors any more than Wylder liked giving them out.

Too often, it turned out there were strings attached.

Since I'd fled the restaurant last night, I'd been living moment to moment. I had to start thinking more clearly about the future. And part of that meant figuring out how to take care of myself so Wylder wouldn't have any grounds to call me a burden.

As I changed into the clean clothes, I moved my engagement ring and the cocaine-scented fifties from one pocket to another. The sight of the ring made my jaw clench, but Kaige was right. I'd left my purse behind in the restaurant; everything else I owned was in the Katz house that Colt would have thoroughly swept by now. This was the only thing of value I had left, so I had to use it. It'd definitely give me enough cash to buy plenty of essentials so I wasn't relying on Noble charity or scavenging drug money.

There was just one thing I couldn't replace with cash. I'd find a way to get that back as soon as I could. The fifties should even pay my way. The rest... The less I thought about my old life, the better.

My stomach rumbled. It had to be way past lunch, and I'd recovered enough from the stink to rediscover my appetite.

I made my way back to the kitchen without running into any of the guys. Sighing with relief, I headed for the fridge. I wouldn't be surprised if Wylder walked in and demanded I get started on his next task for me. If I didn't get anything into my stomach first, I'd probably hit him in his stupidly perfect face.

I found some leftover pasta in the refrigerator and put it in the microwave to heat. While I waited, a girl I vaguely remembered from the party walked in. It was the blonde who'd been shimmying on the edge of the pool table I'd just cleaned.

The look on her face was of absolute fury. As she came to a stop in front of me, planting her hands on her hips, I could feel the venom coming off her in waves. How the hell could she hate me that much when I had no idea who she even was?

"What the fuck are you doing here?" she demanded.

I blinked at her innocently. "What do you mean?"

She sneered. "I mean *here*. In this kitchen, in this house. You were at the party last night, weren't you? Why didn't you leave? Do you want me to show you the way out?"

"As a matter of fact, I'm a guest," I said.

She looked down at my modest T-shirt and smirked. Her own deep V-neck top was skintight and dipped practically to her nipples. "If you're going to try and seduce the guys, that's not going to work."

I rolled my eyes. "Good thing I have no interest in seducing them then."

She scowled. "I know girls like you. But trust me, they don't last here very long."

What exactly was her problem? "I don't give a flying fuck about what you think of me," I said. "You're welcome to try to kick me out, but somehow I think you'll find yourself *knocked* out instead. Give it a shot."

The girl gaped at me in disbelief. The microwave pinged, announcing my food was ready. I dipped into the slightest of mocking curtsies. "Now if you will excuse me..."

I tried to move toward the microwave, but she blocked my path. "No way."

Annoyance crept in. She was wasting my time—and getting between me and my food. I'd dealt with plenty of girls like her all through high school: all talk, no action. If she really wanted a fight, I was happy to give her one. But I didn't think she'd enjoy the result.

"You're blocking my way," I said coolly.

"Oh yeah? What are you going to do about it?" Her voice had grown increasingly high-pitched through our short conversation. And man, she was standing so close to me I could smell her strong perfume. How much of that crap had she doused herself with?

I shrugged. "Oh, I don't know. Maybe I should ask your boyfriend why you're so obsessed with defending his honor. Which one of them is it? I mean, you must be dating at least one of them if you're getting this worked up about it, right?"

Her expression twitched. With savage satisfaction, I knew I had hit a nerve.

The girl got right up to my face, her straw-pale hair swinging, spit practically flying at me. "I protect what's mine. And I don't let any bitch just walk in here and pretend she knows what she's doing. So you better take the fuck off with that attitude or else..."

Instead of finishing her threat, she poked me on my arm, right over my bullet wound. I winced at the needle of pain that shot through the muscle.

I balled my fists at my side. "Wrong move, bitch."

I was about to punch the living daylights out of her, consequences be damned, when a voice spoke from behind me. "Gia, back off."

The girl who was apparently named Gia looked toward the door and faltered. "Oh. I was just— Wylder wouldn't want her—"

Rowan ambled into the room, his expression mild. "Wylder knows she's here. He told her she could stay, for now." Had an edge come into his voice with those words? "Do you want to take it up with him?"

Gia stepped away from me. "I don't trust her. You can tell him that. I've met enough girls to know trouble when I see it."

"Right now I'm pretty sure you're the one making the trouble," Rowan said. "Get out of here, and leave Mercy alone."

His voice stayed casual, but there was a hint of steel underneath it that I'd never heard before. Whether because of his own authority or simply his association with Wylder, Gia shut her mouth. She gave me one last look and surreptitiously flipped me off before scampering out of the kitchen.

Rowan stopped in the middle of the room as if he thought it was better not to get any closer to me. "Gia's a bitch to pretty much everybody who isn't Wylder," Rowan said. "It's nothing personal. She's annoying but mostly harmless."

Was he seriously trying to make conversation? After everything that had happened? "Thanks for the tip," I replied with dripping sarcasm and returned to my meal.

I expected him to leave, but he stayed there, watching me take the plate of pasta out of the microwave. I set it on the island and found a fork, but I couldn't just dig in with him as an audience. "*What?*"

"I didn't say anything," Rowan said, but he stepped closer. His eyes were hooded, his expression almost unreadable.

For a second, I found myself searching for the guy I'd known all those years ago, the boy with eyes that sparkled the moment they found mine in the crowded hall of the high school and the easy smile grazing his lips that made me want to know everything about him. How much of him was left under that nonchalant façade he was putting on?

How much of him had ever been real to begin with?

"If you don't want anything, you could let me eat in peace," I said.

He snorted. "Is that what you came here for? To find *peace*?"

"You know why I'm here. Why *you're* here, I don't have a clue. But frankly, I don't care. So run off to your master, since we both know you never gave a shit about me."

His eyes flashed, but I forced myself to focus on my food, jabbing a piece of penne with a little more force than was strictly required. I'd eat, and then I'd get out of here if he wouldn't.

"I only came in because I saw how Gia was going at you," Rowan said after a moment.

"I wasn't worried about Gia," I said. "So if you're waiting for a thank you, it's not coming. I was handling her by myself just fine, and I most definitely didn't need your help."

"Right," Rowan said in a voice that held far too much meaning. "Because Mercy Katz never needs *anyone's* help."

I glared at him, but images from the seventh-grade field trip when we first started talking rose up in my mind despite my best intentions.

My classmates hadn't known everything about my father, but they'd gotten enough of the gist over the years to be nervous of me—and resentful of the fact that I made them nervous. At the museum that day, someone had dared me to climb inside an antique wardrobe. Refusing to show any fear had mattered more to me than the fear I had very definitely been feeling.

As soon as I'd climbed inside, they'd jammed something to hold the door shut. I could still remember the snickering, the footsteps fading away, and the expanding realization that I was trapped, in the dark, just like—

The walls had begun to close in on me. No amount of shoving got me out, and after what felt like an hour, I curled into a ball, muttering to myself to try to hold back the terror sinking its talons into my mind. I'd been crouched there, shaking, when the door had yanked open and a head topped with ash-blond hair had appeared in front of me.

Rowan had come to the junior high from a different elementary school. I'd barely noticed him before. But when I couldn't stop rocking, he'd squeezed in there with me, grasped my hand, and talked about all the ridiculous things he could say about the kids who'd locked me in until my panic attack receded.

I'd never trusted anyone at school before. Never really trusted *anyone*, full stop. But Rowan... Rowan had convinced me he was worth it.

And then he'd thrown all my loyalty and love in my face.

Rowan took another step toward me, the movement bringing me back to the present. There was something in his eyes, a low kindling fire, one that might have been anger or desire or both.

"You shouldn't be here," he said, his voice low.

"Really?" I said. "And who the fuck are you to tell me what I should or shouldn't do?"

He flinched. As if *I'd* hurt him. Me, the one who'd given him everything from my first kiss to my virginity. The one who'd spilled all my darkest secrets to him, always expecting him to run away, more reassured every time he didn't. I'd thought his love meant I was more than just my father's daughter, a worthless girl.

But he'd run away after all. He had no claim on me now, no right to try to tell me anything about how to live my life. He'd thrown that away when he threw *me* away.

"It's for your own good, Mer," he said.

"My good or yours?" I stood up, my food forgotten. I'd lost my appetite.

Rowan's eye swept down my body and then up again as if he'd been looking for something he hadn't found. Like him, I'd changed too, a lot of it in ways he couldn't see.

"This isn't going to end well," he said finally.

I snorted. Yeah, it was definitely himself he was worried about. What did my being here cost him? "What are you so afraid of?"

"I'm not afraid," he snapped. "Not anymore."

What did he mean by that?

Fuck it, it didn't matter. I didn't have to play his games. I brushed past him. "You just don't want to deal with the fact that I'm here or to face up to what you did all those years ago."

"That isn't true," he said as I headed for the door. "I did what had to be done. I don't feel any regret."

My heart stuttered at his words. It turned out Rowan Finlay still had the ability to hurt me.

When I didn't speak, he kept going. "Walk away from all of this. Your dad is gone; you can start fresh. Maybe this is a good thing for you, just what you needed."

He had some fucking nerve. "My freedom shouldn't have come at the cost of innocent lives. Besides, you lost any right to give me advice when you vanished on me." I spun to face him again. "I never had a normal life, and I never expected to get one. Who says I'd want one anyway?"

I turned on my heel and stalked out of the kitchen.

Kaige

I COULDN'T SLEEP. AGAIN. OF COURSE, THAT MIGHT have had something to do with my drinking habits. The staff kept the mini fridge in my bedroom well-stocked with energy drinks, and I was in the habit of guzzling them throughout the day whenever I had the urge. My last one had been just before dinner, and a restless buzz was still tickling through my veins.

At least it was a pleasant night to be up. A warm summer breeze licked over me where I lay swinging in the hammock tied between the trunks of two of the biggest trees around the side of the Noble mansion. Crickets chirped in an erratic melody. A smattering of stars and a half-moon peeked between the leaves overhead. Ridiculously peaceful. Maybe I'd manage to drift off for an hour or two right here.

The shadows around the edge of the house shifted, catching my attention. I sat up slowly, my eyes narrowing, my instincts kicking into gear. The unmistakable form of a body darted past the shrubs lining the front walk. Was somebody trying to break in?

But no—the figure was headed away from the house. Whoever it was moved stealthily, folding into the shadows so deftly that if any of the men who patrolled the grounds at night had looked that way, they must have missed it. Interesting. A worthy opponent.

I smiled to myself, all possibility of sleep vanishing under a jolt of adrenaline. I hadn't had a mission in weeks, and honestly I'd been dying for an assignment. I missed the rush that came with it, but Wylder had me keeping a low profile after what had happened with Titus. He didn't want to give anyone the chance to accuse me of screwing up a job until my name was cleared.

I clenched my teeth at the thought. I didn't care about proving anything to anybody except him, but it would be nice if people didn't think I went around murdering my colleagues—no matter how much of a prick they were—for no good reason.

Tracking the figure's movement, I stayed still on the hammock. When the person dashed from the bushes toward the brick wall that framed the sides and back of the yard, I squinted to get a better look.

It was a woman. Her hair was tied back in a braid, and she was wearing clothes that covered all of her body except her arms, but there was no missing the shape of the perky mounds on her chest outlined against the faint moonlight.

I was so arrested by that delightful sight that it took me a second to recognize who it was.

Mercy Katz cast a glance up and down the road before jogging out of sight past the wall. Huh. Where was the Claws' princess heading in such a hurry and so secretly? I got to my feet, itching to find out.

I couldn't deny that Mercy had caught my eye the moment she had walked into the party, her chin raised, fearless and demanding Wylder's attention. There weren't many people in this county who'd talk to the heir to the Nobles that way. Most of the women around here started babbling or simpering the second he was in their vicinity. If I hadn't respected the guy so much, I might have found it annoying. But hey, there was always plenty of action for me too.

Loping after Mercy, I reached toward my phone. Should I alert Wylder that his "Kitty Cat" was on the prowl? Maybe she'd given up all hope of him joining her revenge plan after all. I wouldn't really have blamed her after the mind-numbing chores he'd been putting her up to. Just today, he had made her pull out the weeds in the back lawn using just her hands. I shook my head, my mouth twitching with amusement when I remembered the death glare she'd shot his way.

But she'd followed through, as gorgeous and defiant as ever. She seemed pretty serious about proving herself.

What if all that had been for show, and she had ulterior motives after all? She could be sneaking off to meet some co-conspirator.

After a moment's debate, I left my phone in my pocket and continued after her. I'd look like an idiot if I raised the alarm for no reason, and half of Ezra Noble's staff saw me as an idiot already. Anyway, I'd find out more if I saw where she went first.

And a chase would be more fun.

Around the fence, I caught sight of her farther down the street, heading toward the corner. I hustled after her, setting my feet as quietly as I could and keeping close to the trees at the edge of the neighbors' lawns so she wouldn't notice me.

It was harder to hang back far enough heading down the steep slope that led to the busy downtown streets below the hill. I let Mercy get more of a lead, but my gaze never left her.

Just as she reached the bottom, where traffic was whizzing by, she raised her hand. My muscles started to tense with the thought that she might have had plans to meet someone behind our backs, but a moment later, a striped car pulled up to the curb. She'd only been flagging a cab.

Of course, that cab could be taking her somewhere Wylder would want to know about. As she popped into the back seat, I hustled the rest of the way down the hill.

Thankfully, there were plenty of taxis cruising around downtown at this time of night, hunting for bar-goers who needed a safe ride home. I spotted one about to zip right by me and dove into the street in front of it.

The tires screeched, the hood tapping my thighs as it just barely stopped without knocking me over. I grinned at the driver through the windshield, my adrenaline spiking just the way I liked it.

"Y-you almost died," the cabbie stammered.

"But I didn't." I bounded around to dive into the back. "I need a ride. Follow that yellow-and-green taxi that just stopped at the lights up ahead. I'll pay you double if you step on it."

Money could grease plenty of wheels. The driver got over his shock just like that, and in moments we were rumbling after Mercy without her any the wiser.

To my surprise, Mercy's taxi headed out of the city and into the Bend. Wouldn't Colt's men be on the hunt for her there? My suspicions prickling to the surface again, I leaned forward in the seat as if I could figure out Mercy's intentions if I stared at the car hard enough. What was she doing walking back to the den of the tiger?

Wylder didn't bother doing much business directly in the Bend, but I was pretty sure the part we'd ended up in was former Claws' territory. Mercy's taxi stopped in a residential neighborhood, and I asked my cabbie to pull over at the other end of the street. After handing him a wad of cash, I got out and covered the rest of the distance on foot.

Mercy had disappeared into the backyard of a big brick house farther down by the corner. I frowned, venturing closer. Movement flickered in the shadows, and then suddenly she was bounding off the high branch of an oak tree onto a second-floor balcony.

All right, so the girl had some climbing skills. She was part-cat after all.

Smirking, I stayed in the shadows to watch. She landed on the balcony railing so lightly I couldn't hear the impact and sprang toward the door there without hesitation. From the looks of it, she'd done this a million times. With a quick jiggle of the handle, she disappeared inside the house.

I eased into the yard. The house looked empty, no lights on, no vehicles in the driveway. An obvious explanation occurred to me—and was confirmed a moment later when I spotted a beefy guy lurking by a car on the other side of the cross-street in front of the house.

No one was home, but the place was under surveillance. Why had Mercy figured it was worth the risk of coming back here?

But she'd managed it without the heavies staked out in front noticing her. After about fifteen minutes, she reappeared and launched herself back onto the tree. I couldn't see exactly how she made it down. Stepping back against the hedge next door, I let her hustle past me, a leaf she hadn't noticed snagged in her dark hair. Then I stalked after her, a smile curling my lips in anticipation.

Probably looking for a busier spot where she could hail another cab, she set off at a brisk pace. After a couple of blocks, I figured we were far enough from the house to avoid the notice of what I assumed were Steel Knights sentries.

With several swift strides, I caught up to her, tucking my hand around her elbow as I reached her. "Well, fancy running into you here."

She startled, slamming her hand against my chest before her gaze had found mine. Recognition lit there, followed by a mixture of wariness and irritation. Not exactly the response I'd want to provoke in her, but we could work on that.

"Fuck, you scared the living daylights out of me," she hissed, jerking her arm out of my grasp. "What are you doing here?"

Still smiling, I stepped closer, forcing her back against the wooden fence of the nearest yard. I set one hand on either side of her, just an inch from her shoulders. Her eyes darted to the side, and I could see her calculating her chances of escape: very slim.

I hadn't been quite this close to her before. Her scent hit my nose, like some kind of wildflowers that had caught on fire. Pretty and fierce at the same time. Perfect for the woman in front of me.

"I should be asking you that," I said casually. "You came to the Nobles for help. Of course your movements are going to be monitored, especially when you leave the house in the middle of the night like some kind of thief."

She scowled at me. "I had no idea that place had become my prison or that I wasn't allowed to leave."

"I wouldn't say it's a prison, but we have to take precautions. A lot of people would like a piece of the Nobles." I cocked a brow at her. "Why on Earth would you come back to the Bend in the middle of the night when somebody is trying to assassinate you? Whatever brought you here must be nothing short of world-ending."

"It's none of your fucking business," she spat out.

I leaned closer. "I think it *is* my business. You made it mine when you came to us for help."

Mercy huffed in response, but I could see her pupils dilating. She shifted, visibly swallowing, her body just inches from mine. Was that a tiny tremor running through those delicious curves?

My grin widened. "Does the kitten like to be dominated?"

"Fuck you," Mercy said, but she didn't make any move to struggle. My hands slid down the fence, brushing the sides of her arms, and her breath caught just slightly. Ah ha. She might be pissed off about that, but she liked it too.

I resisted the urge to see how she'd react if I trailed my fingers over the mounds now straining against the thin fabric of her T-shirt. As much as I was enjoying the moment, I did have a job to do. "Now tell me, what are you doing here? Or do I need to haul you back to Wylder and let him ask the questions?"

At first she didn't answer. My hands skimmed down to the level of her waist, and I gave into the impulse to splay my fingers over the sides of her full hips. She tipped toward me just a bit before reining her response in. Jesus Christ, this girl was built generously in all the right places.

"So, hauling it is?" I said, both teasing and serious.

"We don't have to bring anyone else into this," she bit out. "I was just stopping by my house—or at least, what was my house. I had something there I wasn't willing to leave behind."

"Didn't we talk about this? You don't need to stick

your neck into harm's way—just use that bastard's engagement ring to get whatever money you need."

She grimaced. "There are some things money can't buy, you know." She was quiet for a beat before she rummaged in her pocket and then held up something in her hand. I inspected it under the moonlight. It was a silver bracelet, too tiny to fit Mercy's wrist and cheap-looking—the kind you'd give a kid. The words *Little Angel* were engraved into the plate clasped to the chain.

I blinked at her with genuine confusion. "You risked your life for *that*?"

Mercy stuffed it back into her pocket with a scowl. "I don't expect you to understand. My mother gave it to me. It's all I have left of her."

I stared at her for a few seconds, and she didn't flinch away from my gaze. She was telling the truth. I took a step back, giving her a bit of space, a twinge of guilt running through my stomach.

I'd been playing around, trying to provoke her, when this whole expedition meant a hell of a lot more to her than I could have guessed. Now I felt like an ass.

Silence stretched between us. I groped for words and said the first thing that came to mind. "I do understand."

She snorted. "Right."

"No, really. I—I didn't have the greatest relationship with my dad, but I've still worn his dog tags since the day he died."

Her gaze dropped to my chest. "Are they invisible dog tags?"

I glowered at her. "No. I fucking lost them

somewhere a couple of months ago. But until then—
Anyway, the point is I get it. If I knew where they were,
even if it was behind enemy lines, I'd go for them too."

Her tone softened but stayed wry. "Maybe you
should look harder then."

I didn't like the direction this conversation was
going in. I'd wanted to get under her skin, not the other
way around. I took another step away and raised my
chin toward the road. "Let's head back before people
start questioning where you went."

Her eyebrows arched, but her tone turned hesitant.
"You're not going to rat me out?"

I laughed. "Do you want me to?"

She shook her head, looking unconvinced.

"Come on, let's get some sleep. Not together of
course. I mean, unless you really beg." I added the last
part with a chuckle, and she punched me in the arm.

"Fat chance of that," she muttered, but right then, I
knew I was going to find a way to have her.

8

Mercy

A SCRAP OF THE CURTAIN BEING JERKED ASIDE WAS followed by a blare of sunlight on my closed eyelids. I groaned, shielding my face against the sudden brightness, and rolled over on the bed.

When I looked up, I found myself staring right into Wylder's striking green eyes. He was leaning over me, his face just inches from mine. At the sight, I woke up completely, with a jolt that made me hit my head hard against the headboard. I winced.

"What the hell do you think you're doing?" I snarled, rubbing the sore spot.

"You seem to have forgotten, so I'll politely remind you. This is my house." Wylder offered a lazy smirk and stepped back. "If you don't enjoy my hospitality, you're welcome to shack up somewhere else overnight."

I made a face at him. "I don't exactly have anywhere else to go." Not even my own house really belonged to me anymore, not with Steel Knights thugs staked out on the street outside. "And shouldn't you be happy to have me at your beck and call?"

The edge in my voice didn't appear to faze Wylder at all. If anything, his smirk widened. "Oh, don't worry, I am."

"Rise and shine," Kaige declared from behind him. Before I knew what was happening, he'd scooped me right out from under the covers and up into his arms. As he carried me toward the door, I squirmed in his arms, twisting this way and that until his grip loosened.

Landing a solid kick, I spun from his hold and onto my feet—a little too easily considering his bulk. Annoyed by the suspicion that he'd let me win and by that cocky grin he was now aiming at me, I shook a fist at him. "Try to carry me off again and the next thing getting carried will be your ass into a morgue."

A laugh exploded out of him. That wasn't the reaction I'd been going for. "You'll think it's less funny when you find out how serious I am," I informed him.

Wylder tsked. "Careful, the kitty cat hasn't been declawed after all."

I bristled all over again. "Don't call me that."

Wylder just kept smirking. "Come on, you've made us late for breakfast. And I, for one, am absolutely starving."

I followed them to the kitchen where Gideon and Rowan were waiting, talking to Anthea. Rowan was wearing one of what seemed to be his usual suits, looking overdressed next to all the other guys in their jeans and casual button-ups.

Gideon had a cup of coffee in his hand, stroking the handle as if he was protective of it. His tongue flicked out over the silver ring that protruded from one side of his lower lip. I couldn't help tracking the movement. There was something weirdly sensual about it that provoked a response I didn't entirely like low in my belly. Even with his bizarre blue hair and cool eyes, Gideon was just as good-looking as the others in a remote, alien sort of way.

I looked up to see Anthea observing me like a hawk and quickly averted my gaze.

There was nothing cooking on the stove yet. Even though I was wary of her, Anthea was a damn good chef, and the thought of her French toast was making my mouth water. I glanced around. "What's for breakfast?"

"I don't know," Wylder said. "Why don't you tell us, since you're the one cooking today?"

I took a few steps back. Abso-fucking-lutely not. "I can't cook. At all." That wasn't technically true. I had to make myself food all the time, but only basics like a PB&J sandwich. No way was I up to Anthea's level. And I could just tell she'd jump on any reason to criticize my efforts.

Wylder shrugged. "Too bad. You're going to today. So, chop, chop. Get to it."

I suppressed a sigh. The ache in my fingers after the many weeds I'd yanked out of the lawn yesterday were all the reminder I needed that what Wylder wanted, Wylder got—unless *I* wanted to forget my whole revenge plan and spend the rest of my life in hiding, stewing ineffectually over Colt's betrayal. Fuck.

Well, if he didn't like my breakfast, he'd have no one to blame but himself, now would he?

I reluctantly stepped behind the stove, even grabbing a polka-dotted apron that was hanging from a hook on the wall. Everything in the kitchen seemed so harmless and homely, it almost didn't feel that it belonged in a house belonging to Ezra Noble, the gang boss revered by everybody in Paradise Bend.

"I think I want bacon," Wylder said after he seemed to ponder over it for a few seconds. "What about you, Kaige?"

The brawny asshole grinned with a gleam in his eyes that suggested he was remembering our secret adventure last night. At least it seemed like he'd kept his mouth shut about that like he'd said he would. He tapped his chin cheekily. "I like the sound of an onion and cheese omelet."

"I've already eaten," Anthea said with a hint of disdain.

Gideon didn't bother looking up from his coffee. "Whatever they're having. Food is just fuel."

"I thought *I* was deciding what's for breakfast," I said. "Who said anything about taking orders?"

"Rowan?" Wylder asked, ignoring me.

Rowan shrugged. "Bacon and eggs works for me too."

Somehow it irritated me that he hadn't asked for anything else, like he was trying to cut me a break I hadn't asked for. Gritting my teeth, I stomped over to the fridge and retrieved an onion, a block of cheese, a carton of eggs, and a package of bacon. I knew at least enough to figure out that the onion should go in first.

I found a cutting board and a knife and started chopping away. It took all of three seconds before my eyes stung with tears.

Wylder stepped up behind me. "That's not how you do it."

I scowled. "Will you let me work?"

Wylder smiled, feigning innocence. "I'm just trying to be helpful, since you said you weren't much of a cook and all."

I nearly rolled my eyes out of my head. "No thanks. I'm sure I can figure it out on my own."

The asshole reached for my hand anyway. For one instant, I thought he would pry the knife right out of my hand. Instead, his fingers curled around mine over the handle. A thrum ran through my body as his strong hand flexed, adjusting his grip, holding me in place with his other hand settling on my waist. Warmth washed through me all down my side.

"I don't think you can, Kitty Cat," he said in a sexy, bossy voice that left me breathless despite myself. My insides clenched. He was trying to take charge... and I kind of wanted to let him, damn it.

From the corner of my eye, I noticed Rowan straightening up to get a closer look. When I glanced at him, daring him to say something, he went back to fiddling with a delivery menu someone had left on the island.

Wylder's breath tickled hot down my neck. "I think

I need to teach you how to chop up onions nicely. You see, cooking is an art."

I contained the shiver that ran down my spine at his proximity. I wanted to turn around and shove him away, while another insane part of me had the urge to pull him even closer just so I could soak up all of his heat.

"If you don't create the perfect base, nothing you make is going to taste good." As he spoke, he directed my hands back to the cutting board and slowly chopped the first few slices, his actions almost sensual. I bit my lip as his hips brushed mine. He practically had me locked in an embrace. His leather-and-brandy scent filled my nose, and I might have leaned into him just the slightest bit—

Wylder stepped away with a sly look on his face that I wanted to smack right off it. "See, not that hard, right?"

I glared at him. He knew exactly what he'd been doing to me. Still grinning, he took a seat on the kitchen island next to Kaige, who was watching me appreciatively.

"I could get used to seeing you in an apron," the bigger guy said.

I waved the knife at him. "In your dreams, maybe."

Once the onions were sizzling, I cracked the eggs one by one, trying to remember how I'd seen my grandma cook for me whenever I went to her house. I was aware of everybody's stare on my back—especially Kaige's, whose hot gaze made my stomach knot. Anthea seemed to be studying my every move as if she were going to write a report on my performance.

Rowan and Gideon stayed in the periphery. Any time my gaze slipped over Rowan, he was scowling almost as if he was annoyed to be there, spinning a pen between his fingers.

After I'd beaten the eggs with a fork, I rummaged in the kitchen cabinets, searching for the pepper and salt. Then I scrambled to turn down the heat, since the onions were quickly heading from lightly browned to blackened. I'd never hear the end of it if I burned this meal.

"For somebody who doesn't know how to cook, you're doing it quite well," Anthea observed dryly. I didn't quite know what to make of her. I definitely didn't get friendly vibes from her.

Somehow I didn't think she meant her words as a compliment. It was hard not to wonder what tricks she had up her sleeve that were deadlier than her little truth serum. "Thanks," I muttered.

As I started to toss the eggs in the pan, Kaige took a deep sniff of the air. "Smells great."

"It's just onions and eggs."

"With a hint of you," he said with a wink. "That's what makes it better."

A smile tugged at my lips despite myself. First Wylder was getting to me, then Kaige—what the hell was wrong with me? I wiped the smile off my face, replacing it with a frown.

These guys were my potential allies—nothing more than that. They sure as hell weren't my friends. I'd been slaving away for the past two days without much sign of anything changing.

When the omelet was done, I scraped it onto plates in four portions. Then I popped several strips of bacon onto the pan. Feeling pleased with how well I'd stayed on top of things so far, I threw a few pieces of bread into the toaster oven for good measure.

Anthea came around the counter to inspect me. I pushed the bacon around the pan with the spatula, trying to fry it as evenly as possible. That was the goal, right? If I remembered right, Grandma's trick had been to hold the pan a bit higher than the flame and then toss it with a flick of her wrist.

I grasped the handle, but for a moment the memory of my grandmother in her kitchen gripped me so vividly I couldn't move. A burning sensation crept up through my chest to the back of my eyes.

Before I could get a hold of myself, Anthea brushed past me, her shoulder hitting mine. The force of it made me stumble. A few drops of hot oil splashed into my skin. I hissed in pain and almost dropped the pan.

I shoved it back onto the stove and flipped on the tap. The cool water washed over the stinging of the much more literal burn, making me wince.

"I'm sorry, I didn't realize you were so distracted," Anthea said, not looking even a little bit apologetic. No way had that been an accident. She'd been trying to screw with me. What had I done to her to make her hate my guts?

Rowan was on his feet, but he stayed by the island as Kaige, who'd also hopped up, offered me a towel to dab at my sensitive skin.

"Thanks, but I'm fine," I said, keeping my voice even.

"You need ice?" Kaige asked.

Wylder yawned. "Didn't you hear her? She said she's fine. I think you burnt the bacon, Kitty Cat."

What an absolute asshole. I immediately switched off the stove and worked at prying up the over-fried bits of the bacon.

"I'm starving. Serve the breakfast," Wylder ordered as if it wasn't his aunt's fault I'd gotten sidetracked. When I glared at him, he raised his eyebrows. "What are you waiting for?"

I turned away. I couldn't let his heckling bother me. Nothing that happened here mattered as long as it led to Colt getting crushed under an onslaught of Noble rage.

I slapped the plates down on the island in front of each of the guys and stepped away, grabbing a piece of toast and slathering peanut butter on it for myself. Wylder pretended to gnaw on a particularly difficult piece of bacon. "I've had better."

"It's not totally awful for a beginner," Kaige offered with a smile.

Rowan looked a little pained, which might have been because of my presence or his feelings about my cooking. Gideon wolfed everything down between delicate sips of his beloved coffee without a word. At least the food appeared to have been edible.

Just as they were finishing up, the big guy with the shaved head who'd hassled me while I was cleaning two days ago appeared at the door. He was carrying a lit cigarette on his lips which he slowly took a drag of.

A cloud of annoyance appeared on Wylder's face. "You know no one's supposed to smoke in here, Axel."

"Says who?" Axel asked with a challenge in his voice. "This isn't your part of the house."

Wylder remained unfazed. "The rule is no smoke around me and my men, *anywhere* in *my* house. If you're in the mood for criticizing, why don't we talk about how you still haven't gotten Trent back in line?"

Axel muttered a curse and threw the cigarette to the floor, where he crushed the butt with his shoe. Instead of leaving, he stepped farther into the kitchen.

"You're one to talk. What have you done to solve the issue?" The older man's gaze fell on me. "Meanwhile you're letting strangers walk all over the house."

"Why should I do your work for you?" Wylder said. "And she's here for a reason. As a matter of fact—" A slow smile came over his face. "It might be your lucky day after all. I know just the way I'm going to fix that little problem."

I eyed him, already knowing he was going to drag me into some new scheme I wasn't going to like. He grinned back at me. "How'd you like to get out of the house for a bit, Princess?"

"To do what, exactly?"

"Patience, patience. All will become clear." He stood up. "Stay here and clean up while I get the details sorted out."

Just like that, he walked out of the kitchen, beckoning

for the other three guys to follow him. Prick. I aimed my middle finger at his retreating back. Kaige chuckled, but he left his plate on the island like the others did as they all headed out at their boss's bidding. Anthea shot me one last narrow look and stalked after them.

Axel's phone rang, and he walked to the far corner to talk in a low voice. I liked his company even less than the others', but whatever.

When I went to grab the plates, my hand stopped over the flyer Rowan had been toying with. He'd been doodling on it too. A little pen sketch had expanded the flower logo for the restaurant into a whole garden of blooms trailing around the border.

He'd always been so good at drawing. Apparently a few things hadn't changed. Before I could second-guess the impulse, I snatched up the flyer and folded it into my pocket.

Instead of washing the dishes, I just dumped them in the sink and ran some water over them. Let Wylder complain if he wanted to.

Axel ended his call and looked around the room, glaring at me as if annoyed that I was the only one left. "Where the hell did Wylder head off to?"

Did he think I was somehow the Noble heir's keeper? "I don't know. He said he'd be back." Of course, he hadn't mentioned whether whatever details he had to sort out would take minutes or hours. I wouldn't put it past him to leave me sitting here waiting for the rest of the day.

But looking at Axel, a light bulb went off inside my head. I needed all the information I could gather to get myself an edge around here, and he definitely knew a few things I'd be interested to hear more about.

People tended to say more if they figured you already knew what they were talking about. I forced a smile way sweeter than he deserved. "Hey, no hard feelings about the other day. I get how concerned you'd be about strangers after what happened to the Titan."

Axel's expression stayed wary, but he didn't bite my head off for bringing up the subject, which was a start. "What's it to you?" he growled.

"I just mean it's kind of hard for me not to worry when people are going around killing each other around here. Why the heck would Kaige go off on one of Ezra's own men?" I shook my head disapprovingly.

Axel didn't correct me, which meant my guess that he'd been talking about Kaige being the culprit was right. "Good question. Maybe you should ask the kid who's covering for him."

I tipped my head like the ditzy girl he no doubt saw me as. "As if Wylder's going to tell *me* what really went on. He obviously cares more about protecting his friends."

That remark seemed to hit the right spot. Axel let out a disgruntled sound. "It's clear as day who must have done it. Who else could have tossed Titus over the goddamn fire escape?"

So the Titan—or Titus—whatever his name was— had been thrown off the fire escape to his death? What a way to go. "Yeah," I said carefully, leaving space for him to fill in the blanks. "I mean, after all, Kaige is just so..."

"No one else could have overpowered him," Axel burst out. "The young guys and their stupid tempers— all riled up because Titus laid it to him straight about what the rest of us think of his 'boss.' Kaige practically killed him right then. Threatened to put him in a grave for daring to speak up, and guess what? He did."

Mercy

AXEL'S LAST WORDS HAD BARELY FADED FROM THE AIR when Wylder strode back into the kitchen. He glanced from me to Axel and frowned. "Having a little chat?"

"She's smarter than she looks," Axel said, nodding at me. I groaned internally. Obviously he was happy that I seemed to agree with his theories about Wylder and Kaige, but why the hell did he have to say that?

Now that he'd dropped that little bomb, Axel ambled out. I hoped at the next party he stepped in vomit *and* sat on someone's chair turd.

"I see you've made friends," Wylder said dryly.

I folded my arms in front of my chest. "So, what, I can't talk to people?"

"Talk to my men as much as you like. Axel is an idiot. But I'm guessing you could tell that. What were you hoping to get out of him, Kitty Cat?"

I swallowed hard. Wylder definitely wasn't an idiot,

no matter how big a prick he was. Or how big his prick probably was.

Focus, Mercy.

I couldn't tell him that I was asking questions about Kaige and how he was involved in this Titus guy's death. That was obviously a sore spot for him. I groped for the most obvious answer. "I was just asking him about your father. I haven't gotten to meet the old man yet, after all."

"He's out of town on business," Wylder said coolly. At the mention of his father, his eyes turned frosty. Okay, another sore spot. Clearly we had plenty of awful parents to go around between the two of us. No big surprise. If there was a Venn diagram of qualities that made for great gang leaders and fantastic fathers, the circles would barely overlap.

"Where did he go?" I asked.

"What's it to you?"

"I don't know. I figure if I'm asking for the Nobles' help, I should probably loop in the man in charge at some point."

Wylder snorted. "Trust me, you don't want to be anywhere near Ezra Noble. *If* I decide your cause is worthy, I'll handle that side of things. Forget about that for now. I have something for you."

I studied him suspiciously. "Does this have something to do with whatever new job you dreamed up for me?"

"So quick to catch on." Wylder stalked up to me like a tiger on the prowl, stopping just a little too close for my nerves—or my hormones—to stay quiet. "You're tired of cleaning duty, aren't you? Ready for some real action? Well, you're getting your wish. There's an important meeting in a couple of hours. I'll have a dress sent to your room. Wear it and be ready."

I scowled. Was he about to dress me up and parade me in front of people? "I'm not going to a party as your escort."

A laugh spilled out of him. "Trust me, Princess, that's not what I had in mind." With that he whirled around and left, leaving me seething. What was he up to this time?

I went back to the guest room and paced the length of it. Before long, somebody was knocking at my door. I threw it open to reveal the same woman who'd brought me the tee and sweats the first night. Today she had a sequined dress in her hands. Even without seeing it unfolded, I could tell it was absolutely hideous.

"Mr. Noble says to wear this," she said and thrust it and a cosmetics bag at me. Before I could ask any questions, she scurried away.

When I opened the bag, lipsticks, glitter, and mascara fell out of it. Despite Wylder's sarcastic assurance, this stuff definitely had an escort vibe. Holding up the dress to my frame, I shuddered. The thin strips of fabric would cover my nipples and crotch and not a whole lot else.

But he wanted me to say no. This was yet another test. I wasn't here to cater to my dignity, but to avenge all those bodies bleeding out on the restaurant floor.

I discarded my casual clothes, slipping my childhood bracelet and the flyer with Rowan's sketch out of the pants pocket. After a moment's hesitation, I tucked them both into the make-up bag, which was the closest thing I had to a purse. I didn't want to leave the bracelet out of my reach again, and the doodle, well... Call it silly, but there was something vaguely comforting about the idea that I hadn't been *totally* wrong about the guy I'd thought I'd been so close to.

Standing in front of the full-length mirror, I shimmied into the dress. When the silver of it caught the light, it gave a glow to my otherwise pale skin. Unfortunately, way too much of that skin for my liking was on display.

Might as well make the best of it. Aunt Renee had given me lessons in make-up until I'd been able to pull off the kind of look that could stop a man in his tracks, if that was what I was going for. These might not have been the exact cosmetic items I'd have picked, but I could work with them.

When I was done, I stepped back to inspect myself in the mirror again. With the deep red lipstick and my hair falling in loose waves across my shoulders, I could have given a lesser goddess a run for her money, if I did say so myself. Even the bandage around my upper arm looked almost like part of the costume. It was a fierce, avenging warrior goddess they'd get.

I smirked to myself. Wylder's intention of humiliating me was going to backfire on him big time.

Just then, the door burst open and Kaige strode in.

"We can't be late—" He broke off mid-sentence when his eyes landed on me. His feet stalled just inside the doorway, his jaw going slack. If I didn't know any better, I'd think I'd left him speechless.

I waved a hand in front of his face. "Earth to Kaige."

He blinked, and a smile crossed his face that was both sexy and predatory. "I don't know—from the looks of things, I've landed in heaven instead."

When I scoffed at the cheesy line, he walked right up to me. His fingers skimmed down my back, only just grazing my skin but leaving a trail of heat in their wake. Suddenly all sorts of parts of me were waking up in ways I didn't like. *That* wasn't how this was supposed to go.

Kaige tugged a lock of my hair, twisting it around his finger possessively. "You look...wow."

I shook off my body's reaction to him as well as I could. "Thanks."

He held up a pair of heels. "I brought shoes. If you don't like them, blame Wylder."

They were stilettos, the spikes at least three inches high and sharp as needles. Lovely. I made a face but took the shoes from him. Looking on the bright side, if somebody decided to get handsy with me, I could get in both a kick and a stabbing at the same time.

Thankfully I'd gotten in my practice with towering heels at my father's various formal events. When he bothered to bring me along, he wanted to be able to show me off. The heels clicked against the floor as I followed Kaige downstairs to the foyer where Wylder and Rowan—but not Gideon, I noted—were waiting. They looked up simultaneously.

Rowan's stance stiffened. Instead of looking at me, his gaze seemed to latch onto Kaige, whose hand had settled on my upper back. I was deeply aware of it, along with the other pair of eyes watching me.

Appreciation lit on Wylder's face, his gaze roving over me. He inspected every part of my body as if he could see right through my skin-tight dress.

"Look at that," he said in a husky voice. "Kitty Cat cleans up well."

A rush of pleasure climbed up my spine at his compliment. I clamped down on it, mentally cursing myself. I'd have been happier that I'd clearly struck the mark with him if my stupid body wasn't betraying me at the same time.

I walked toward the boys, flipping my hair behind me. "Here I am. What's the big event?"

Rowan turned toward the door, tearing his eyes away from me. "The people we're going to meet today will be mouthy and defiant. Talking nicely hasn't worked so far. This is going to take force. Are you sure you want in on this?"

Force? With me dressed like this? What the hell were we actually doing here?

But Rowan's tone made me raise my chin. All my life, I'd never backed down from anything. He knew it well. "Of course. I'm ready."

Wylder explained everything in his car. He drove a deep-blue Mustang, which even though it was obviously an older model was sleek and pristine. "Trent has been causing a lot of trouble lately. Your job will be to go in and rile him up, giving us an excuse to step in."

"What's he done?" I asked curiously.

"He hasn't paid his tithe," Kaige said from the seat

next to me. Wylder drove the car while Rowan sat beside him. "And he's been mouthing off, acting like he shouldn't have to pay tribute to the Nobles. We need to stamp out his little rebellion before others get ideas."

My father had a special room in our basement, made for people he wanted to punish. Old images flashed in my mind's eyes, souring my mouth.

Wylder was nodding. "You go in, ask for the money, and get him to lose his shit. He won't take you seriously—"

I rolled my eyes. "Why? Because I'm a woman?"

Wylder raised his eyebrows at me in the rearview mirror. "You're a woman, and you're dressed like a hooker. I think the second part is what'll really do the trick."

I glared at him and noticed Rowan watching me surreptitiously. The set of his mouth told me he was annoyed for some reason. I reached into the make-up on my lap and pulled out the doodled-on flyer.

Yeah, it reminded me that the boy I'd loved hadn't all been a lie, but right now I just wanted to get a reaction out of him.

I waved the paper carelessly. "Found this in the kitchen. Hey, Kaige, what's your favorite animal?"

Rowan turned fully in his seat, his jaw tightening even more as he must have recognized the paper. Kaige rubbed his square jaw, pretending to think hard. "I would have to go with a cat." He gave me an impish smile.

I rolled my eyes. "Something else."

"Fine. Can I say dragon, or are mythical creatures not allowed either?"

"I can do that." Making a few swift creases, I tore the flyer into a square. Rowan almost flinched. Just a doodle, but he didn't like me manhandling it, now did he?

"What are you—" he began, and then he seemed to catch on.

I deftly formed a series of folds, smoothed the sides to give it a final shape, and then held it up. "Ta-da!" I offered the origami dragon to Kaige.

"Damn, girl," he said, taking the fragile figure out of my hand. "You'll have to teach me how to do that."

"What will I get in return?"

He waggled his eyebrows. "Anything you want."

"It's a childish game," Wylder announced.

I wrinkled my nose at him. "Let's see you do it then."

He met my gaze in the mirror, and I had to keep myself from squirming at the look in his eyes. "I'm good at everything I do, so I'd imagine I could handle twisting around a bit of paper if I wanted to bother."

I had the itch to kick the back of his seat but controlled the flicker of anger. Instead of giving in to it, I leaned back into the seat. "So where are we headed?"

"People call it the Park," Rowan said tersely.

"And where is that?"

"It's the covered parking lot of a mall," Wylder filled in. "Trent and his main bunch like to hang out there. He's decided to make us come to him. We're going to make him regret that."

Right. And I was the bait. I held back a grimace and peered out the window. A question that'd been niggling at me ever since I'd come down to meet them rose up again. "Where's Gideon?"

Wylder's eyes narrowed. "Fights aren't his strong point. He doesn't normally come along for these kinds of jobs."

"The great Wylder Noble has someone on his team who can't hold his own in a brawl?" I said in mock disbelief.

"What Gideon can or can't do is none of your business," Wylder snapped as if I'd gravely offended him.

Kaige chuckled and ignored the evil eye Wylder shot at him. "Don't mind him. He's just over-protective. Gideon helps out plenty in his own way, with the computers and everything. He gets more done with his brains than I do with these guns." He flexed his biceps. "He's got a lung condition; it acts up if he pushes himself much physically."

"I did say it's none of her business," Wylder reminded him.

I remembered his grousing at Axel over the cigarette. "Is that why nobody's allowed to smoke in the house?"

"You're damn right." Wylder clenched the steering wheel harder. "I protect my own."

"We're here," Rowan announced with what sounded like trepidation.

We pulled into one of the empty parking spots in the lot. This end of the space clearly didn't get used much by your average mallgoer. A few abandoned cars stood sprawled across more than one spot, one missing a door, another with its roof dented in. Spray-painted graffiti mottled the concrete wall nearby. The sound of raucous voices carried from the other side of a couple of parked vans farther across the lot.

"Trent and his crew will be over there." Wylder pointed to the vans and then turned to me. "You know what you have to do?"

"It's not exactly a complex plan. Go in, ask Trent to pay up, listen to him insult me a bit, and then watch the three of you swoop in and kick his ass."

"Right," he said, a hint of sarcasm in his tone. "Trent isn't dangerous, but he thinks he is, which makes him a little unpredictable. So stick to that plan."

I glowered at him. "Like I said, I've got it."

Rowan jumped in. "The first sign of trouble, and you—"

I cut him off. "I *am* here to cause trouble, aren't I?"

Before any of them could lecture me more, I shook out my hair and pushed open the door. I was aware of the three pairs of eyes watching me in the closed space.

"See you boys later," I said as I stepped out of the car.

The guys followed me, moving more quietly. They'd hang back by the vans out of sight until they had all the excuse they needed to take their target down several pegs. I took brisk steps, my stilettos rapping away on the concrete.

The faint notes of hip-hop music drifted toward me.

The smells of cheap weed and cheaper beer saturated the air.

As I came around the vans, I found a loose circle with half a dozen guys in ripped jeans lounging in plastic chairs. A woman in a short dress was sitting on one man's lap, batting her eyelashes.

"Which one of you is Trent?" I demanded, jutting my hip out for good measure. If I was going to play a role, I'd damn well sell it.

I'd already guessed the leader of these goons was the dude with the goatee and the beer gut whose chair was just a little larger than the others. He looked me up and down with an open leer while a couple of the other guys let out whistles of approval. "That'd be me. What are you looking for, honey?"

As I sauntered over, I added a little sway to my stride. I planted myself right in front of him. His eyes lingered on all those gaps in the dress, his tongue slicking over his chapped lips with a lecherous grin. Ugh.

"I'm looking for money, Trent," I said, giving him a sickly-sweet smile. "You owe the Nobles quite a lot, and you haven't been paying up."

A rush of murmurs and a little laughter spread through the crowd. Trent scoffed at me. "And they sent *you* to collect it?"

"Damn right, they did. Now are you going to hand it over or what?" I made a grabby gesture with my hand.

"Forget it." Trent leaned back in his chair, propping his feet up on a crate. "I don't owe the Nobles shit. I'm my own man now."

I cocked my head. "I don't give a crap about your delusions of grandeur. I just want the money you owe. Now stop acting like a pussy and pay up."

That riled him up good. His eyes flashed, and the others fell silent. He kicked aside the crate and sprang to his feet. "Talk to me like that again, bitch, and you'll be the one having delusions."

I wondered if he had any idea what that even meant, because that threat hadn't made a whole lot of sense. I sighed. "Well, if you want to do this the hard way, that can be arranged. But are you sure you want me embarrassing you in front of your dickhead friends?"

One of the guys let out a grunt of protest. Trent held up his hand, openly seething. "What exactly do you think *you're* going to do, you trumped-up whore?"

I let another smile, much sharper, cross my lips. "Let's not get to that. Imagine what your master will say if he hears that one of his lapdogs has forgotten who's in charge? If that ego inflates any more, your head might explode."

"I'm not a lapdog," Trent roared. He reached into his jeans, and before I could blink, he was pointing a gun at me. "You're going to die, bitch."

Did he think he was the first man to ever aim a pistol at me? I eyed it calmly, my pulse only stuttering momentarily.

I could handle this. I'd faced so much worse than he could imagine.

Trent jabbed the gun at me. "What do you have to say about me now, huh?"

I fluttered my eyelashes at him. "Now you're a dog

with a gun."

Wylder was probably intending to rush in here the second the asshole released the safety. But I had other ideas. He wanted to see what I was made of? I could kick plenty of ass all on my own.

Before Trent could react to my insult, I snatched his wrist and twisted so swiftly the gun tumbled from his fingers. As the men around him leapt to their feet, I finished him off by yanking him toward me—right into my knee, which happened to be ramming straight at his crotch.

He started to crumple, and I bashed my elbow into his nose for good measure. The bone crunched with a spurt of blood.

Oh dear, I'd stained this pretty dress. What a shame.

When I shoved him away, Trent fell to his knees with a groan. One of his men charged at me, but before I could give him a taste of the medicine I could deliver, a huge form barreled into him.

Kaige toppled the guy with a swift body-check. "Thought you might need some help," he tossed over his shoulder to me as he spun to face another incoming attacker.

Around me, a larger fight had broken out. Rowan tackled a man to the floor while Wylder took on two at once. I watched as his well-built body shifted from side to side between them. He knocked one to the ground, and when the other came for his shoulder, he turned and grabbed him by the neck. With one quick heave, he slammed the other guy into the hood of one of the vans.

"Don't you fucking dare," he snarled.

My pussy clenched as I watched him. There was something undeniably hot about Wylder dominating his enemies. Not that I'd ever admit that to him.

Kaige looked down at Trent, who was still hunched on the ground. Blood flowed down from his nose onto his T-shirt. The other guys stumbled off.

Wylder spit on the ground next to Trent in disgust and then looked up at me again, his face twitching. With surprise, I realized he was trying not to smile. He actually looked impressed for a change.

"That was fucking *hot*," Kaige said. "Don't mess with Mercy." The gleam in his eyes made my stomach wobble in a way I wasn't sure was totally wise.

I cleared my throat. "I'll let you guys clean up," I said, and spun toward the car.

Kaige caught my arm before I made it two steps. "I think I need a little more inspiration first."

Before I could ask what he meant, he slid his fingers along my jaw and tugged me into a kiss.

The press of his firm lips sent a flare of heat through my entire body. I clutched his shirt instinctively, my mouth already moving against his, urging him on.

Kaige's tongue teased over the seam of my lips and slipped into my mouth. Fuck, he was good at this. It was definitely unwise. It was a horrible idea. But I couldn't bring myself to shove him away.

Kaige started to ease back, and I yanked myself away too, my cheeks flushing. His sly smile made me wish we hadn't stopped. "Wow," he murmured.

Yeah, that about summed it up. Hell. That definitely hadn't been part of *my* plan at all.

10

Mercy

As I took another step away from Kaige, still reeling from the kiss, I noticed Wylder watching us with narrowed eyes. His fists were balled at his sides, his body pulled taut, radiating tension. But if he had something to say, he just walked right past us.

Part of me felt relieved that he hadn't acknowledged the kiss. At least he wasn't accusing me of trying to make a move on Kaige.

I hadn't been the one to initiate the moment, after all, despite how much I'd liked it. Kaige was still grinning. "Damn," he said. He swiped his thumb across his lips and sucked on it as if savoring the lingering taste.

My cheeks flushed like I was some kind of naïve virgin. For fuck's sake.

But maybe it was a little understandable. Other than a few brief pecks, I hadn't done anything with Colt during the year of our engagement—or with any other guy, since it hadn't seemed smart to treat our impending marriage *that* much like it was only business. He hadn't pushed, and I'd been happy to wait to get more intimate after the knot was fully tied. We'd still been building the trust between us.

But he'd probably been laughing it up with different girls every night while I'd been stuck in a dry spell. I was certainly thirsty now.

Rowan walked over with a stack of bills in his hand, providing a welcome distraction. Wylder glanced at him. "You got everything he owed?"

"And a little extra in asshole tax," Rowan said.

"Well, now the prick knows better than to bite the hand that feeds him. Or a cat that's baring her claws." Wylder's gaze slid to me, and I'd have sworn that impressed look flickered in his eyes for just a second before he pointed everyone toward the car.

He reached it first and tugged open the front passenger seat. "In you go, Kitty Cat. You sit with me."

Was he trying to keep me and Kaige apart? The bigger guy came up behind me, cocking his head. "Everything okay?"

Maybe I'd rather not be sitting too close to that buff body anyway. I hopped in as if it'd been my idea anyway. "Yeah, fine."

Kaige's expression darkened, but he didn't argue. Rowan accepted the change in seating with a pursing of his lips. As Wylder started to drive, the silence hanging over us felt thick enough to spread on toast.

I sank back into the seat, which was annoyingly

comfortable, and pretended not to notice the awkwardness. When Wylder turned up the hill to the mansion, I couldn't take it any longer. "So, you saw what I can do. I held my own. Can we get on with making my ex-fiancé pay already?"

Wylder gunned the engine to roar up the steep slope and swerved neatly around the corner. He parked the Mustang in the driveway and stalked toward the house without a word.

I had half a mind to throw one of my heels at his head as I scrambled after him. "Aren't you going to say something? I swear to God if you've changed your—"

He whirled around so suddenly that I crashed into his hard chest. He caught my arms to steady me and just as quickly let me go with a jerk. His smile was stony. "I didn't promise anything, Kitty Cat."

The nerve of this asshole. "Listen, you—"

Just then the skinny blonde who had confronted us in the kitchen pranced out of the house. I racked my brain to remember her name: Gia.

"Wylder, I've been looking for you all over," she said, clinging to his arm. He looked annoyed but didn't ask her to let go.

Gia glanced toward me, eyeing my dress with malice. "Where are you coming from wearing a dress like that? Are you that desperate for attention?"

I rolled my eyes. Her dress wasn't much better, and she'd picked that one out herself. "FYI, it isn't very nice to slut-shame other girls. It's almost like *you're* the one begging for men's approval."

Gia scowled at me. "Why do you always have to be a bitch?"

"I'm simply reflecting back what you've given me to work with," I replied with mock sweetness.

The girl's eyes narrowed and she looked about ready to throttle me. I almost wanted her to try.

"I don't think you want to start a fight with Mercy, Gia," Kaige said, walking up beside me. He put his arm around my waist, and Gia stiffened. Jesus, did she think she owned Wylder *and* Kaige? Did this girl have a thing for all the guys here? "She just came back from breaking a man's nose. Possibly also his balls—we didn't stop to check."

Gia's eyes widened, and she seemed to shrink against Wylder as if seeking his security. Drama queen. "Yeah, I don't want any of that," she said in a shrill voice.

Wylder actually looked at her as if she were some kind of wounded animal. Jeez, did men really buy into that?

Kaige grinned at me, stretching his arms to admittedly impressive effect. "I feel like this calls for a raid into the liquor cabinet." He poked Wylder's shoulder. "You've been promising that Grey Goose for a while now."

Wylder rolled his eyes. "Fine, but only if the princess retrieves it."

I set my hands on my hips. "You still haven't made good on your word."

"What word exactly did I give you?"

I let out a huff of frustration. He hadn't said exactly

that getting the money from Trent would be what it took to finally get his help, but what more proof could he possibly need of my "worthiness"?

Anger surged up inside me. I'd had enough of this shit. "Do you want me to prove myself as the gang princess or your freaking maid? If you even for a second mistook me for the latter, let me remind you that—"

Wylder spoke over me. "Spare me. You know you need my help—you're a desperate little kitten. That's why you're here following my orders like the good girl you are."

"You have no idea what I am or what I can do."

"I think I've got a pretty good idea." Shaking off Gia, he took a step toward me. He might not have been quite the hulk Kaige was, but he still towered over me. As if I was going to let him scare me.

His eyes flickered down to my mouth, and he wet his own lips as if in anticipation. I found myself following the path of his tongue. Okay, maybe fear wasn't the emotion he was trying to strike here.

I balled my hands into fists, my glare daring him to try me.

"Woah, woah, woah," Kaige said, stepping in between us. "No brawling until I get the drink I was promised."

Wylder just chuckled. He spun on his heel, and I didn't have much choice but to follow him and the other guys into the house.

Wylder led the way to a lounge room near the kitchen. To my annoyance, Gia followed us to the doorway. He turned to her there. "Don't you have anywhere else to be?"

She peered at him coyly through her eyelashes and reached for his arm again. "I'd rather be here."

He pried himself out of her grip, much to my satisfaction. "We've got work to do. Take a hike."

Gia made a face, but she couldn't exactly argue with him. She gave me one last dirty look before she pranced away. Good riddance.

Kaige was already standing in front of a liquor cabinet behind a built-in mahogany bar, rubbing his hands together eagerly. It was packed with bottles of just about every kind of liquor I could imagine and then some. The Nobles kept a nice stash, I'd give them that.

"Go on," Wylder said. "Find the Grey Goose."

I brushed past Kaige to step behind the bar, running my hand along the smooth surface of the polished wood. Even more bottles were stashed under its countertop. There was enough classy booze in this room to party for a year straight without feeling your face.

I spotted the bottle easily and held it up. "Just vodka straight? I could do something more interesting with this."

Wylder looked faintly amused. "So you know your liquor too, huh? What was that about being a good girl? Maybe I'll have to revise my opinion."

"Like I give a shit about your opinion on that subject," I retorted mildly, grabbing a couple more bottles and a few of the glasses stacked off to the side of the bar.

"Kind of a shame to cut that stuff with anything else," Kaige said.

"Fine, you can have yours neat. I'll save my skills for the boss." I let sarcasm drip from that last word.

There was a little fridge with lemons and an icemaker, a saltshaker perched on top of it. I was set. With several brisk motions, I poured Kaige his Grey Goose, slid the glass across the bar to him, and got to work on my concoction for Wylder.

I was freestyling, but that was how I'd found I worked best after I'd branched out from learning all the typical cocktails the people at my father's gatherings would want to inventing my own. No one had ever cared that most of that time I'd been too young to legally drink myself.

People's lips got pretty loose around the bartender, even an unofficial one. It'd been one more way to glean all the secrets I could, searching for an advantage. For a way to ensure Dad never got to lay a finger on me again.

The guys watched, Wylder still looking amused, Kaige practically swooning as he savored his vodka, and Rowan's expression mildly surprised. I'd picked up this hobby not long after I'd parted ways with him.

As I tossed a dollop of this and that into the glass, Anthea and Gideon walked in. Her eyes narrowed. "What's our runaway princess doing now?"

"Repaying my host for his kind hospitality," I said tartly. I finished mixing and nudged the glass toward Wylder. "Drink up."

He considered the drink with obvious curiosity and

picked it up to swirl it in his hand. Just as he was about to take a swig, I called out. "Wait."

He froze. Kaige and Rowan looked at me, their bodies tensed as if they were about to spring on me any second, like I was the one who concocted poisons around here.

I extended a saltshaker toward him with a smirk of my own. "I think I forgot to add the salt."

Kaige laughed, and I felt the tension leave the room. Even Wylder chuckled. He threw back a gulp and then blinked with obvious surprise. "I've never had that before, but it's good."

"My own recipe," I said, propping my elbow on the bar.

He raised an eyebrow at me. "What's it called?"

"Hadn't named it yet. Just made it up five minutes ago." I tapped my finger against my lips. "In honor of its inspiration, how about we call it an Asshole on the Rocks?"

Kaige snorted so hard I thought a little Grey Goose might have shot up his nose. Wylder glowered at me. He did throw back more of the drink, though. Point to Mercy.

"Anyone else?" I asked, already putting together another.

Gideon ambled over, his gaze mild. "I'll give it a try."

Anthea stayed noticeably silent, hanging back from the bar. I had no problem simply ignoring her. As I mixed Gideon's drink and one for myself, because I'd like a taste too, Wylder drained the rest of his glass and leaned his elbow on the counter. "I wonder how your fiancé dealt with that tongue of yours. Or maybe the problem is that he didn't?"

He was close enough that his breath tickled over my hand when I poured out a splash from a bottle of gin. "What do you mean?" I asked, as if I couldn't already tell this was going in a bad direction.

He shifted even closer, trailing a finger down the side of my arm. I resisted the urge to flinch backward like a coward, gritting my teeth at the heat his touch stirred up.

Wylder's eyes gleamed. "You're practically drooling for it. Couldn't Colt Bryant satisfy you in bed? Although I guess a woman like you would be hard to please."

"Oh, and I suppose you figure you're the man to do it?"

He leaned back with his typical smirk. "Maybe that's why you really came here, begging for my help." His voice was full of innuendo, sending more heat through my body even though he wasn't touching me now. I couldn't help but think of how he'd fought the guys back at the parking lot, so swift and powerful. Imagine that strength put to work on my body in much more enjoyable ways...

I jerked myself out of the reverie. All this game-playing had gone on long enough. I drew the one ace I had. "You know what I think? You're just making me merry-go-round in an attempt to distract yourself from the real problem."

"And what's that?"

I looked him straight in the eyes. "Titus's death."

I was taking a hard gamble, one that could go very, very badly. Farther down the bar, Kaige stiffened.

Wylder's eyes turned cold. "What do you know about that?"

"You think word doesn't get around? I've heard things." I turned to Kaige with a flicker of sympathy for his obvious discomfort. "Things I find hard to believe, as convincing a case as certain parties might have made."

"Kaige had nothing to do with it," Wylder snapped. I'd hit a nerve, just like I'd meant to.

I shrugged. "There's no point dancing around it. If you tell me your side of the story, maybe I'll have some insights."

Wylder scoffed. "What kind of insights?"

"I figured out plenty already without even trying, didn't I?"

Wylder grimaced as if he didn't want to give me credit. "You found out some. Not even half of it, I'd bet."

I shrugged. "Then why don't you fill me in while I make you another drink? What could it hurt?"

Wylder stayed silent, but he didn't say no, which meant he was coming around. I grabbed another glass. This time I added a more generous amount of vodka, tweaking my recipe slightly. All the better to loosen his tongue.

Anthea pushed into the guys' midst, her arms crossed. "Are you sure getting her involved in this is wise?"

Kaige studied me warily for a moment, but his shoulders had relaxed. "I don't see the harm."

Wylder finally spoke, his voice light but with a hint of an edge. "It *has* been two weeks since you started investigating, Aunt Anthea, and we're nowhere near the answer as far as I can tell."

Anthea bristled. "There's little to no evidence. I told you, I need more time." Then she looked up at me accusingly as if I were the one questioning her competence.

But Wylder had made his decision—in my favor. As I passed him his second drink, he nodded to Gideon. "Why don't you do the honors?"

Gideon tapped his fingers against the bar counter as if counting out the facts. "Titus, also known as 'the Titan,' was one of Ezra's best men. Two weeks ago he was found dead on the back lawn. He appeared to have fallen from the fire escape platform on the third floor after the railing broke."

Axel hadn't mentioned the railing. "Then why does everyone seem to think he was murdered?"

"The railing *was* broken, but on closer inspection, it was clear it'd been sawed through and treated with chemicals to make it look as if it'd rusted out instead." Gideon's tone stayed totally matter of fact. "Oh, and he was dead before he even hit the ground anyway. His neck had been snapped first."

He pulled out his phone and turned it toward me. The photo on the screen showed a guy sprawled limply on his back. Axel crouched next to the body with an angry expression. Even in his prone position, Titus was obviously huge—at least six and a half feet tall and a good two hundred and fifty pounds minimum, all muscle. His veiny arms looked ready to pop. Like Axel, his head was shaved.

Shock rippled through me. Somebody had managed to break this giant's neck.

"That must have taken one heck of a powerful person," I said.

"It sure as hell wasn't me," Kaige muttered. After a pause, he couldn't seem to help adding, "If it'd been a fair fight, I wouldn't have minded taking credit. To date, no one's beat Titus in a brawl."

"But *someone* did. Someone who managed to kill him." Possibilities were already running in my head. It had to be somebody with massive upper body strength. As narrow as the neck was, it took a lot of effort to snap it, not to mention getting access to that area in the first place unless his attacker was equally tall.

Without thinking, my eyes drifted to Kaige. He was the picture of innocence. But could I really trust him? It was true that I hadn't seen anyone else who came close to the Titan in size and strength around here so far.

"People are pointing the finger at Kaige because just a few days before Titus's death, the two of them got into a spat," Rowan said, speaking up for the first time.

Kaige smacked his fist on the counter. "I had no choice. The bastard decided to come after Wylder, questioning his authority, getting right up in his face. I'm not going to stand around while anyone disrespects him."

Wylder nodded. "Kaige was standing up for me."

"By going ballistic?" Anthea said. "And it wasn't just that. Multiple people heard you threaten to *kill* the guy."

Kaige frowned. "Whose side are you on exactly?"

"I'm just stating the facts."

"It was an empty threat," Kaige said. "I was pissed off, but I'm not a big enough fool to go after one of Ezra's men. That'd be a death sentence for *me*."

"Titus had threatened to kill you too," Anthea pointed out.

"Just spouting off like I was. I forgot about it by the next day." Kaige grimaced at her. "I told you already, I didn't kill Titus. I hated the old bastard, but he didn't die at my hands."

The circumstantial evidence against him wasn't exactly hope-inspiring, though. Was he annoyed by the discussion because he really had nothing to do with it or because he knew what a proper investigation would unearth?

Wylder was observing me as closely as I was watching Kaige. "So, what do you think of all this, Kitty Cat?"

"It's a strange case," I admitted.

Kaige groaned. "I'm sure everything will be fine if Anthea stops pointing out the reasons it could be me and actually manages to exonerate me."

Anthea scowled at him. "Ezra gave me a job, and I intend to do it to the best of my abilities. Stop doubting my judgment."

Wylder shook his head. "It's not enough. We're running out of time. Dad will be home soon, and Axel and the others will be pushing for retribution as soon as he does. Maybe that means it's time to bring in reinforcements." He arched his eyebrows at me. "What do you think, Kitty Cat? Are you up for the job?"

I blinked at him. "What?"

"You wanted a proper deal, right? Well here, I'll give it to you. You figure out who actually killed the Titan, and I'll take down Colt Bryant for you, no further services required."

Gideon

AT WYLDER'S WORDS, THE GIRL'S PIERCING BLUE EYES widened. In my head, I referred to her as the girl because she was a temporary guest in our life. When she was gone, I would simply delete her from memory like I did most useless information.

Or at least that was what I told myself.

My gaze drifted over the silvery lines of the dress Wylder had forced her to wear—and the copious amounts of smooth, pale skin that showed through the gaps in the fabric.

"You're serious?" she said to Wylder. "No changing your mind once I've done what you asked me to, yet again?"

My best friend looked back at her with the kind of calm I knew hid a whole storm of emotion inside him. "If you can clear Kaige's name, I'll make Steel Knights' blood rain from the sky for you, no questions asked."

She raised her chin. "Forgive me if I'm not sure I can just take your word for that. You're asking me to go after a known killer, without any idea who that killer is. That's a little more dangerous than confronting some dork with a gun."

Wylder walked around the bar until he was standing toe to toe with her. The girl, to her credit, didn't even flinch. Wylder frowned, as if he had wanted her to cower, but when she stood her ground, he simply reached for the paring knife she'd cut the lemon for our drinks with. When he held it up, she still didn't try to move away. She didn't break eye contact for a second.

There weren't many people Wylder couldn't manage to scare when he wanted to. She definitely wasn't much like the other girls around here.

He flipped the knife in his right hand and carefully punctured the skin of his left thumb so that a bead of blood trickled out of it. I hissed under my breath before I could catch the sound. What the fuck was he doing? A blood promise among criminals like us wasn't something you could walk away from, not without losing all faith in your word going forward. But Wylder was offering one anyway.

"I mark my words with the honor of my blood," he said.

The girl's eyes widened for a second. She knew he wouldn't make an offer like that without meaning it, and we all stood here as witnesses. I wanted to haul Wylder's ass out of the room and ask him if he knew what the hell he was doing giving the word of his blood to this unproven quantity.

Finally, she nodded and shook hands with him. It was done.

"Wow," Kaige said, sounding bewildered. Wylder had done this for him, in the hopes of establishing his innocence. I just hoped he knew where to draw the line.

The girl took a step away from Wylder. "I'll try my best to find out who the killer is."

"Just don't get murdered in the process," Wylder said casually as if he hadn't just given her the most solid oath any of us could make. He turned on his heel and walked out of the kitchen.

The others followed suit. The girl paused to put away the alcohol, ignoring the empty glasses we'd left on the bar. I guessed cleaning up wasn't her job anymore.

When I moved to go too, she cleared her throat meaningfully. "Hey."

I glanced back at her. "Yes?"

She paused, looking a bit awkward, which wasn't unusual. No one ever seemed to know exactly how to talk to me—except Wylder. He never acted like there was anything to be uncomfortable about. Like there was any reason to think that I didn't belong here.

Then she raised her eyes, and the full force of that bright blue gaze burned into mine. "You had someone bring me a clean outfit the other day, didn't you?"

The wheels in my head spun, but I knew she was right before I'd even quite remembered it. She'd looked so bedraggled coming up from the first task Wylder had given her... It hadn't been fitting for anyone who was running with the Nobles even on a small scale. I'd simply ensured she didn't tarnish his image through his association with her.

"It was nothing," I said evenly.

"It wasn't." She held my gaze, no awkwardness left, and it occurred to me that her initial hesitation might not have had anything to do with me but with her own pride. No one who lived this kind of life tended to be very good showing open gratitude. "I appreciated the gesture, whatever reasons you had for making it. I just thought I should say that."

I didn't like the unexpected list of my stomach at her words. Why should it matter to me whether she thanked me over some brief remark to the staff or not?

"Don't mention it," I said, my tone coming out brusquer than I'd intended, and strode out of the room before I could dwell too much on the trace of disappointment I'd caught on her face at my response.

Back in my office, I sat down in front of my expansive computer setup, but the image of her face, those eyes pinning me in place, lingered in my head. Without any conscious direction, my mind produced another image—of her peeling the strips of that silvery fabric down her shoulders to reveal her breasts...

My cock stirred. Fuck. I swore under my breath and shook any thought of Mercy Katz away. To distract myself, I made my way to the complex espresso machine I'd had installed in my office. I couldn't work without caffeine—and it had to be caffeine done right. Maybe it would jolt me back to the mindset I needed.

With a meditative air, I set the machine running to my typical specifications and watched the dark liquid fill the mug. There was something grounding about the steady stream and the rising of the coffee against the pale sides. When it was finished, black, sugarless, and perfect, I sipped it while eyeing the aquarium that filled most of one wall across from my computer. The gliding motions of the fish grounded me too.

There was a knock on the door. Wylder peered in before I had a chance to answer. "Chess?"

I nodded. We kept up our running games a couple evenings a week, whenever Wylder wasn't too occupied with other work. I'd thought the girl's arrival might have put those on hold until the matter of her revenge request was settled. Apparently not.

Wylder sat down in one of the chairs by the table that held our partly played-out game, holding a snifter of amber liquid he'd brought with him. Kaige might salivate over the Grey Goose, but Wylder liked nothing more than the most expensive brandy he could get his hands on, drunk the old-fashioned way.

I raised a brow. "Haven't you had enough already?"

He chuckled. "Apparently not."

I shook my head and sat down next to him, considering the arrangement in which we'd left the pieces. I was winning. But then, I nearly always was. And if I wasn't, the tide turned soon enough.

"It was your turn," I reminded him.

Wylder rubbed his mouth, giving me a wry look. "Are you sure you're not giving me an extra turn in the hopes I'll offer a little more of a challenge?"

He'd need at least a dozen more moves for that. "Nothing's stopping you from studying up on the game a little more, you know. Or paying more than five seconds' attention to where you put your pieces."

He laughed. "I think even if I spent a year buried in chess books, you'd still beat me every time. That's okay. I like watching how you take me down."

Someone else might have seen that as a sign of suspicion. I knew Wylder had only admitted it because he trusted that I'd never turn on him in actuality. It was an honor, having that trust.

Beating him in chess once a week, not quite so much.

He took his move, shifting a pawn. I brought out my knight. Wylder squinted at the board for a second and then sent his bishop whipping several spaces.

I'd be able to take it now. I wasn't sure if he didn't realize or simply didn't care.

He watched me as I decided whether I wanted to bother or if there was an even better move available. "Do you have anything to say about what happened earlier?"

I shrugged. "You can make whatever promises you want to whomever you want."

Wylder snorted. "Come on, you obviously disapproved."

Fine. "We don't know her. Yes, we questioned her extensively, and her story has checked out so far, but we both know looks can be deceptive. She is the Katz heir."

"With no family left."

I shrugged. "Maybe that makes her even more dangerous. She has nothing left to lose."

Wylder paused. "I have considered that."

"Have you?"

"Yeah." He took a long, hard sip of his drink and put it on the table. "Concentrate on the game."

We played for several more minutes, Wylder's defeat becoming ever more inevitable, before he spoke again. "On a scale of one to ten, how likely do you figure she is to get to the bottom of the Titus thing?"

"Only the tiniest fraction more than zero," I said without hesitation. "Nothing is ever impossible, but she's a gang princess, not Sherlock Holmes."

Wylder chuckled. "That doesn't sound so promising."

"Well, it doesn't matter," I said. "We don't have anything to lose by letting her take a shot. She's just a tool anyway, right?"

"Right," Wylder said, but I could tell from his tone that wasn't entirely the truth. He was obviously more invested in her than I thought he should be. The knowledge that he was lying to me about that investment sent a prickle down my spine.

Of course, in a way I could understand his fascination. Her body with all its curves, as if it'd been made to lead men's minds astray. The way she let her hand linger against her skin now and then, I could already track which spots must be most sensitive.

A vision flashed through my mind of pinning her beneath me while I found every sweet spot that would make her moan. The side of her neck, definitely, right at the base where it met her shoulder. And the crook of her jaw just below her ear...

"What are you thinking?" Wylder asked, pulling me back to reality, and I realized I'd gotten hard beneath the table. A flush crept over my face that I fought to dispel.

"Nothing," I said, and made a hasty move that left a careless opening for Wylder. Not that he was likely to notice. As surreptitiously as possible, I adjusted my position in my chair, willing certain parts of my body to calm down.

Women didn't affect me like this. I couldn't allow this one to. My job was protecting Wylder in every way I could, and no one, no matter how pretty their bright blue eyes were, was going to threaten the security I'd worked so hard to construct.

Mercy

Standing on the back lawn not far from where Titus must have hit the grass, I peered up at the fire escape that zigzagged across the mansion's rear. I couldn't make out a whole lot from down here. The ladder to the second-floor section wasn't reachable from the ground, and the sun glared off the metal bars, stinging my eyes.

The promise Wylder had made came back to me, and with it the image of him slowly sucking the trickle of blood from his finger. My stomach fluttered at the memory. It was probably one of the sexiest things I'd ever seen, and there shouldn't have been anything even remotely sexual about it.

I shook my head to clear it. He'd given me his terms, and now I had to meet them. Even if I didn't have much of a clue how to accomplish that. Examining the scene of the murder had seemed like the most obvious place to start.

Heading inside, I got to enjoy the rush of the chilly air conditioning for the climb to the third floor. A large window at the end of one hall opened to the fire escape. I guessed that was how the Nobles' patrols climbed out to survey the yard from above. Titus would have had to squeeze to get out there.

I clambered through it back into the summer heat, grateful that the sweats and tee I'd put back on meant I wasn't flashing anyone who might have walked by below like I would have in that ridiculous dress. My shoulder twinged when the bandage brushed against the frame, but the bullet wound seemed to be healing nicely. It barely hurt when I moved now.

The third-floor section was only wide enough for three or four people to stand side-by-side. Maybe two if you were as big as Titus. A chunk of the railing *was* missing partway down.

I crouched next to it and examined the surface, running my fingers down the length of where the metal had broken off. Flecks of rust stuck to my finger. The broken ends definitely looked corroded. I checked the floor. There was a little sheen of dust but not enough to make a proper footprint. Well, by now a lot of people must have come out here to investigate anyway.

The lawn was a good thirty feet below me. Hardly anyone could survive that fall.

Especially with their neck already broken.

A loud screech behind me startled me so badly I

nearly jumped out of my skin. My foot slipped, my body swaying dangerously close to the precarious drop.

A hand shot out and snatched the back of my shirt, yanking me away from the gap in the railing. I stumbled to the side and whirled around with a hitch of breath.

"Careful there," Anthea said. She climbed out of another, smaller window—its pane must have made that screech as she'd opened it—and onto the metal platform beside me. The thin smile that curved her lips suggested she was more amused than concerned by my near fall.

I narrowed my eyes at her. What the hell was she doing sneaking up on me? I curled my fingers around the more solid railing next to me.

Anthea hopped up and down a couple of times, managing to make the floor beneath us wobble. "It's a very old structure, you know," she said conversationally. "I'm not sure it was the wisest for Titus to be coming out onto it in the first place. Unfortunately, my brother isn't very keen on renovating. He doesn't want strangers on his property." She fixed her penetrating gaze on me.

I took a moment to study her right back. Other than the red in her hair and the proud slope of her nose, she didn't share a whole lot of features with her supposed nephew. But then, gang leaders had a habit of getting around. Especially with the age gap, chances were she and Ezra Noble didn't share a mother. Which made her, what, Wylder's half-aunt?

"What are you doing out here?" I asked, trying to keep the accusation out of my tone. I didn't want to seem like I was paranoid or show that she'd rattled me.

She shrugged. "I thought you'd need some help."

I highly doubted that she'd come here out of the goodness of her heart. But two could play at this game. I pushed my mouth into a smile. "That's fantastic. I had some questions, so I'm glad you're here."

Anthea looked surprised that I'd decided to take her up on the offer. She leaned back against the side of the house. "Shoot."

I ran my hand along the railing, tapping the broken edge. "How exactly did you know this wasn't an accident? Like you said, it's a pretty old structure, and it *is* obviously rusted."

Anthea tsked and pointed to a couple of whitish marks, so tiny I'd never have noticed them on my own. "You see that? Some kind of chemicals have been poured on the metal to accelerate the process of corrosion. They sawed out a chunk of the railing and doctored it afterward so it'd look accidental."

I examined the marks. "What does a person use to make metal rust just like that?"

Anthea shrugged. "The easiest would be a combination of hydrogen peroxide, vinegar, and salt. It'd take just a few hours."

"And who around here would know that?"

"Anyone who can run a quick Google search," she said dryly.

Okay, so that wasn't going to be my big clue. I glanced at the window Anthea had climbed through and then the one I'd used. "So, someone knew Titus would come out here on his patrol. They prepared the area ahead of time. Then they caught him while he was on the platform, broke his neck, and pushed him off."

"Right, simple as that."

I ignored her sarcasm, frowning. It *was* simple, actually. The real problem was how anyone had managed to do the "simple" task of overpowering Titus in the first place. Even if they'd snuck up on him like Anthea had with me, who could have gotten a good enough grip on his neck and managed to snap it without him tossing *them* over the edge instead first?

Maybe the real question wasn't who could have but why anyone would have wanted to.

I glanced at Anthea again. "Do you have any suspects?"

She arched a brow. "As far as I'm concerned, everybody is a suspect."

"Is Kaige included in that?"

"He's innocent until proven guilty."

Her voice tightened with those words, a hint of a frown creasing the corners of her mouth. I didn't think she liked that there was so much suspicion on him. "You don't think he did it, no matter how much evidence there is."

She aimed her frown at me. "He and Wylder are like brothers. I've practically seen him grow up. He can fly off the handle pretty easily, and he'd kill to defend Wylder in the moment, but I can't see him arranging some elaborate murder plan when no one's in immediate danger."

"Then why are you investigating him at all?"

She lowered her petite form to sit on the windowsill.

"If I don't remain neutral, the investigation will be tainted. My brother wouldn't like that."

I worried at my lower lip. If she didn't think Kaige could have done it, I had to admit I was inclined to believe her. "Isn't there *anyone* else who could have taken Titus on? Who else was around that night?"

"It's a pretty busy house. Some of the top guys live here most of the time, and there are always associates coming and going. And then there are the groupies, not that they pose a threat other than by venereal disease."

I held back a laugh, picturing how Gia would have responded to that assessment. "Are there a lot of 'groupies' who hang around here?"

Anthea made a dismissive wave. "A few of them. It's a steady rotation as they realize no one here is going to want them for more than a quick lay and they move out to make room for the next round. But my brother lets them have a room so they're on hand should any of the men want to... partake of their services."

From the bitterness that had crept into her voice, I wondered if her mother had been one of the groupies. We might have had that in common. Whoever my mom had been, Dad definitely hadn't bothered to marry her or anything official like that. She'd been nothing more than a broodmare to him.

I wasn't trying to make an enemy out of Anthea— well, more than we already were—so I didn't pry on that subject. I was debating my next question when she spoke up again.

"You don't belong here."

"What?"

She stood up again, stepping close enough that I had to back up, starkly aware of how little space was left behind me. One quick push, and she could heave me over the railing just like that.

"Forget your revenge, forget vying for Wylder's favor, and get the hell out of this house," she said in a low voice. "Kittens don't last long in a place like this."

I snorted. "Is that a threat?"

"I could make it one. Let me be very clear: I don't want you here."

I folded my arms in front of me. "Oh yeah? So what's stopping you from showing me the door?"

Her jaw clenched. "It's not my house, and Wylder has decided to entertain your delusions. I have plenty of other resources at my disposal, though."

"You're a Noble too. You have seniority over him, don't you?"

A sharp guffaw spilled out of her. "And you're a woman too. I think you know well enough how men in this life see us."

"You have some kind of position here," I had to point out. More than my father had ever allowed me.

"Oh, sure, my brother makes use of my unique skill set. That doesn't mean he gives me any authority outside of that."

"And your job is poisons?"

She gave me a sharp little smile. "Any kind of killing that can fly under the radar as an accident or illness to prevent further investigation. Both identifying them and dealing them out."

The hairs on the back of my neck stood on end. But

then, every man in this mansion was probably a killer several times over. Why not the main woman of the house too?

I forced my tone to stay casual. "That's how you knew about things like this rust concoction?"

"Exactly. My truth serum is only scraping the surface of what I can deal out, little girl."

I bristled automatically, but I held my tongue. She was trying to unnerve me, to get me to snap. I wasn't going to give her the satisfaction.

In my silence, she stepped closer again, stomping her foot hard enough to send a vibration through the platform. "As I said before, you shouldn't be here. We've already established that the railings don't hold, haven't we?"

If she wanted to intimidate me into running scared, it wasn't going to work. I held my position. "I actually like it up here." Sunlight danced on my skin, and the clean, fresh air filled my lungs. I didn't feel as caged as I did inside.

That was why I liked parkour too. Apart from the fact that I was naturally good at it, I could shut my mind off completely when I climbed and bounded, letting my body work on autopilot.

Anthea cocked her head with a knowing look I didn't like at all. "No, it isn't the sky you're afraid of but what lies beneath the ground, isn't it? No one likes being shut away inside a space they can't escape from." Her gaze dropped to my hands.

My arms froze at my sides. "What are you talking about?" Flashes of memory from years ago, images I had buried deep inside me threatened to cloud my vision. The rotting scent, the sting in my fingertips, my throat hoarse from screaming.

"You okay?" Anthea said innocently. "You look a little pale there."

She couldn't know. She was just taking whatever jabs she could. "I'm fine," I bit out.

"I suppose we'll see about that." She turned back to the window she'd come out through. "Well, this has been an enlightening conversation. Let me enlighten you a little more. The last person who really pissed me off was my former husband. Former because he's three years dead. And that's not a coincidence."

She shot one last smirk over her shoulder at me. "Wouldn't it be a horrible pity if somehow you ended up meeting the same fate?"

Mercy

My conversation with Anthea left my nerves jumping all over the place. Back in the house, I did my best to shake off the uneasy sensation crawling over my skin after her last words. She wouldn't come at me *that* hard while Wylder was still on board with having me around, right?

One thing was clear: if I was going to get to the bottom of this murder before she decided it was more important to get me out of the way, I couldn't do it alone. And I knew exactly the man who'd have the most answers at his fingertips.

It took me a while to figure out where Gideon's office was, even asking a couple of staff where he worked. The mansion was huge, and there were just so many fucking rooms here with ornate handles and oak doors. It was hard to pick one from the next.

I'd just tried another that led into a broom closet of

all things when Kaige appeared at the other end of the hall. He held a steaming mug of coffee.

"Hey," he said. "I was looking for you. Thought you might need this after all the craziness this morning."

The craziness that had included our scorching kiss. My stomach did a little flip that had nothing to do with nerves. At least, not the nerves Anthea had provoked.

"Uh, thanks," I said, accepting the cup from him.

"You're very welcome." He flashed me a smile. Was he always this charming or was he simply trying to get into my pants?

If that kiss was anything to go by, maybe I shouldn't be stopping him.

"What are you thinking?" he asked with a sly grin as if he knew exactly what was going through my head.

I shoved away those completely unnecessary thoughts. "Uh, I was actually looking for Gideon."

Kaige frowned. "Why are you looking for him?"

"He seems to make a business of knowing everything about everyone else's business. I figured he might be able to fill me in on a few more details to prove your innocence."

"Well, I can't complain about that." Kaige beckoned me with a finger. "Allow me."

I followed him down the hallway to yet another door I couldn't have differentiated easily from any of the others.

It opened before he could knock on it. Wylder stood on the other side. When he saw Kaige and me together, an odd expression crossed his face. I remembered how he had looked when he'd caught us kissing this morning. Displeasure flitted across his face. "What are you doing here?"

Without answering, I walked past him into the room.

The office wasn't all that big, considering some of the massive rooms in this place. There was a desk with an elaborate set-up involving several monitors and two keyboards, plus a monster of a computer underneath. At the other end of the room, a huge aquarium covered the entire back wall.

"Jesus," I muttered under my breath. Colorful fishes swam around in the water, several of them as large as my hand, the rest just tiny slivers of bright reds, blues, and yellows. I wasn't a fish enthusiast, so I couldn't have identified any of them for sure... but the bigger ones with a metallic sheen to their scales and jutting lower jaws had a vicious look to them. Were those actual *piranhas*?

Why not? What else would a fucking gangster keep in his fish tank?

Gideon was sitting in a wheeled chair in front of his computer setup, Rowan leaning against the edge of the desk a couple of feet beyond him. My ex glanced away when I met his eyes. The guy I'd come to talk to hadn't bothered to look up in the first place.

I ventured farther in, tapping the surface of a small table beneath the narrow window between the desk and the aquarium, the only other furnishing in the place. A chessboard, several pieces still scattered across it, lay on the table. "Didn't finish your game?"

Kaige had stepped in behind me. He chuckled. "Wylder and Gideon always have a game going on."

Gideon still didn't look up, but he did acknowledge that point with his voice. "Wylder says it keeps his mind sharp."

"So far it hasn't gotten sharp enough for him to win a single game, as far as I know." Kaige grinned at his boss, who knuckled him half-heartedly.

"I'm pretty sure I could beat *you*," Wylder said.

Kaige held up his hands. "Which is exactly why I know better than to play."

It was kind of warming in a weird sort of way, watching them banter. I didn't think my father had ever been that comfortable even with his brothers. He'd seen everyone around him, even family, as a potential threat.

And the first time anyone had convinced him to let down his guard, that bastard Colt had made all of us pay for it. My teeth gritted, and I turned to Gideon. "I need some answers."

He finally raised his head, his expression unreadable. "To what questions?"

"For the investigation," I said. "Exactly who was here the night Titus died, what their role is, whether any of them other than Kaige might have had a beef with the guy."

His mouth twitched with what looked like annoyance. I guessed I'd probably interrupted him in the middle of something. "I've checked everything," he said. "So did Anthea. If there was anything that obvious, we'd have found it already."

"While I'm sure that's true, I need to start

somewhere." I waved my hand vaguely. "Eliminate the obvious so you can see what remains, or something. Isn't that how detectives are supposed to work?"

Wylder snorted. "So now you're a detective?"

I jabbed a finger at him. "You're the one who put me up to this. If you want to skip that part and go straight to decimating the Steel Knights, be my guest."

"But why should I when it's so much fun watching your pert little ass scurry around at my bidding?" He smirked and tossed a remark to Gideon as he turned to leave. "Don't give up the goods too easily!"

Gideon eyed me for a long moment. I had the impression he might be staring right inside my skull— and that he wasn't all that impressed with what he was finding there. I shifted my weight from one foot to the other, and Rowan, naturally, decided to play hero.

"I can take you through—"

Gideon held up his hand with a jerk. "No. She should have the most accurate info, and I'm the one who can provide that." He blinked slowly, and a hint of a smile touched his lips. "But Wylder's right. She should have to work for it. We can't have someone messing around with Kaige's fate who isn't totally committed."

A shiver ran down my spine. "And what exactly do *you* expect me to do?"

He pointed past me to the aquarium. "Stick your hand in the tank with my school of piranhas. As long as it's fully dunked, I'll keep talking."

He kept the lights in here dim. The eerie glow of the computer screens lent his sharp features a grace that was almost angelic, but clearly he was just as devilish as the rest of these pricks.

"Are you kidding me?" I sputtered.

"Do I sound like I'm joking? Simply getting your hand wet shouldn't be too hard for the heir to the Claws."

I held back a growl and marched over to the aquarium. Stick my hand in the water. No big deal. He wouldn't ask me to if he really thought the fish would *eat* it, would he?

"Just so you know," he called after me with no apparent concern, "I can't remember whether I've fed them today. They might be a bit hungrier than usual."

Fan-fucking-tastic.

"Gideon," Rowan said, but his protest only hardened my resolve. He should see just what Mercy Katz was made of these days too.

"It's fine," I declared. There was a low step stool next to the aquarium cabinet. I stepped onto it so I could easily lift the lid over the tank.

The filter hummed. The piranhas swam by with flashes of their silvery scales. I swallowed hard and dipped in my hand.

The water was warmer than I'd expected. I watched the fish carefully, braced for a response to the disturbance.

The tiny, colorful fish scattered. The piranhas glided onward. I held my fingers as still as possible, wary of making any sudden movements. "Okay. I did it. Start talking."

Kaige and Rowan both stood frozen, looking nearly

as tense as I was, but neither of them doing anything further to intervene. Gideon ran the show in this room.

The blue-haired guy had swiveled all the way around in his chair now. The reflected light glinted off his lip ring. He flicked his tongue over it and grabbed his tablet off the desk. "Ask away."

I tipped my head toward the hall. "Who was staying in or came by the mansion around the time of Titus's death?"

"Ezra, Wylder, Ezra's closest associates, and the three of us."

"And Ezra's closest associates would be..."

He rattled off several names that meant nothing to me, as well as Axel's. One of the piranhas flitted past my hand so close its scales slid against my fingers.

I clenched my jaw against a flinch. My fingers remained unchomped.

"Who else?" I demanded.

"Ezra had a meeting with a few of the lesser underlings." Gideon mentioned a few more names. "A couple of members from the Mont X crew came by. And, of course, the groupies and the cleaning staff are pretty much always around."

Mont X. I recognized the name—they were a small outfit on the fringes of the Bend. "What did the Mont X guys want?"

Gideon shrugged. "We weren't part of that meeting, but chances are they were offering Ezra more access to their territory in exchange for his backing in some business endeavor."

"And did he give them it?" Maybe Titus had intervened and pissed them off—

But Rowan's nod cut off that line of thinking. "They left looking happy, so I think that's safe to say."

Gideon cut a glance at him as if he resented anyone else intruding on his role as purveyor of all important information. At the same moment, another scaled body glided just beneath my fingertips, its upper fin tickling my skin.

Another piranha getting cozy with me, and I still hadn't lost so much as a nibble of flesh. My arm was getting a little stiff propped against the tank, but an unexpected thrill shot through my chest, like the rush I got when I pulled off a particularly dangerous parkour move.

Gideon had dared me, and I was rising to the challenge. Just like I'd keep doing until Colt and his men were nothing but crumbs crunched under my feet.

"That's everyone?" I asked, my head coming up a little higher.

Gideon eyed me. I couldn't tell whether he was pleased that I was passing his test or annoyed. "Those were all the people who could have had access to the fire escape, as far as we know."

Kaige nodded. "And some of them, like the Mont X guys—they left before the actual murder happened."

"There's always a chance someone we didn't know about slipped through our security," Gideon admitted with obvious reluctance. "No system is infallible."

Well, that didn't help me at all. "Okay, forget that,

then. Who had Titus pissed off lately, whether you know they were near the house that day or not?"

"Plenty of people, I'm sure," Gideon said coolly. "He did a lot of work enforcing the Nobles' authority. But he was very good at it. I can't imagine many people would have thought it worth the risk of carrying out a grand plan to get revenge just on him, one that would have put them in far more danger than he ever threatened them with."

Kaige snorted in agreement. "Most of these crews are like Trent's. You saw what wimps they were."

"Hey, I'm trying to come up with a convincing story for how it could be *anyone* other than you," I reminded him. But I had to admit I was grasping at straws here. I snatched at another one. "Who was the last person who talked to Titus before the murder?"

"Other than the murderer, that appears to be Axel," Gideon said. "They were both on patrol that night, and they're friendly, so they talked a bit before setting off to cover their respective routes. He didn't tell Anthea anything useful, though."

Damn. Frustration raked through me, and my fingers twitched of their own accord. I snapped back to stillness, my pulse hiccupping.

Two of the piranhas swam closer. Were their teeth jutting even more avidly from their brutal jaws?

They flitted past my hand and continued through the tank. A rush of adrenaline replaced the fear in my gut.

What was the worst that could happen anyway? If they took one chomp, I'd just pull my hand out. The pain would only be momentary. There was a kind of power in knowing that I was tempting fate and doing it despite that, not letting the instinctive fear control me. *I* decided when I was done here.

"Do you know exactly when Titus died?" I asked. "I assume people noticed pretty quickly." A guy that big wouldn't have hit the ground quietly.

Gideon nodded. "People ran over to see what was going on as soon as they heard him fall. That was eleven thirty at night, from what they've reported. He started his patrol a little before eleven on the first floor, so he definitely couldn't have been dead all that long before he was shoved. I'd assume they happened nearly simultaneously."

That would make sense. Why would the killer want to hang around with his body, risking getting caught, rather than getting on with their scheme to make it look like an accident? I glanced at Kaige. "And you don't have any alibi for that time?"

He held up his hands with a crooked smile. "I was in my room asleep. Without company, sadly. I didn't even know the prick had kicked the bucket until I came down to breakfast the next morning. No one thought to accuse me until later that day once they got the autopsy and examined the railing by daylight."

Obviously if he'd had proof he couldn't have been there, this wouldn't be a problem to begin with. At least I had a small window of time to focus on now.

The water currents rippled against my skin. I glanced down at the piranhas, but my fear was completely gone now, replaced by the almost giddy sensation that'd been building in me. I found myself welcoming it.

Gideon was watching me closely, and I didn't know if he could tell that I wasn't afraid anymore. But there was something in his eyes that I could almost swear was grudging respect. I'd have enjoyed it more if the hint of admiration on his striking face hadn't sent a twinge of attraction right between my legs.

Damn these assholes and their ridiculous attractiveness.

"Anything else?" he asked.

I considered. "We're assuming the murderer must have come through the house, right? Because it'd be a lot easier to get out onto the third-floor platform of the fire escape that way, and it's not likely they could have run for it out on the lawn with everyone hurrying out to check Titus's body."

"We've found no evidence that anyone scaled the fire escape from outside, and no one saw anyone fleeing the scene."

Fair enough. I nibbled at my lower lip, with a flicker of satisfaction when both Gideon's and Kaige's gazes shot straight to my mouth. "I'd still like to see any surveillance footage you've got of the yard, just in case." I hadn't seen any cameras inside the mansion, naturally. Ezra wouldn't want his business activities being recorded, even by his own people. Too easy for someone to exploit that for their own gain.

"I've looked over it carefully, and so has Anthea," Gideon said, but he was already turning toward his screens. "You can take your hand out and come have a closer look."

"Thank you ever so much," I said with snarky formality, and closed the lid on the tank before wiping my wet hand on my pants. More adrenaline tingled through me as I shot the other guys a fierce smile.

They'd figure out soon enough that I could take anything they threw at me and still come out on top.

14

Mercy

THE SECOND TIME I LEFT THE NOBLE MANSION, I
didn't bother to sneak. No one had *said* I wasn't allowed
to leave, and I was planning on sticking to Paradise City
this time anyway. I needed to get out of that place to
clear my mind and let everything I'd learned hopefully
settle into something I could make sense of.

I also needed to stop relying on borrowed clothes.
One less thing for Wylder to hold over my head as he
was so fond of doing whenever he could.

I returned just as dusk pinkened the sky, carrying a
few shopping bags. Kaige had been right: pawning off
my engagement ring had given me a sizable chunk of
change—and no small amount of satisfaction to boot.
Thanks to a thrift store down the street from the pawn
shop, I had a decent array of jeans and shirts I could call
my own, as well as a wallet to keep the rest in. A
convenience store farther down had supplied me with a

burner phone I had to think might come in handy. That was all I needed for now.

I'd never been able to earn any money of my own without Dad taking it over. I wasn't going to spend this windfall all at once.

As I began to climb the staircase to the guest room, a screechy voice called out from behind me. "Well, well, well, look who we have here."

I turned around to face Gia, who was scowling at my bags. Great, my favorite person in the house. And considering Anthea was also living here, that was saying a lot.

I suppressed a sigh. "What do you want?"

She curled her painted-red lips in a sneer. "Whose credit card did you steal to buy all of that stuff?"

"News flash: I don't answer to you." I spun around and continued up the stairs, figuring we were done, but apparently she was feeling particularly irritating today. Her strappy sandals tapped against the hardwood. She caught up with me just as I reached the second floor.

"Don't think I don't know what you're doing here. Acting like the victim, trying to get the guys all wrapped around your finger."

Oh, she was one to talk. I whirled on her. "I have no interest in wrapping the guys around my *anything*, like I've told you before. The only person obsessed with them here is you."

She glowered at me. "You think you can steal them out from under the people who've been there for them so much longer, all because you have some stupid sob story. Please." She jerked her chin toward my bags. "And now you're stealing who knows what else from them. It's obvious trash like you can't afford these things."

My patience was fraying fast. Anger bubbled up inside me. I was *looking* at the trash, and I was starting to think it was time I took her out. "You have no idea who I am."

"Oh really?" Gia jutted her hip to one side. "Who are you exactly? A whiny little bitch who thinks she can sidle up to the guys and suddenly she'll be part of their circle? Doesn't matter what crazy ideas you have—a whore is still a whore."

I dropped my bags. "You—"

"Ladies!" Kaige ambled down the hall toward us. He looked between Gia and me. "What's this about?"

"Your groupie is accusing me of stealing," I said. In more ways than one, none of them true. "I think you need to put her on a leash."

"You bitch." Gia took a step toward me.

Kaige pulled her back by the arm. "That's enough."

Gia blinked at him, immediately looking like a lost puppy. I sputtered a laugh, remembering how just seconds ago she'd been accusing *me* of pulling a poor-me act. "But Kaige," she simpered, "she—"

He cut her off, clearly unmoved by her performance. "You've been hassling her since she showed up. Shouldn't dish it out if you can't take it, you know."

"Kaige, you don't understand." Her hair flipped over her shoulder as she turned to look at me. "This cunt was strutting around acting as if she owns you."

Any good humor in Kaige's voice fled. His eyes

flashed, and he shoved her away. "Don't you dare call her that. You're lucky she hasn't already beat you down."

Gia hugged herself. "I was just trying to protect you," she insisted.

"Get lost, Gia. Now." Kaige gave her a look of utter disgust and turned away. "I don't want to hear another word."

An expression of dismay crossed Gia's face. Her lips quivered and then pressed together, her eyes closing for a second as if she was trying hard not to cry. Huh. I didn't think that was an act. He wasn't even looking at her now. She seemed to be... genuinely upset.

I almost felt bad for her. Almost. Gia was still a bitch, and if I wasn't going to put her in her place, I was glad someone else had.

She peered at Kaige a second longer and then darted away, swiping her hand across her face. Well, maybe if she hadn't been such a pain in the ass, he'd have liked her more.

"What the hell is her problem anyway?" I muttered as she disappeared down the stairs.

Kaige shrugged. "Don't mind her. Wylder was in a good mood the first night she showed up, and she thought him being a little friendly meant he was hers for life or something. Give 'em an inch..." He shook his head wryly, the usual sly gleam returning to his eye. "And how could she possibly help being jealous of a stunner like you?"

I rolled my eyes, ignoring his flirtation and the flicker of heat it sent through me. "So she's after

Wylder, is she?" I said, grabbing my bags and turning toward my room.

Kaige ambled alongside me down the hall. "Pretty much all the girls are."

"Heir to the Noble legacy and the top prize," I said dryly, and considered what I'd just seen. "She seemed pretty upset having you tell her off, though."

"I suppose I make a decent second choice." He waggled his eyebrows. "And I can't completely blame her for being possessive about what she wants. We must protect what we intend to belong to us."

"What's that supposed to mean?" I looked up at him, practically having to crane my neck to meet his eyes when he was this close. He was just so freaking tall.

Which was why most of the people around here assumed he'd killed one of the Nobles' own. Who else was big enough to have a chance at taking on Titus? No real alibi, plenty of justification that even he'd admitted to, even if he'd dismissed their fight... *Could* he have done it? Was the charming smile a front for a ruthless killer?

I didn't want to think so, which was definitely a problem.

Kaige stopped, halting me with a hand on my waist. As he leaned in, his musky, manly smell washed over me, and my heart skipped a beat despite myself. His hand reached out to touch a strand of hair that had come loose from my ponytail. Instead of tucking it behind my ear, he played with it, twirling the lone strand between his fingers.

"Only that when I see something I want, I make sure I get it," he said.

It took me a second to remember what question he was answering. "Great," I said, willing my voice to stay steady and wincing inwardly at the breathiness that crept into it anyway. I wiggled the bags I was still clutching. "I've just got to put these away..."

"What's in the bags?" He refused to step away, his hand dropping to my jaw and then stroking a slow, sensuous path to my neck. I almost curled into his touch. Shit.

I forced myself to ease back a step instead, but I couldn't go any farther—my shoulders hit the wall. "Just some clothes. I took your advice about the ring."

"I have plenty of good advice on all sorts of topics." He grinned, prowling closer again. "Now I can't help wondering exactly what all is in there. You must have needed more than just T-shirts and jeans. Are you a plain beige girl or black lace? Or maybe you go for scarlet?"

My underwear, he obviously meant. I had actually popped into a store to grab a couple packs of new panties and new bras to match—because who wanted to buy those used?—one set beige, one set black. But I sure as hell wasn't telling him that. Especially now that his voice had dropped to that suggestive whisper. It seemed to dance on my skin, leaving goosebumps in its wake.

He tapped his finger under my chin, setting off even more sparks. "What's your favorite color, Mercy?" he asked, making the simple question sound unbelievably dirty.

I licked my lips unintentionally. "It is red, actually."

His rich brown eyes darkened with desire. "You know what they say about girls who like red..."

"I don't."

He leaned even closer, his warm breath washing over my cheek. "No matter what kind of front they put on, underneath they're dying to get it rough and hard. What do you think, Kitten? Under all that toughness, is there a little freak just waiting to be taken?"

My stomach clenched. Images of him dominating me in all kinds of ways flashed through my mind, and I'd swear lust momentarily short circuited my brain. So it wasn't really my fault that before I could form any kind of response, Kaige stole whatever words might have tumbled over my lips with his own mouth.

He kissed me slowly at first, easing me back until I was pinned between him and the hard wall. The bags slipped from my hands, but I didn't give a shit. His tongue traced my lips before seeking its way inside. As it twined with mine, he deepened the kiss. It was hot and insistent and oh, fuck, I could feel my insides turning to putty.

I clutched at the collar of his shirt to try and bring him even closer to me. He grabbed my hips, squeezing them as his tongue explored my mouth, making me moan against him. With a firm grip that sent an eager quiver through me, he nudged my legs apart and settled his thigh in between them. The pressure made me want to grind against him like a bitch in heat.

Damn, he was good at this. Good enough that I couldn't quite remember why I'd been so resistant a few moments ago. I dug my fingers into his shirt, plundering his mouth right back, and reveled at his groan. He rocked his thigh against just the right spot—

And a loud cough from farther down the hall brought me crashing back to reality.

Kaige pulled back just a few inches—which was far enough for me to see Anthea stopping a short distance away, her arms crossed and her fingers tapping the sleeve of her sundress. Somehow she looked as fierce as a tiger even in clothes that would have suited a '50s housewife.

"Got lost on your way to the bedroom?" she sneered.

I shook myself, recovering my sanity. Kaige offered Anthea a lazy smile, barely affected by the fact that she had stumbled on us making out. In fact, I was pretty sure he was enjoying it.

A flash of cold hit me at the thought of how this interlude would look to her, and I shoved him away from me. I hadn't been trying to seduce Kaige or any of the other three, but Anthea already had her mind made up against me. I'd probably just confirmed the worst of her assumptions.

Kaige stepped back at my push with a chuckle. "Woah, easy there," he said in that playful voice of his. It only set my temper more on edge. Why had I let his smooth, sexy talking get to me?

Anthea walked even closer, her heels clicking against the polished tiles. "Am I interrupting something?" She looked down at my shopping bags which had scattered around us, the clothes spilling out of them.

I bent down and began to collect them, stuffing the contents back in as quickly as I could.

Kaige winked at me. "We were just having a little fun."

I bit back a grimace. The movement of my lips brought back the memory of the kiss. They were still tender. God, if she'd waited just a *little* longer to come prancing down here—

No, it was better that she'd intervened. I needed a clear head, and Kaige certainly wasn't helping with that. Especially when he slowly wiped his mouth with a teasing swipe of his thumb.

"It isn't what it looks like," I said as I stood up.

Anthea scoffed. "Pretty sure I saw his tongue shoved down your throat. But okay, I'll hear your excuse anyway. What exactly is going on?"

"Nothing that was my idea. This guy started the whole thing. I was *about* to put a stop to it."

Kaige just continued to grin at me. It was obvious that he knew just how much I had enjoyed our interlude. "Aw, come on. I'm not that bad a kisser, am I?"

Not at all. I chose to ignore that remark. Turning away from Anthea's skeptical gaze, I marched the rest of the way to my room.

"We can pick up where we left off some other time," Kaige called after me, and damn if my pussy didn't twitch at the suggestiveness in his tone.

"What do you think you're doing?" Anthea snapped at him in a voice not quite low enough for me to miss it.

"She's helping clear my name," Kaige said, unperturbed. "Besides, a kiss never hurt anybody."

The thing was, it'd been more than a kiss. And it'd felt like a promise of many more things to come.

I closed the door to my room behind me and sank to the floor, bringing my fingers to my lips. They were tender to the touch. My panties were soaking wet.

I was in so much fucking trouble.

"What's wrong with you, Mercy?" I asked myself. "You can't let dick distract you."

So what if it had been over a year since I'd last gotten it on with anyone? I'd been around plenty of guys during that time without wanting to jump their bones in a fucking hallway.

"Fuck." I took off my shoes and then stalked to the bed, thinking maybe I'd let off some steam all on my own. I was about to flop down on the mattress when I noticed a piece of paper on the floor. It drifted closer on the breeze that slipped through the open window.

It was a lined paper like kids used in school, slightly crumpled, with a drawing covering most of its surface. The lines were haphazard, almost childish themselves, obviously not drawn by any great artist. Even Rowan's half-hearted doodle had shown more skill, so this definitely wasn't his. The rough sketch showed the face and shoulders of a girl with cat ears drawn over her hair.

Very funny. It was obviously meant to be me, Princess Katz the Kitty Cat. But who had drawn it, and why leave it for me to find?

I picked it up to get a better look at it, and my fingers tightened, creasing the paper. Any lust that'd still been coursing through my body vanished in an instant under a wave of horror.

At a glance, I'd thought the line by the girl's neck had been a shirt collar. Instead it was a gaping wound, blood pouring down from it. Someone had drawn me and then imagined slitting my throat.

And they'd wanted me to know it.

15

Wylder

BAM, BAM, BAM.

Every shot hit the target smack in the middle of the chest. I adjusted the gun in my hands, the feel of the butt heavy but comforting against my palm, and aimed at the head next.

Bam, bam, bam. Another perfect tattered hole. Smiling, I switched on the safety, removed my earplugs, and set the gun on the table next to the array of other weapons.

I picked up my phone and added the model to my list of mastered guns. Testing the new makes that came in, especially 9mms, on our personal range was one of my favorite activities. All the chaos that came with this life fell away with the muffled blare of the shots and the jolt of the kickback. Simple, direct, powerful. Exactly the way I aimed to be in all things.

A voice carried across the lawn from behind me. "Wylder."

I looked up to see Gia sashaying toward me. She almost tripped on a dip in the grass when she neared me, but I made no attempt to reach for her.

I let my expression darken. "What are you doing here? No one except the official crew is allowed on the range."

The ditz giggled and twirled a strand of her blonde hair. "It's fine. I'm not scared of guns." The way she eyed the weapons arranged on the table suggested otherwise. "Are you practicing?"

"Checking out some of the merchandise. I don't need practice." The first time my father had brought me out here, I'd been six years old. And he'd ridden me even harder after—

I dismissed that thought before it could rise all the way to the surface.

Gia giggled. "I'm sure you've got great aim. I'd love to watch you work."

"Sorry to tell you I was just finishing up."

As I moved to sweep the guns back into the crate, she sidled up to me, running a finger down my neck. I grasped her hand and pushed it away. I'd only tolerated her fawning earlier for Mercy's sake. The look on the Katz's princess's face when Gia had practically climbed onto me had been priceless.

She curled her lip into a pout she probably thought was sexy. "If you don't like that, why don't you tell me what you would like?"

I ignored that question. "What do *you* want, Gia?"

"I was just hoping to get to know you better," she said, putting both her arms around my shoulder.

I had the strongest urge to roll my eyes. I could see through her bullshit from miles away. She was no different from the countless girls who walked in and out of my life—just particularly desperate. She was after the power and protection that came with being a Noble woman, either as a mistress or something more permanent.

It was no good telling her that this life would slowly strip her of her dignity and respect—either they never believed it or they didn't give a fuck. It wasn't even *me* she wanted, just my proximity to power.

If I pushed her away hard enough, she'd find someone else to latch onto without more than a moment's regret. The whole thing left a sour taste in my mouth.

"Wylder!" somebody called out. Mercy was striding toward us, moving like a force of fury and spitfire. When she saw Gia hanging off my arm, her face tightened.

A twisted sort of satisfaction coursed through me. To piss her off, I pulled the other girl closer. Even Gia looked shocked for a second before she snuggled against me.

Unfortunately, Mercy didn't look fazed. And the defiant energy radiating off her was having way too much effect on my cock.

She slammed a piece of paper on the table with so much strength I practically hit half-mast just like that. "What the fuck is this supposed to mean?"

Down, boy, I thought at my least obedient body part, and frowned at the paper. It held a pen drawing, rough and amateurish. "Why am I looking at this?"

She set her hands on her perfectly curved hips. "The great Wylder Noble can't figure it out for himself?"

My gaze lingered on the cat ears and then the vicious gouge along the figure's throat. Hmm. Before answering her, I turned to Gia. "I need to deal with this, babe," I said with a smile. "See you later?"

Gia sighed. Beside me, Mercy's fists balled at her sides. Toying with her was fast becoming my favorite activity.

Gia unstuck herself from me reluctantly and sauntered away. When I turned to Mercy, she was looking at me with barely hidden disdain. It almost made me laugh, but I managed to keep a straight face. "That's the company you enjoy keeping?" she said.

I shrugged and picked up the paper. "Are you applying to be a cartoonist? I'll say you need more work."

"I didn't draw it," she snapped. "Obviously. But that's definitely supposed to be me in the picture." She pointed at the cat ears.

I pretended to be shocked. "The resemblance is astounding."

She let out a huff. "Wylder, I'm serious. I found it in my bedroom—someone left it for me to see. This feels like a threat."

I cocked my head at her. "What do you mean?"

"I mean someone wants me gone—most likely in a body bag."

"I hardly think we should take cartoons so seriously."

She ignored my jibe. "Think about the rest of the company you keep. Are any of them likely to toss sketches into people's rooms as a joke?"

She might have had a point there, not that I was going to admit as much to her. "All right, let's hear what you have to say then. Who do you think left it?"

"My best guess would be Anthea," she said without hesitation. "She's already all but threatened me to my face. I could see her wanting to intimidate me into leaving. Not that it'll work."

A frown crossed my face for the first time. My aunt had done *what* without checking with me first? I held my annoyance under wraps. "Whatever else she's done, this doesn't look like Anthea's work to me. She doesn't play kiddie games."

"Maybe it was Gia, then."

I snorted. "Then you really have nothing to worry about. You'd take her down in five seconds flat, Princess."

I probably shouldn't have admitted that thought out loud, but thankfully Mercy seemed to be too distracted to notice the compliment. She glowered at the drawing. "I don't like it, that's all."

An idea unfurled in my head, my smile returning with it. I let my voice drop lower. "I can think of something that would help you feel safer."

Her gaze jerked up, suspicious... but not without a certain heat. Oh, the Claws' princess might have had shields up all around her, but she wasn't unaffected by me, not by a longshot.

"What did you have in mind?" she asked tightly.

I motioned to the table. "Can you use a gun?"

Her gaze followed my gesture, taking in the array. Her posture stiffened slightly, but she nodded. "I haven't in a while, but I know the basics."

Of course she did. Her father would have been an absolute failure if he hadn't even given his daughter a basic grounding, whether he'd considered her a proper heir or not.

"No time like the present to refresh those skills." I picked up a smaller model of gun, checked to see if the clip was loaded, and handed it to her. "Go on, try it out."

Mercy blinked at me in surprise. "You're putting a gun in my hands while you're standing there unarmed?"

"If you even think of pulling it on me, you'll be dead in less than two seconds."

She ignored my words and instead peered down at the guns again. Her hands hovered over each before she set down the one I'd given her and grasped one that was bigger. "I think I'm going to go with this."

Interesting. Ambitious. I liked that more than I wanted to. "Are you sure?"

She shot me a baleful look. "I wouldn't have said it if I wasn't. Now what?"

I grabbed a pair of earplugs from the case on the table and handed them to her. "Assuming you value your hearing." Then I nodded at the targets on the opposite side of the range, each showing the outline of a head and torso filled with concentric lines narrowing in to a bull's eye on the chest and forehead. There were three other than the one I'd already blasted away. "Pick one and try to hit a bull's eye."

Mercy hesitated, but only for a second. She marched over to stand in front of one of the targets, giving me an excellent view of her ample behind. That body was all soft curves, a major contrast to her personality.

She fired the first bullet before I could stop her. The force of the recoil made her stumble. I caught her shoulders before she fell. She looked up at me and then at my hands where I held her.

"Your stance could definitely use some work," I said before she could shake me off. Of course, I *had* to lean especially close so she could hear me with the earplugs in. "Allow me." I fixed her arms and angled her body toward the target. "You must hold it firmly but not too tightly. All your muscles can't be engaged, or it'll kick you back harder than it has to. You need to be able to hold your ground."

"I know that," she said through gritted teeth, elbowing me.

I tsked at her. "Easy, Kitty Cat. You might know how to use a gun, but your technique still sucks. Your old man obviously slacked off in your training." I ran my hands down to her waist, something I'd been wanting to do for a long time. She went very still as my hands skimmed her body. Hell, she smelled fucking amazing, the acrid scent of gunfire mingling with something darkly floral.

My cock hardened in my pants all over again. It

would be so easy to lay her flat on the table and take her right there. From the soft hitch of her breath, I wasn't sure she'd even protest before her normally hostile words turned into sighs of pleasure.

Reining in that urge, I slid my finger over hers on the trigger. "There you go. And then you fire."

We squeezed together. The first bullet hit the target at the edge of the chest bull's eye. Mercy stared in shock for a second.

I forced myself to let go of her and stepped back, letting her take charge. She promptly finished the entire round, firing five more bullets in quick succession, each closer to the center than the last. It was unbelievably hot, and my jeans were feeling way too tight. This girl— this *woman*...

Mercy lowered the gun and popped out her earplugs. I took on a smooth, unaffected tone. "Very good."

She shot a glare over her shoulder at me. "I don't need your approval. I'm glad to improve my skills for my own sake."

"And so you should be." I gave her a sly smile. "And since I helped you get there, that's why you should always remain grateful to me."

"Thanks," she said, giving me the middle finger at the same time. I held back a laugh. She placed the gun on the table and pointed to the paper drawing again.

"Are we still on that?" I asked, amused.

"This is important," she said. "Tell Anthea if she *is* the one who left this, to—"

"I already told you. Anthea had nothing to do with it."

"You can't know that for sure. What would it hurt to bring it up?"

I shrugged. "It's not my problem."

Her jaw ticked. "You're making this difficult on purpose."

"No, you are." I walked right up to her, grinning at the momentary widening of her eyes when I had her locked against the table by my body. "My patience is limited. If you really want my help, you'd better focus on the problem at hand instead of stupid pranks. Or is there something else you want from me, something that needed a silly excuse to seek me out?"

My eyes dropped to her pouty lips. I wondered how she would look with them closed around my cock, worshipping it.

She glanced up, her gaze zeroing on my mouth. Fuck, the heat in her eyes almost made me come undone. My hands itched to pull her up to the table and sink my tongue in her hot mouth. I wanted to know if she tasted like violets as much as she smelled like them.

Without realizing what I was doing, I reached for her face, grazing my fingers along her chin. For just an instant, she leaned into my touch, her eyelids fluttering.

The next second, she was yanking away from me, horror written over her face. Frustration shot through me, but I quickly replaced it with a sardonic smile. I didn't want to let her see just how much this small rejection stung me.

"What happened?" I taunted. "Did the Big Bad Wolf scare you?"

Instead of answering me, she turned and stomped back toward the house. My cock throbbed in my pants, reminding me that even if she hadn't won this round, I hadn't exactly won either.

"Don't worry, Kitten," I murmured. I wasn't one to force women or to chase after skirts. They came to me because they knew I'd deliver what *they* wanted. It was never the other way around.

I could play the long game. There'd come a point when she'd no longer be able to resist what so much of her was already begging for.

16

Mercy

Even though Gideon had said Axel hadn't offered any useful information about Titus's death, I'd seen for myself how invested the guy was in his friend's death. So when I spotted him out in the front yard the next day with a few of his buddies, drinking and smoking cigarettes Wylder wouldn't have allowed most places inside, I figured it couldn't hurt to talk to them. I couldn't exactly end up with fewer leads than I already had.

I made my way toward them, squinting in the hot late-afternoon sun. The sharp scent of nicotine-laced smoke tickled my nose.

Axel gave me an amused smirk when he saw me approach. "We're being joined by royalty. Here's the infamous Claws princess."

So word about my identity had spread around here. Wonderful.

I ignored his bait. "I need to speak to you. Ideally alone."

He snorted. "You can do it here. There's nothing I'd say to you that these guys can't hear."

The other men were practically leering at me. My knuckles itched to land square on somebody's nose, but I forced my voice to stay even. "Fine. I wanted to ask you about Titus. I heard you were the last person who talked to him before he fell."

Axel's face tightened. He threw the cigarette butt to the ground and crushed it under his heel. "Before he was pushed after being murdered, you mean. What about it?"

"Did he say anything to you about any run-ins he'd had earlier that day? Anyone who'd been hassling him recently?"

"No one was stupid enough to hassle the Titan," Axel said. "That's why he was Ezra's favorite to send in when any of the lowlifes in the Bend got too cocky. But no, he didn't seem concerned about anyone in particular. The only person I know he'd had a beef with was that attack dog of Wylder's."

Kaige. I tried another angle. "He didn't seem at all distracted?"

Axel scowled at me. "He took his job seriously."

"I mean, he must have been at least a *little* distracted if somebody was able to ambush him."

Axel jerked around to fully face me, the veins practically popping out of his tattooed head. "I don't like you implying that he got killed through his own carelessness. If that hotheaded prick hadn't gone fucking crazy, nothing would have happened."

"Why are you asking so many questions?" one of the other guys asked.

I didn't think they'd respond well to the idea that Wylder had me investigating to clear Kaige's name, so I just shrugged. "I'm curious. Since it seems like I might be sticking around for a while, I'd kind of like to figure out how a person makes sure they *don't* get murdered."

Another asshole snorted. "Steer clear of Kaige Madden. And get any delusions about joining the Nobles out of your head. Just because your family kicked the bucket doesn't mean there's an opening for some ghetto princess. I wouldn't aspire to anything higher than the big man's bed."

The others snickered, and I gritted my teeth. "You definitely won't find me anywhere near yours," I retorted.

He took a step closer, purposefully looming. "You'd be *lucky* to get a taste of this."

It might have been four to one, and they might have all had a good fifty pounds on me, but I couldn't stop myself from making a gagging sound. The guy bared his teeth like he was going to bite my head off, and I readied my fists, adrenaline racing through my veins. Maybe I'd get a chance to introduce him to my mean right hook. At least that'd mean a little action.

Then a far too familiar voice called out from across the lawn. "Hey, let's all take a step back."

I whirled around to find Rowan walking toward us,

his stance casual but his eyes intense. The other guy stiffened, but he didn't make a move. Obviously he knew better than to challenge Wylder's inner circle openly.

"Did Wylder tell you to babysit her?" Axel sneered. "You should do a better job."

"I just think we can give a better impression to one of the Nobles' guests than getting into a fight with a woman over a few comments," Rowan said calmly. "None of our egos are that fragile."

He did have a weird way with them that somehow deflated the tension. I guessed Axel couldn't exactly argue with his statement. Axel flicked his gaze toward me for just a second. "I've said all I'm interested in sharing. Beat it." He and his group ambled a little farther across the lawn, falling back into their original chatter.

Rowan reached as if to touch my shoulder and then drew his hand back. "Are you okay?"

I glared at him. "I was perfectly fine. I've spent more time around guys like this than *you* have." Why was he always annoyingly around just when I appeared to need help?

I turned toward the mansion, meaning to stalk back inside, but one of the things Axel had mentioned wriggled up through my mind. Ezra had sent Titus into the Bend to lay down the law when things got particularly bad. Gideon had mentioned something about that too. The start of a plan unfurled in my head.

Rowan was still watching me. "What are you up to now?"

"Just finding ways to fulfill the job your boss gave me," I said. "I'd rather do it without spectators."

He looked as if he might have said something more, but then he just shook his head and walked away. Good. I didn't want to find out what he'd say if he realized I was heading back to my hometown.

Technically, going into the Bend right now was dangerous. Colt probably still had the Steel Knights on the lookout for me. But I knew that place better than the back of my own hand. The streets were my home. I'd just stick to Claws territory, keep my head low, and there'd be nothing to worry about.

I slipped into the house just long enough to grab my new hoodie, which was a little hot for the current weather but would help me avoid notice, and a switchblade someone had left on a side table. Their loss, my gain. I tucked the knife into the hoodie's pocket and stuffed the hoodie under my arm for now. No need to draw attention around here before I was well on my way. Kaige had already spotted me taking off once before.

And speak of the devil, as I crossed the lawn, guess who came sauntering out of the garage, his gaze immediately zeroing in on me. Shit.

Kaige grinned when he saw me. "I hope you're not being a bad kitty and running off on us again."

Annoyance shot through me at his riff off Wylder's nickname, but I shook it off. I wasn't going to waste time here. Besides, just the sight of him made my lips tingle as the memory of our hot and heavy make-out session crowded my head. "I was just heading out to look into something that might help clear your name."

One corner of his mouth curled upward. "Need a ride? It'd save you spending your ring money on another taxi. I'm done with my car for the day."

I blinked, startled by the unexpectedly generous offer. The cab ride to my house the other night hadn't been cheap. "Yeah, that would be perfect, actually."

"Follow me," he said, and had to add one of his sly winks. "We could even warm up the engine before you go."

I rolled my eyes, but I followed him as he returned to the garage, which was a two-story building with a huge metal door. Kaige tapped in a code, and the door yawned open to reveal a sprawling bay. There were several cars haphazardly parked next to each other. I recognized Wylder's Mustang. There was a night-black Jaguar next to it, which I wouldn't be surprised to find out belonged to him too.

"One of the few areas where I'd disagree with Wylder is his taste in cars," Kaige said as if he could read my thoughts. "He's more of a style over substance man."

I followed him into the bay. "So which one is yours?"

He pointed to a sleek dark blue Audi. I walked up to it and ran a finger down the hood. It looked like a car Kaige would drive, not too flashy but with an undeniable presence. Just like him.

He leaned against the car and eyed me with some interest.

"What?" I asked.

"I didn't say anything."

"You're really going to let me drive off in this thing, no further questions asked?" It was hard to believe it'd be that easy.

Kaige shrugged. "You're going to try to get me out of trouble. I kind of owe you, don't I?" A lazy grin crossed his face. "Anyway, Gideon has all our cars outfitted with his fancy tracking devices and all that shit. You wouldn't get far with it if you tried anything sneaky."

I hadn't been planning on it, but that was good to know in case I ever had the urge to turn car thief. I held out my hand. "All right then. Where's the key?"

He pointed to his jeans pocket. "Right here. Come and get it."

I narrowed my eyes at him, knowing exactly what he was doing. Undeterred, I hung my hoodie from a side mirror and marched up to him. He watched me through hooded eyes, his smoldering gaze tracing a path slowly from my legs to my face.

I made a grab for his pocket, but he dodged and snatched the key out before I'd gotten to so much as grope his muscular thigh. I raised an eyebrow. "Give it to me."

Kaige grinned and held the key up high. "You'll have to try harder than that."

I stood up on my toes and reached, but he was just too damn tall. I'd never win this fight fairly, so I made use of my own bodily assets. Leaning in, I pushed my tits against his hard chest and then did a wiggle so that his body was deeply aware of the soft mounds. Kaige froze.

I took the opportunity to yank his hand down and grab the key. But maybe that was all part of his plan too. Before I could skip out of reach, he closed his arms around me. "Where do you think you're going?" he rumbled. "I'm not done with you yet." Then he ducked his head and caught my mouth with his.

Some small part of me wanted to push him away like I had in the hall. But it was a *very* small part, and the rest of me was screaming to just enjoy this moment already.

I deserved this, didn't I? I sure as hell didn't owe my ex-fiancé anything. And maybe if I let loose some of the sexual tension that'd been building inside me, my hormones would quit going haywire over Wylder's antics. I didn't really trust him *or* Kaige, but between the two of them, I'd rather put my body in Kaige's hands any day.

Those thoughts whipped through my mind, and I gave in to my desire. As Kaige's mouth ravaged mine, I gave back just as good.

There was nothing gentle about the kiss. One of his hands reached up to grip my ponytail while the other grasped my waist, almost digging into my skin as he pushed me against the hood of the car. Without breaking the kiss, he put his arms under my ass and effortlessly pulled me on top of the firm steel.

My arms encircled his neck. Our tongues danced to gain control over the other, and nobody was ready to back down. His teeth grazed my lips and then nipped, with a pinch of pain that only made the pleasure of the kiss spike hotter. I moaned, my pussy clenching hard. Oh, we were going to heat up this engine all right.

I put my legs around him, tugging him closer. The feel of his hard cock digging into my inner thigh almost unraveled me.

Kaige abandoned my mouth long enough to mark a trail down my neck, kissing and licking. I gasped softly as his lips bit down on my earlobe before slowly sucking on it.

One of his hands reached up from my waist to skim along my side and finally cup one of my breasts. He massaged it greedily, sending giddy tingles all through my chest. "Fuck," he muttered. "I've got to have a taste of these."

Without wasting an instant, he picked up the hem of my shirt and pulled it up over my arms, almost tearing it at the seams. Kaige tossed the shirt to the side and turned to me. As his gaze roamed over my tits, his hungry brown eyes turned almost black with lust.

I hadn't had a lot of choice in the store I'd found, and my breasts were practically spilling out of the thing. My hard nipples pressed eagerly against the thin cotton material.

Kaige pulled on one before leaning over and sucking it into his mouth. I pressed my palms against the hood for balance. Even through the cotton, the feel of his hot mouth made my pussy impossibly wet.

He pushed the strap down to reveal one mound. Flicking the nipple with his finger, he looked up at me, his gaze scorching. Without breaking eye contact, he devoured the bare nipple as if it were the best meal he'd ever had.

Fuck, he was turning me on so badly. He kept shooting those lustful glances at me as he alternated between sucking on my nipple, nipping it between his teeth, and laving it with his tongue again. I growled at the myriad of sensations, each better than the other. My mind had lost the ability to think.

I pulled his face back up to me and kissed him hard. Kaige groaned into the kiss before pushing me away, panting. I blinked up at him.

"What?" I asked, my voice coming out so thick and husky I hardly recognized it.

Instead of answering, he pulled out a condom from his jeans, rolling the foil between his fingers. The question was clear in his eyes.

Despite my earlier resolve, I hesitated. But I knew my body needed this. It was practically screaming at me for release. What could a quick roll in the hay—or, well, the garage—hurt? Fate owed me a little distraction after everything that had happened in the past week.

Only an idiot would say no to it.

I took the packet from him and ripped the foil open. Kaige beamed at me before leaning in to kiss me again.

In a tangle of urgent movements, I yanked off his shirt and he started unbuttoning the fly of my jeans. Together, we helped him out of his own. I ran my hands along the hard planes of his chest, his muscles flexing under my fingers, the vines tattooed all across them rippling.

"Like what you see?" he asked. I chose not to answer.

His hand brushed against the sensitive skin of my thighs, skimming upwards. I held my breath as he reached my slick core. He stroked me and then slipped a finger in, and I practically exploded right there.

"You're so wet already," he whispered, curling another finger inside me. "So wet for me."

I'd be gushing in a moment. As the waves of bliss swept over me, I clutched hard at his shoulder so that I wouldn't slip off the car. He continued to kiss my neck as his fingers worked inside me. My eyes rolled up, and I ran my fingers down his bare back.

As his deft fingers flicked my swollen clit, I couldn't help crying out. My hips moved against his hand of their own accord, swaying with his rhythm.

"Easy, Kitten," he said gruffly, reaching down to roll the condom over his hard dick. I set my fingers over his and slid them along his length. His cock twitched in our combined grasp, as huge as the rest of him. I groaned at the size of it.

As soon as he was sheathed, he stepped between my legs and in one fluid motion, plunged into me. My body bucked against his. I stretched with his girth, shivering at the heady mix of pleasure and pain.

He thrust hard and rough, just the way I needed it. "Do you like that?" Kaige murmured. "Do you like my cock inside you?"

I gasped in answer, which was easier than admitting that yes, I did, very fucking much. With each thrust, he started swirling his hips so he hit the perfect spot inside. Damn, he was good at this.

Another moan slipped out of me, and Kaige brushed a teasing thumb over my lips. "Shhh, Kitten. You wouldn't want to get too loud. The walls echo, you know, and who knows who might come in to check on things."

The thought of somebody walking in on us—especially Wylder—shot a burst of excitement down my spine. A part of me wanted him to watch and seethe, knowing he would never own me like this.

Kaige eagle spread me on the hood, keeping a hand on my shoulder as he continued to pump inside me. Somehow the friction at my back heightened that between my legs.

He reached down between us and found my clit even as he continued to stroke into me harder and faster. My body jerked against his as both his finger and his cock found exactly the right spot at the same time. The orgasm climbed in me, careening toward a crescendo, and then I was flying on it.

My body sagged against the hard metal, but Kaige didn't let me recover from my first orgasm before he flicked my clit again, setting off another swell of ecstasy just like that. The crest of pleasure was even bigger this time. Everything around me hazed out with the blaze of bliss.

Kaige followed me with a guttural sound, his body jerking more erratically. He slumped too, almost collapsing on me, our labored pants intermingling with each other. A drop of sweat from his forehead rolled down to my body. He followed the trail to my tits, sucking on my nipple one last time before he pulled out of me.

Jesus fucking Christ. My legs still shook from the aftermath of the second orgasm, and my thumping heart was threatening to burst out of my ribs. When had sex *ever* felt that good?

Kaige tossed the condom away into a bin by the wall and pulled up his jeans. I dropped to the ground and almost lost my footing. I'd had good dick in my day, but I hadn't felt after-effects quite like this. Kaige knew his way around a woman.

And he was fully aware of that fact. "You okay?" he asked slyly as he caught my shoulder to steady me.

I nodded, getting a grip on myself. It'd just been sex —fantastic sex, but still only sex. And it'd probably only seemed so freaking fantastic because I was coming off the longest dry spell of my life.

Turning away from Kaige, I collected my clothes. He watched me lazily as I got dressed. His black hair stuck damply to his scalp, and he looked almost boyish as he stood, greedily drinking in the sight of me. My pussy started throbbing again as if it was ready for round two.

Oh, fuck no. It wouldn't do me any good getting hooked on this guy. We'd had a bit of fun, but I wasn't going to let it mean anything at all.

Mercy

Kaige tossed me the car key, which I caught easily. "That was one hell of a detour," he said with a grin.

"Thanks," I said, ignoring his innuendo. Yes, we'd just had mind-blowing sex, but his ego clearly didn't need any stroking on that score. It was time for me to get down to work.

Kaige gave me a strange look as I climbed into the Audi. You'd have thought he'd be happier about my easy-going approach. I mean, we'd just had our first hook-up on the hood of his car. Presumably he hadn't thought we'd be holding hands and whispering sweet nothings next.

I started the engine and smiled. This beat a taxi by a mile.

Kaige hit the button to open the garage door for me, and I thanked him with a little wave as I cruised past. I pulled out of the driveway and swung the car around the corner to careen down the steep hill that led into the center of Paradise City. As the car zoomed toward the bend, I leaned back in the buttery leather seat.

It smelled like Kaige—musky with a bit of a spicy bite, like ginger or something. To my annoyance, the scent set off a flare of heat low in my belly. When I squeezed my thighs, I could feel the lingering wetness between them.

Okay, maybe a *tiny* part of me hoped our hook-up would turn out to be more than a one-time thing.

As Paradise City's pretty streets gave way to the Bend's grittiness, a twinge of homesickness rippled through my chest. I knew each and every corner of the place. Before my formal education had even begun, Dad had made me memorize the street names and the by-lanes that ran past them. I'd made so many nooks and ledges my own, sneaking in my parkour practice when I could. This neighborhood had been *mine*, and now Colt had me running scared.

He'd pay for that like he would for so much else.

I found a quiet street in Claws territory and parked the Audi there out of view, because even if it wasn't especially flashy, a car this nice would draw the wrong kind of attention. As I stepped out, I pulled on my hoodie, yanking the hood up to hide my ponytail and shadow my face. The sun was starting to sink, thank God, because one minute in these clothes and I was already sweating.

There were a few bars in the neighborhood where

disreputable types tended to gather. I headed toward the nearest one. Passing my favorite diner, Joe's Morning, a whiff of pancakes-for-dinner filled my nose and made my mouth water. Whenever I'd been feeling low, I'd stop by here.

Movement caught my eye. Up ahead, a grey car had stopped in the middle of the street. Three guys got out. One was swinging a baseball bat idly, though there definitely wasn't anywhere to play around here, and they all had red bandanas tied around their upper arms. Red bandanas with an emblem of a knight's helmet on them.

I froze. I hadn't expected to run into a whole squad of Steel Knights in the middle of Claws territory. With a lurch of my heart, I ducked into the closest alley, clutching the switchblade.

They didn't seem to be at all interested in a young woman walking down the street, though. They stalked right past my alley with a thrum of energy around them that told me something was about to go down. Frowning, I edged closer to the mouth of the alley to watch.

The guys marched up to the barber shop right across from Joe's. The leader rapped on the door with his bat.

A few moments later, a man poked his head out, his eyes wide. "What's going on here?"

"Where's our payment?" one demanded. "We sent out a message a few days ago. Now we're here to collect."

The man stared at them, bewildered. "I already paid my tithe to the Claws."

"The Claws are gone and dust," one of the Steel Knights replied. All three of them looked younger than me. That and their exaggerated swagger made me think they had to be new recruits. "These streets belong to us now."

My jaw clenched at his words. I was about to take a step forward when I remembered where I was—*who* I was. If I blew my cover, I was as good as dead. One little knife wouldn't do much good against the guns they were all undoubtedly packing.

But who the hell were these pricks to claim this territory as their own? The Claws leadership had barely been dead a week, and Colt was already mass-recruiting to fill the gap?

Not just recruiting but terrorizing the people who didn't fall in line as fast as the Steel Knights wanted.

"I—I don't know about this," the man stammered, and one of the guys grabbed him by the collar. As he dragged him out onto the sidewalk, the one with the bat smashed the shop's front window with a brutal swing.

I flinched at the shattering sound. Panicked people down the street started rushing away without making too much noise.

This wasn't exactly a new sight around here, but the streets were almost safe once each gang had established their territory. The Steel Knights were changing the very face of the Bend.

The guy who'd grabbed the shop owner shoved him down on his hands and knees. The man's shoulders shook. "I'll get your money. Please, this is my livelihood. Please."

His begging fell on deaf ears. When the guy with the bat stepped inside the barber shop, more smashing sounds followed in his wake. The third Steel Knight grabbed a can of gasoline from the car.

No. Anger built up inside of me like a whirlwind. My hands itched to find a gun or anything else to end this senseless violence, even if I had to use violence to do that.

The guy with the gasoline went into the shop and returned empty-handed with his bat-wielding colleague beside him. I knew what was going to happen, and I knew I couldn't stop it without risking everything, but I couldn't will myself to look away.

The apparent leader pulled a lighter from his pocket. "Let this be a warning to anybody who decides to cross the Steel Knights," he announced to the street at large. "We're the kings of this territory now. Everything here is ours."

With that, he flicked on the lighter and threw it through the store window. A terrible orange light spilled out, flames lashing at the frame and roaring higher inside. The owner, crouched on the pavement outside, started to sob.

The Steel Knights took turns kicking him. "Next time we ask you to pay up, you'd better have it ready or else."

After a few more jabs, they got back into their car and drove away. The sound of a fire engine's siren wailed in the distance. I knelt by the wall, trying to regain my breath as rage expanded inside my ribs until it felt like a splintering force.

My family hadn't even got a proper burial yet, and Colt's people were rampaging through my home, tearing it to shreds.

When I'd managed to calm the fury inside me enough, I walked across the street to where the fire was still raging. The man was weeping, beating his closed fist against the pavement. I crouched down next to him and took out a wad of money, most of what I had left from selling my engagement ring.

I'd bought everything I could use for now. He needed it a hell of a lot more than I did.

"Here," I said. "Take this."

He looked up at me with tear-filled eyes. He might have recognized me—Dad had made me a semi-public figure, dressing me up and dragging me to events. Showing off the daughter he sneered at in private.

"I'm going to make this right," I promised. The man nodded, but I couldn't tell if he believed me.

There was nothing else I could do but walk away. But I wasn't leaving it behind, not really.

The farther I went, the more evidence I saw of the Steel Knights claiming this territory. Fresh graffiti marked the walls. More guys with the knight emblem bandanas prowled the streets. There were plenty of people who'd pledged loyalty to my father still alive around here, but apparently no one was willing to push back without a leader.

I guessed I couldn't totally blame them. I'd gone running for help—they hadn't had the same option.

By the time I reached my intended destination, an old brownstone building in the warehouse district with a crooked banner that announced its name was Rookers, my stomach was churning with even more anger than before.

I entered the dimly lit room to the smell of old whiskey and smoke. The place was fairly crowded even though it was early in the evening. A few guys circled around a table were playing poker with chips, and others were occupied at the snooker table placed to the side. Twangy country music played over the speakers.

I walked up to the bartender, an old man who was cleaning the glasses. He didn't look like he was interested in serving anybody, but I took a place on one of the empty bar stools anyway. A guy sitting a few places down swirled a glass of amber liquid in his hand.

"What do you want to drink?" the bartender snapped.

So much for customer service. I considered the cash I still had on me, which wasn't much. But I definitely wouldn't make any friends here if I didn't cough up a little dough as a paying customer. "Gin and tonic. Strong." I needed it to drown out my fury over everything I'd witnessed outside.

A few moments later, he passed me a glass. I drank it slowly, letting the burn of the alcohol seep through my body. My other hand dropped to the pocket of my jeans, where my fingers traced the outline of my childhood bracelet.

Little Angel. Was that how my mother had seen me? I sure as hell wasn't an angel now, and that was a good thing. Bitches got things done. Angels... Maybe they ended up like her, either run out of town for fear of her life or buried in a grave somewhere.

Dad had never given me a straight answer about where she'd gone when she'd disappeared, but even at six, I'd been able to tell he was upset that she hadn't given him another kid. The boy he wanted that he'd never gotten.

Considering how many women he'd tried with, that'd obviously been *his* fault. Not that he'd ever have admitted it.

When I'd almost finished my drink, I tossed out a casual remark. "Say, I heard Titus used to stop by here now and then. Have you seen him lately?"

The bartender frowned. "Who?"

"A big guy," I said. "*Really* big. Some people called him the Titan. I wanted to talk to him about something."

The man grimaced. "From what I've heard, he's dead, girl. A pretty thing like you doesn't want to mess with that business."

"Oh my God." I pretended to be shocked. "How did he die?"

The man farther down the bar glanced over at me. Uneasiness made the back of my neck prickle. I turned my head so my hood would shield more of my face from his nosiness.

"From what I heard, he got drunk and took a fall," the bartender said. I guessed that was the story Ezra Noble preferred to have spreading around rather than that someone within the gang had murdered one of his top guys.

"Seems like a strange way to die," I ventured, watching the bartender's reaction.

He swiped his rag over the countertop harder. "You never know. He certainly didn't have many friends around here. A person's sins can catch up to them eventually."

Vague and noncommittal—playing it safe. He knew how things worked in Paradise Bend.

As if any of us here didn't have plenty of sins to our name. Man, if this place was any type of Paradise, it was definitely the crooked kind.

I kept my tone neutral. "Is there anyone here who he might have talked to at all? Maybe they could give me a hand with what I was going to ask him about."

"I can't think of anyone, but around here, he's more likely to have been breaking bones than hanging around to chat." He turned his back on me, conversation over. I wasn't getting anything else out of him, but I didn't think he knew any details about the murder anyway.

I looked around, wondering who to try next. The snooker guys seemed to be as good a bet as any. I slipped off my stool and sauntered over to lean against the table.

I wasn't exactly a sexpot in this hoodie, but one of them looked up after taking a shot and gave me an unrestrained leer. I forced a smile. "You play really well."

He smirked. "Thanks. I haven't seen you around here before. Looking for some... action?"

"Buddy, pay attention to the game," one of his friends said with a sigh.

"This isn't my scene usually, but I come by every now and then," I said, trying to keep him engaged. "I think I have seen you before—were you playing with Titus?"

One of the men snorted. "The Titan? He never touched a cue in his life—except maybe to break it over someone's head."

I bit my tongue. Wrong tactic. But Titus clearly had a reputation around here. No one seemed to have any specific personal animosity toward him, though.

From the corner of my eye, I noticed the man from the bar now lingering in the corner. Was he trying to listen in on our conversation? A chill washed through me. Had he realized who I was?

I was probably being paranoid, but my gut told me that I would rather be safe than sorry. This place felt like a dead end.

"Thanks for your time, gentlemen," I said and ambled off as if I wasn't in any hurry. Outside, I glanced at the reflection on the window of another storefront and saw the man follow me out. Picking up my pace, I took off toward a row of old warehouses, most of which were in terrible condition.

After walking for a few blocks, I glanced around and found the man had vanished. Crouching as if I needed to tie my shoes, I scanned the area for the space of several more heartbeats. When I didn't see any sign of him, I exhaled in relief. False alarm.

The grumble of a large vehicle brought me back

onto my feet. Slipping into the deepening shadows of a doorway, I watched an armored truck approach. What the hell was *that* doing here?

I caught a glimpse of a red bandana around the arm of the guy in the passenger seat. The Steel Knights were behind this too. The truck had to be carrying something important. Drugs? Weapons?

As it disappeared around a turn, I made a split-second decision to follow it, breaking into a sprint to catch up. I had to figure out what they were up to. We couldn't take down Colt if we didn't know everything he was preparing.

The armored truck was moving slowly as if the driver was concerned about jostling its contents too hard. That was an ominous sign. I managed to keep up with it in short dashes between bits of shelter, never letting myself get too close. When it veered into Steel Knights territory, the hairs on the back of my neck rose, but I was committed now.

After several more blocks, the truck swerved to pass through a low gateway. Behind a crumbling brick wall around a courtyard, the dingy form of another warehouse loomed. As I came up on the wall, the truck's engine cut off somewhere inside the compound and a man started shouting commands.

Itching to take a closer look, I slunk over. I hitched myself up using the few loose bricks that stuck out of the wall. It was an easy climb. Keeping my head low, I peered over the top.

Men were ferrying huge crates from the rear into the warehouse. A tall man stepped out of the back of the truck, and my blood ran cold. I didn't know his name, but his face was burned into my memory. He'd been with Colt the night of the rehearsal dinner—he was the one who'd shot my grandmother.

"Hurry up, we don't want to dawdle around all day," he hollered.

One of the men heaved his crate out faster, and it slipped from his grasp. As it crashed to the ground, its lid jolted off.

"You idiots," the man snarled. "Can't even do one thing right."

I squinted to see the crate's contents. It looked like guns, large ones nestled in straw. Lots of them, from how many I could make out and the size of the crates.

They must have been bringing in hundreds. What the fuck did they want with so many weapons all of a sudden? It almost looked like they were planning for a major assault.

Against who? Hadn't taking down the Claws been enough? How much of the Bend did they want—and what made them think they'd need an army's worth of firepower to get it?

Unless...

My stomach twisted. I dropped down the wall before I could be spotted and hurried in the opposite direction.

I needed to get back to the city, back to the mansion, and tell Wylder and his guys what I'd seen. This could be even worse than I'd thought.

I hurried past several blocks of buildings without registering much. I was so lost in my thoughts that I almost didn't notice when I bumped shoulders with somebody on the sidewalk.

"Watch it," a familiar voice snarled.

I whirled around and found myself staring at Gia, a thin jacket covering most of her skinny frame and a small duffel bag clutched against her side. My shock was mirrored in her eyes.

"What are *you* doing here?" she squawked before I could ask her the same thing. She whipped a knife out of her jacket and brandished it at me. "Are you stalking me now, you fucking bitch?"

Whoa, talk about going from zero to one hundred in an instant.

"Why the hell would I stalk a pathetic excuse for a human being like you?" I shot back. "I didn't even see you until you smacked into me."

"*You* bumped into *me*. I knew you had to be some kind of psycho. Get the fuck away from me!"

She waved the knife, but I didn't flinch. Maybe it was time Gia found out exactly what happened when you went around throwing insults at the wrong people. I didn't even bother reaching for the switchblade in my pocket—just my fists against Gia seemed like an awfully unbalanced fight.

"I have just as much right to be here as you do," I said evenly. "So why don't you scamper off and leave me to my business?"

She scoffed. "If you don't take off *right* now, I'm gonna—"

I didn't get to find out what she was going to threaten me with—and how hard I was going to laugh at the thought—because just then a cool, hard voice rang out from behind me.

"If it isn't my lovely fiancée. Come to pay me a visit?"

My body turned to ice. I spun around and came face to face with Colt Bryant.

18

Mercy

Gia slowly lowered her knife, her gaze flicking from me to Colt and clearly evaluating him as a greater threat. The bulge of a gun showed clearly at his hip. "Who the hell are you?" she asked, but her bravado had gone thin.

He flashed bright, vicious teeth. "The man who owns these streets—no one you want to mess with. I'd like to speak with my fiancée *alone*."

Gia hesitated for only a second before darting away. Colt immediately returned his full focus to me. He circled me like a shark does to its prey.

As I stood face to face with him for the first time since our rehearsal dinner, conflicting impulses tore through my body. The bastard looked so fucking *smug*. Fury unfurled in my chest, urging me to hurl myself at him and rip out his throat with my bare hands if that was what it took. But the—smaller, but insistent—

sensible part of me pointed out that he'd probably put a bullet in my brain before I even touched him. My chances of destroying him were way better if I lived to return with proper reinforcements.

I considered bolting after Gia—or in any direction, really—but before the thought could solidify in my head, several Steel Knights men closed in around us. I stiffened, willing back a surge of panic.

This wasn't a chance encounter—Colt had shown up prepared to overpower me. My chances had just dwindled from slim to none. No way could I take on all of them.

"So, you've finally come home," Colt said. "It took you long enough. Got bored of your shiny new friends?"

Did he know where I'd been the past few days? I balled my hands at my sides and then shoved them into my pockets, curling my fingers around the switchblade. If he was going to order my death now, I'd do everything I could to take him with me, hopeless as my chances were.

Colt tracked the movement with eyes that were too keen. He held out his hand. "Whatever you're thinking, it isn't going to work. Give it to me."

Shit. I wavered, and heard the safeties click off several guns. A prickle ran down my spine. I pulled out the folded switchblade and tossed it at him so it smacked into his chest. "Happy?"

"Getting there." He gestured to a lackey, who bent to snatch up the knife. "How have *you* been doing these days, Mercy?"

When I didn't answer, a few of his men snickered. I

gritted my teeth. "Are you having fun toying with me before you gun me down? Ten to one—that's awfully stacked odds for a man who thinks he's such a hotshot."

Colt didn't rise to my bait. "Who said anything about gunning you down? I just wanted to talk."

He chuckled darkly, running his fingers through his thick golden hair. I couldn't believe I'd found him attractive once.

"Keep talking and I'll jam my fist down your throat." I took a step toward him, and immediately all his men jerked their weapons up.

"Stand down, boys," Colt said, raising his hand. "I'm sure my fiancée and I can manage to have a civil conversation."

"Don't you fucking call me that. There's nothing I want to say to you." All I wanted was to choke the life out of this asshole.

"We *will* talk," he insisted. "But this definitely isn't the best spot for it. Come along."

He motioned for me to follow him, and his men drew closer. My skin prickled with resistance, but I didn't have much of a choice. Better to stay alive a little longer and see if I could find an opportunity to escape after all.

When I didn't move right away, one of his men nudged me with his gun. "Walk."

"Don't touch her," Colt said with a warning in his voice. The hint of possession in his tone surprised me. Was he seriously making some gesture toward protecting me after what he'd done?

What did he want to talk about anyway?

With curiosity gnawing at me, I pushed myself forward. We walked for a good fifteen minutes before we reached a part of the Bend which wasn't as impoverished.

Had Colt been down in the warehouse district overseeing the weapons delivery and caught sight of me without me noticing? Or maybe that man from the bar had been some kind of narc after all, identifying me and then running off to tell his master.

Fucking Gia distracting me. I could have been back to Kaige's car by now if it wasn't for her.

Colt's men escorted me inside an old brick office building and up the stairs to the third floor. We stepped through a doorway into an airy open-concept space that smelled of raw wood.

The room was clearly being renovated, beams and chunks of tile scattered around. The breeze carried through the windows, which hadn't been fitted with fresh panes yet. My gaze latched onto one that looked out onto a narrow alley between this building and the one next door, no more than five feet away.

There was my escape route right there, one Colt and his men would never anticipate. I'd mentioned my old interest in gymnastics to Colt once, but never how that had evolved into riskier stunts after Dad had cut off my classes.

Colt motioned for his men to stand guard on the landing outside. "I'd like to talk with her alone."

I eased closer to the window I'd noticed, pretending to be examining the space. The walls at the other end looked recently painted. No furniture had been brought in yet. "What is this place?"

"Just one of my many new bases of operation within my new kingdom." Colt stalked closer to me, and I used that as an excuse to back up in the direction of the window. "Or perhaps I should say *our* kingdom?"

My jaw went slack. Colt was watching me shrewdly. "You killed my family," I spat out. My hand rose to the still healing spot on my arm where one of his men's bullets had clipped me. "You tried to kill *me*. There is no 'our.'"

For an instant, I could have sworn I saw a flash of regret before it was replaced by ruthless ice in his eyes. "I did what I had to do to protect myself," he said. "Your father was going to turn on me as soon as he had the chance."

"Bullshit. He wanted the alliance—it was *his* idea. Why would he work so hard for it only to kill you?"

Colt began to pace. "I can't tell you how your father's mind worked. I only know I've seen more than enough evidence to be sure of it. Our marriage was all part of his plan. As soon as he got a grandson as an heir, he'd have done away with me."

I thought back over all the times Dad had talked about cooperation between the Claws and the Steel Knights. I'd never heard a hint of that kind of malicious plotting. It didn't even make sense. It could have taken years, more than a decade for us to have kids, if we'd had any at all.

If he'd wanted a war with the Steel Knights, why

wait around? He could have married me to some powerless man and hoped to get his heir that way.

Either Colt was making this up to justify what he'd wanted to do anyway, or he was totally delusional.

When I shook my head, Colt walked right up to me and grabbed me by the nape of my neck through my hood. There was nothing gentle about it. "You don't believe it?"

His eyes danced with a terrible light. For the first time, I began to wonder if something was seriously wrong with him.

His gaze dropped to my lips, still slightly tender from Kaige's ravaging just a couple of hours ago. His jaw clenched. Could he tell? Something inside me tightened despite myself.

Colt was an attractive man, his amber eyes like a panther about to pounce. He reminded me of Wylder in some ways—but the truth was, they couldn't be any more different. Wylder had shown me exactly who he was, no pretenses. My *ex*-fiancé had given me nothing but lies.

I shoved him away, and to my surprise, he let me go. "No, I don't," I said. "I knew my father a hell of a lot better than you did, and he was *excited* by all the possibilities of the partnership."

"I know what I've seen," Colt said quietly. "But it's become clear to me that you weren't in on his schemes. We can put the past behind us. Be my queen, and together you and I will rule all of the Bend."

I shook my head. "You're insane." Just a few weeks

ago, his declaration would have woken up butterflies in my stomach, but now I felt nothing but disgust.

"I go after what I want. And *everyone* wants power. Don't lie to yourself, Mercy. You've got to see how much we could accomplish together." Colt paused. "Maybe your father knew what you'd be capable of too, and that's why he tried to break you."

I flinched. "The only person who's lied to me is *you*."

"But I now know that you had nothing to do with your father's plans," Colt said. "Your devotion wasn't false. So let's move on."

"I wasn't devoted to you," I snapped. I'd thought I'd been so calculating, but in the end I'd turned out to be a foolish, naïve girl who thought she could gain her freedom just like that. Ha.

Maybe it wasn't smart of me, but I couldn't stop my mouth from shooting off more. "You know what I think, Colt? What you're telling me is just another load of bullshit. And I'm not falling for it this time." I turned away from him and walked the last few steps to the window. The cooling evening air wafted over, beckoning me.

"What if we could rule all of Paradise Bend, not just the dregs down here?" Colt said, drawing me up short. That sounded all too close to the suspicion that had darted through my mind watching the weapons delivery.

I glanced over my shoulder at him. "What are you talking about?"

"Don't you think it's time the big men on the hill got taken down a peg? Or have you been impressed by those pompous bastards you went running to after all?"

My back went rigid. "How did you—"

Colt shook his head. "Did you really think I wouldn't realize where you'd gone? Even the Nobles can't ensure every mouth stays shut."

Fuck. This was even worse than I'd thought. Not that his stupid plan would get him very far. Wylder wasn't going to give a shit how Colt threatened me.

I raised my chin. "And there's the lie. That's why you actually brought me here—you want me as leverage."

Colt let out a short guffaw. "Hell, no. Mercy, I want you to help me take them down. Go back to them, dig up every weakness you can, trip them up with your wily ways, and lay them on a platter for me. Once the Nobles are out of the picture, we can rule the whole county. Our kingdom will stretch as far as the eyes can see." He swept his hand at the window at the front of the room.

"With the crown on your head and me under your heel?" I retorted.

"I'm not your father. You won't be a commodity; you'll rule beside me. My queen and my equal."

Sudden tears pricked at the back of my eyes. Why did he have to say this *now* after he'd screwed me over in so many ways? It was even better than I'd dared to hope for with him—but I could never trust the man in front of me again. The thought of standing beside him, of letting him lay his hands on me, made me want to vomit.

If I ever touched him again, it'd only be to ram a knife right into his heart.

But as soon as he realized I wasn't going along with his crazy plan, he'd need me out of the picture. My heart thudding, I took one final step and rested my hand on the bare window ledge.

"No thanks. Not if you were the last man on earth. Fuck you."

His face hardened. He started toward me, his hand shooting out to snatch at my arm, but I was already launching myself out into the open air.

For a few tenths of a second, everything slowed down in the whoosh of air and adrenaline. My hands and toes planted against the concrete wall of the neighboring building just as they had so many times in so many less precarious situations.

My muscles responded on what was instinct after years of practice, shoving and spinning me at the same moment. I rebounded off the wall back toward Colt's building, dropping a few feet at the same time. No looking down. Just bouncing back and forth like a rubber ball slowly ricocheting to the ground. I'd scaled three floors going up this way before. I'd just never done it letting my momentum carry me down toward the potentially deadly surface below.

Shouts echoed through the windows above. I ignored them, concentrating on the thrust of my limbs and the rhythm of my breath. Back and forth and back and—

The rough brick scraped the heel of my hand hard enough to draw blood. I sucked in a breath at the sting, my concentration wavering just for a second. But then my feet hit the asphalt of the alley.

I'd made it all the way down. I was free, completely through my own power.

Footsteps were pounding down the staircase inside so loud I could hear them through the wall next to me. Riding the rush of my success, I sprinted out of that alley and into another across the street. Turning here, swerving there, I wove through the streets toward the spot where I'd left Kaige's car, until both my lungs and my calves were burning and I was sure Colt's men hadn't tracked me.

Even if they were still on my trail, I'd be long gone by the time they got here. I leapt into the Audi and tore onto the road heading into Paradise City, clenching the steering wheel tightly to stop my hands from shaking. The one I'd scraped was bleeding a little, dappling the surface of the wheel, but all things considered, I figured Kaige would forgive me.

By the time the bright lights on the hill came into view, dusk had settled over the county. I raced up the slope and sped into the driveway, parking outside the garage since I didn't have the code to open it.

My pulse was still pounding double-time. I threw open the door, peeling off my sweaty hoodie as I went, and rushed toward the house.

Before I'd made it even halfway to the front door, five figures burst out.

"Mercy," Rowan said, oddly short for breath. "Did you go back to the Bend?"

My hackles came up automatically. "What's it to you? You're not my keeper."

Wylder pushed in front of him, Gideon, Kaige, and

Anthea right behind him. One look at the fury etched on the Noble heir's face stopped me in my tracks.

"No, but at the moment, *I* am," he said. "And from what I hear, you not just went scampering home, you've been cozying up to Colt Bryant behind our backs."

Mercy

I froze. There wasn't any question in Wylder's statement. It was an accusation.

Anthea folded her arms in front of her chest. "Don't try to deny it. Gia told us everything."

Of course she had. I reined in my anger, holding myself cautiously. "What exactly did she tell you?"

"That you were out in Steel Knights territory and met with your 'fiancé,'" Wylder said. "Seems like a funny thing for her to make up."

My hands clenched. "She didn't make it up—but it wasn't like—"

"Don't go making excuses," Kaige snarled, shoving past Wylder. "This whole time you've been double-crossing us? After all the— I ought to—" Fury reddened his face, and veins popped from his neck and down his brawny arms. He lunged at me, only brought up short by Wylder grabbing his shoulder.

A chill rippled through me. Who the hell *was* this guy? Kaige's easy demeanor had been replaced by something I didn't even recognize, something feral and wild. If he'd gotten this enraged in his argument with Titus, I could see why Axel and the others thought he could have killed the guy.

How were Wylder and the others so sure he *hadn't*?

But despite my fear, a flicker of heat shot through the chill right down to my pussy. My God, what was wrong with me? He looked savage enough to tear me to pieces, and something about that was turning me on even as I flinched inwardly at having his hostility directed at me. An image flashed through my head of him taking me with all that brutal intensity, hate-fucking against his car in a fiercer version of this afternoon's hook-up.

I shook my head as if I could dispel my reaction. Kaige seemed to take the motion as a denial. "Don't lie to us now," he yelled, loud enough that Anthea winced. "You fucking betrayed us!"

"No, I didn't," I shouted back. "Maybe if you'd let me finish my goddamn sentence—"

"I don't want to hear anything from your stupid mouth." He jerked forward again, and it took both of Wylder's hands to haul him back. The Noble heir watched me coldly.

"We should let her talk," Rowan said quietly. "We have to know exactly what went down, what she told Colt—all of it."

Gideon nodded, his eyes sharply intense and even

icier than Wylder's. "Yes. All the details, quickly." He snapped his fingers.

I drew in a breath, my skin prickling with nervous anticipation. This could go so very badly if they didn't believe me. My muscles in my calves flexed with the impulse to just make a run for it.

But now I wanted Colt and his lackeys destroyed more than ever, and I'd seen incredibly clearly that there was no way I was accomplishing that on my own.

"If *Gia* hadn't been lying, she'd have told you Colt ambushed me. She was right there—she must have been able to tell that I wasn't expecting to see him and that I wasn't happy about it. And then she took off, because all she cared about was saving her own skin."

Wylder scowled at me. "She said he's calling you his fiancée still. That's how we figured out who it was."

I barely restrained myself from rolling my eyes. "Fun fact: I don't have any control over what words that asshole uses. I'm sure as hell not calling *him* my fiancé anymore."

"Still, it's a rather friendly term," Gideon put in evenly. "And Gia got back here almost two hours ago. Where have you been all that time?"

"Colt had a bunch of his men with him. I didn't have the chance to get out of there. He took me to one of his buildings, insisted on talking to me. It took me a while to get away."

Anthea snorted. "And you just waltzed out of what I assume was a heavily guarded building with no problem at all? Sounds too convenient to be true."

Yeah, it probably did. I balked at admitting this skill

to them—I preferred to keep as much as I could in my back pocket—but I had to explain my escape somehow.

"I did gymnastics as a kid," I said. "Until my dad decided it was a waste of time. But I wanted to keep practicing on my own, and while I was looking up training videos, I stumbled on parkour. It was even better—leaping and bounding all over the city, scaling buildings most people couldn't... I broke a few bones in the first couple of years, but I kept at it, and I'm pretty fucking good now, if I do say so myself."

Wylder cocked his head. "A very nice story, Kitty Cat, but it doesn't answer the question."

I glared at him. "It does if you have half a brain. I never talked to Colt about that recreational activity. So it didn't occur to him that it wasn't a good idea to let me get close to an open window. I took a flying leap and rebounded between the building and the one next door all the way to the ground. Ran off before his guys could make it down the stairs coming after me. I know the streets in the Bend pretty well, and we were close to Claws territory still."

Or what'd used to be Claws territory before the Steel Knights had pissed all over it to mark it their own.

"Bullshit," Kaige spat out, but he wasn't pulling against Wylder's grasp anymore. Maybe he'd gotten a glimpse of me using some of those techniques to get in and out of my house the other night.

I set my hands on my hips. "It's up to you whether you believe me or not. Do you need a demonstration or something?"

Rowan was studying me warily. "I never saw you do anything like that."

"Guess you didn't know me as well as you thought. Goes both ways, doesn't it?" I grimaced. "You didn't like hearing about me being in any kind of danger. I didn't think you'd want to hear about *me* putting myself in harm's way."

Anthea tapped her fingers against one elbow. "What I'd like to know is why Colt, who meant to murder you a week ago, decided to bring you around for an extended chat instead of shooting you where you stood."

It was time for the full truth, and I knew it could be an awfully bitter pill for them to swallow. "He figured I'd be more useful to him alive after all. He knows I've been staying here, and he had a proposition for me. He wanted me to join him and take the Nobles down."

Gideon stiffened while Kaige and Wylder swore in unison. "That motherfucker," Kaige said, the growl coming back into his voice. "I'm going to kill him."

"We'll get there," Wylder assured him before he turned to me. "Did you come back here to assassinate us then?"

I let sarcasm drip from my voice. "Right, that's why I just told you everything we talked about. Of course not! I wouldn't have needed to go jumping out windows if I'd agreed with him. I got back here as fast as I could because I wanted to *warn* you." *You fucking idiot*, I added silently, deciding this wasn't the right time to mouth off *quite* that much.

Wylder walked toward me and circled me like he

was sizing me up. "I don't know. It's possible you're playing some kind of game. You want us to believe that you're on our side so we'll let our guard down."

I threw my hands in the air. "Why would I even *want* to side with that prick? He killed my family. He's taken everything I had. I want to see him six feet in the ground, not ruling over all of Paradise Bend."

Wylder watched me like a lion out to scent blood. He slid his fingers over the gun cradled on his hip. Beside him, Rowan shifted toward me. It was barely perceptible, but it almost felt as if he were trying to protect me from Wylder, which didn't make any sense because his loyalty lay to his boss, not to me. When I looked up, I caught a hint of pain flitting through his eyes. Then it was gone.

I fixed my gaze on Wylder again, girding myself. My father might have been a sadistic asshole, but he'd taught me a few useful things, and one of those was never to show anyone fear. *If a man sees he can't make you cower, he might hate you, but he'll respect you,* he used to say.

"You can't seriously be thinking of believing her." Kaige looked at me with pure venom. It was hard to imagine he was the same man who'd made me come harder than I had ever before just a few hours ago. Obviously *his* loyalty to the Nobles came far before any other emotion.

"It sounds to me like she's trying to double-cross us," Anthea says. "I haven't felt right about this since she first set foot in here. What's to say that she wasn't in on some scheme with Colt from the beginning?"

"He slaughtered my family in front of me without a

second thought," I said. "His men put a bullet in my *grandmother*. Like you already pointed out, he tried to kill me. I've still got the stitches." I patted the bandage on my arm.

"You could simply be very committed to your role," Anthea pointed out. "He could have killed you today, but he didn't."

I swallowed a sigh of frustration. "You have to believe me, he's playing at something big here. When I was in his territory, I spotted his men ferrying weapons —enough to wage war on an entire city. They're already preparing to come for Paradise."

"Big dreams for a rat to have," Anthea said with a sneer.

I looked back at her without flinching. "My father underestimated him. Look where that got him."

Wylder eyed me silently.

"With all due respect," Gideon said. "We're not your father. He might have been a major power in the Bend, but that was the limit of it. We've got resources and manpower far beyond any small-time gang."

"Maybe," I said. "But the Steel Knights are already building their own power base, and fast. It doesn't hurt to be careful."

"Starting with you," Wylder said. "If trouble comes knocking at our door, it's chasing at your heels."

"I *declined* his offer," I said. "Even though agreeing might have saved my life if I hadn't managed to escape. Even though *you* haven't done anything for me yet. I hate Colt Bryant with everything I've got in me. I came to you because not only do I want to take him down, I want to crush him slowly and painfully until all he does is call out my name for mercy. Maybe I'll even laugh at the irony."

There was a pause following my words and I wondered if I'd said more than I should have.

"I don't trust you," Kaige said. "There's no way someone like you would have come out of an encounter with Colt unscathed unless he let you go."

Irritation raked through me. I couldn't beg or cajole them. These were hardened criminals. Once their mind was made up, they wouldn't budge.

I shrugged. "Think whatever you want. I've been completely honest."

"You know what I think?" Wylder said. "You're a pretty damn good actress, I'll give you that."

My heart stuttered. If even *he* didn't believe I was on their side, I was screwed. "Excuse me?"

"You're standing there pretending you're some kind of powerhouse when the truth is that you need us. Bad."

I couldn't even deny that. Suppressing a cringe, I lowered my head. "Yeah. And that's exactly why I wouldn't buy into some shitty plan to fuck you over. Haven't I proven I'm not that much of a moron by now?"

He was silent for a moment. Anthea stirred restlessly, probably itching to drag me to the curb—or maybe pour poison down my throat—but she let him take his time.

Finally, he rubbed his hands together. "After this little incident, I think I need to see just how badly you do want my favor. If you think I rode you hard before, you haven't seen anything yet. You want to stick around and get your revenge? Let's start by having you stay in the groupies' room tonight. No private accommodations or special treatment. If that's not good enough, you can go running back to your 'fiancé.'"

I bit back a protest. I didn't want to be anywhere near the girls like Gia who aspired no higher than hoping to get a regular ride on these guys' cocks. But my desire for revenge trumped my ego.

"Fine. Where's the groupie room?"

A smirk crossed his lips, one I longed to knock out with a punch. "You're so smart, I'm sure you'll figure it out."

20

Kaige

As we tramped into Wylder's study, my hands stayed balled at my sides.

This was what I got for letting my dick do the thinking. I'd been too distracted by a delectable ass, those sweet curves, and the eyes that always seemed to be begging me for a fucking. I still remembered how she'd looked when she'd come apart in my arms, keening and moaning. I'd given it to her good, and none of her nonchalance afterward had hidden that.

And me... I hadn't come like I had in her in years.

But none of that mattered now. I couldn't shake the waves of rage when I thought of the deception she'd hidden behind those pretty eyes. She'd told me she was going to investigate Titus's murder, to try to clear my name, and instead she'd driven straight to that jackass in my fucking car...

She was a snake in the shape of a goddess. I didn't

know who I was angrier at—her or myself for falling for her act. What if I'd compromised the Nobles by giving in to her charms?

I paced from one end of the room to the other. "We should keep pushing at her until she breaks and gives away her real reasons for coming here. Then we toss her away." That was all there was to it.

Gideon gave me an analytical look that only annoyed me more. "Why are you so sure she joined forces with the Steel Knights?"

Why did he have to ask that? I couldn't pick apart all the rage whirling inside me. She'd lied to me about one thing, so why not everything else?

"If there's *any* chance she's working with them, shouldn't we assume it's true?" I shot back at him.

He started back at me with his typical cool composure. "I'm starting to think your judgment is skewed by something other than the evidence we've seen in front of us."

If he hadn't been Wylder's best friend, I'd have taken a swing at him. "You don't know—"

Wylder held up his hands, and I cut myself off, the flare of heat inside me as much embarrassment at needing the intervention as anger at the situation. He turned to Gideon. "What's your take?"

The slim guy ran his hand under his chin, a stray finger flicking over his lip ring. "Well, there are classic signs of lying: being vague about the details or laying them on thick like they planned out a huge story, delaying answering questions, touching themselves—"

I raised my eyebrows and motioned to my groin. "You mean like...?"

"No," Gideon said, frowning at me. "What is wrong with you?"

"You're the one who mentioned touching themselves."

He sighed and shook his head. "Small movements like scratching their nose and neck or even playing with their hair, anything that draws attention away from their eyes and makes them feel less self-conscious."

"So was Mercy doing all that?" I had to ask. I'd been so pissed off I could barely remember anything from the confrontation except her eyes piercing mine when I'd gone off on her.

"She seemed fairly calm to me, all things considered," Gideon said. "No excessive fidgeting. She got riled up about the accusations, but she gave her explanation clearly without going on and on about it. Based on that, I'd be inclined to believe her."

"So we're going to decide based on whether she played with her hair?"

Wylder knuckled my arm. "Let the man finish."

Gideon tipped his head in acknowledgement. "We also have to take into consideration what we know about Mercy Katz otherwise. It's clear that the Steel Knights *did* turn on her family and their associates, and family members who weren't even included in the running of the gang were murdered. She shows clear signs of anger every time she talks about Colt. She warned us about him being a threat before we had any reason to consider that. I won't discount the possibility that she could be an extremely gifted liar and master schemer, but I'd place the probability that she gave us the truth at ninety percent or better."

Trust Gideon to put a freaking number on it. But Wylder was nodding as if that all sounded reasonable to him. I glanced at Rowan, figuring I had to get support somewhere, but he was standing rigidly, his mouth in a flat line.

His voice came out flat too. "I told you from the start that I didn't think keeping her around was a good idea, but I don't believe she'd screw us over like this either."

Damn it. "So, what, we're just going to let her slink back in here like nothing's changed?"

"I've already sent her to hang with the groupies," Wylder said dryly. "Considering that Gia's the queen bee down there, I don't think they'll be very friendly. If she sticks around through that, well... We don't beat up on women, but there are plenty of other ways to determine how committed she really is—and to make her regret it if she isn't. If she has anything going on with Colt, we'll find out. We give her nothing and wait to see what we get from her."

I still didn't like it, but I had trouble arguing with his approach. The glint in his eyes said clear as anything that there'd be hell to pay if Mercy revealed any treachery. I guessed it was better having her here where we could rain down that hell if necessary, not running around doing who knew what.

"Fine," I grumbled. "We'll see if she survives the groupies first."

Anger was still thrumming through my veins as I headed out of the room. Flexing my hands, I wandered aimlessly for a few minutes and finally made my way to one of the windows that opened onto the second-floor platform of the fire escape.

The metal slats were still warm from the afternoon sun. Stretching my legs out across them, I stared up at the sky that was coming alive with stars and pulled a joint from my pocket. I knew better than to ever smoke in the house, but no one could complain about me mellowing out when I needed to out here.

My periodic vigils out here had gained me a little friend too. As if on cue, claws clicked across one of the windowsills lower down. With a little mew, the stray tabby cat who'd been keeping me company for the past few months leapt up onto the fire escape. She brushed her furry body against my arm, already purring.

"All right, all right," I muttered, but I was smiling at the same time. She was a greedy little thing. After her first couple of visits, I'd started buying packets of cat treats and keeping them on me. I fished my current one out of my other pocket and opened it while attempting not to wave the joint in her face. Then I sprinkled a bunch of the treats on the interlaced slats of the floor. "There you go. Happy?"

The escalation in purrs sounded like a resounding yes. I took another drag on the joint, letting the soothing high sweep over me, and scratched her striped back.

A creaking sound above me brought my head jerking

up. When I saw a figure poised on the platform above me, my whole body tensed.

"It's just me." Mercy was staring down at me, her blue eyes darkened by the growing dusk. Through the mellow of the joint, it took me a second to figure out why she looked so cautious. Oh, right, last time I'd talked to her I'd been ready to rip her head off.

Maybe I should still be ready for that. I peered up at her. "What are you doing sneaking around up there?"

"I wanted to take another look at the crime scene. Not that it's helped much." She paused. "Got a soft spot for strays, do you?"

"She's lonely. And hungry." I glared through the bars at her, trying to summon more of my previous wariness. "And I guess I have a bit of a problem being suckered in by kittens in need, yeah."

Somehow the comment came out sounding flirtier than I'd meant it to. Mercy's lips twitched to somewhere close to a smile. She hesitated again and then moved to the ladder, easing down it until she reached the platform beside me. She stayed there, leaning against the railing a few feet away from me. At the cluck of her tongue, the cat went scampering over to her.

As she stroked the cat's back, I frowned. "She's usually skittish. I have no idea how she's okay with you doing that when she just met you."

Mercy arched her eyebrows. "How long have you been coming out here to make friends?"

"I didn't come out here specifically to— It's just a habit." I waved the joint. "She happened to come by."

It'd taken me weeks to convince her to let me pet her even briefly. Probably Mercy was getting the advantage of all my past work gaining the cat's trust.

"Habit, you say." Mercy gave me a shrewd look, and I realized what that sounded like. I looked above and could still see the mangled structure through which Titus had fallen.

"I wasn't here when he died," I said tightly.

She shrugged and pet the cat some more, scratching below its neck. The animal seemed to like it, because she leaned into Mercy's fingers and pushed herself even closer. I made a mental note of that.

"What a good kitty," Mercy said to her in a coo that did something funny to my insides, and then looked up at me. "I wouldn't still be checking evidence if I thought the case was closed."

Easy for her to say. She could have been out here searching for clues that would point to me. I straightened up. "Or maybe it's an excuse not to go to the groupies' room. Afraid of what you might find there?"

We held each other's gaze for a few moments. "I'm not afraid of anybody," she said.

"Maybe you should be."

"Of you?"

"Aren't you? Most people are, for good reason." I bared my teeth in a sharp grin.

"But you're a softie under that hard body of yours, aren't you?" she said, definitely teasing now. "Taking in stray cats as your new besties. I bet you've even named her."

Shit. My expression probably gave away that she was right. She laughed—light and almost relaxed in a way I didn't think I'd ever heard before, but I immediately wanted to hear it again.

"Her name's Mittens," I admitted.

"Mittens?"

I scowled. "Is there something wrong with that? She's got those black marks over her front feet like, you know..."

"Mittens," Mercy filled in with a crooked smile. "No, it sounds like the perfect name."

The silence between us felt companionable in a way that niggled at me. I couldn't let her get under my skin all over again.

"You didn't tell me you were going to the Bend," I bit out. "You took my car."

"I didn't say I *wasn't* going to the Bend either," she pointed out. "I didn't want anyone telling me it was too dangerous or some crap like that."

"What did that have to do with investigating Titus?"

She shrugged. "I heard he enforced the Nobles' authority down there sometimes. Figured he might have made an enemy or two who'd have wanted him dead. It was the closest thing to a lead I had that Anthea hadn't already chased to the ground."

"Oh." That... actually sounded kind of reasonable. I gritted my teeth.

In my silence, she pulled a scrap of paper out and started fiddling with it. "What I can't figure out is why *Gia* was out there in Steel Knights territory. Maybe she pointed the finger at me to hide that she's made some kind of deal with them. I could tell she didn't recognize Colt, but she could have been talking to someone lower down the chain of command."

I shook my head. "There's a much simpler explanation. She grew up in the Bend. Her family's still there—her dad's got an auto shop or something. She might be annoying, but she's never given us any reason to think she has bad intentions. And she's been around a lot longer than you."

"That doesn't excuse the fact that she's a colossal bitch," Mercy muttered.

I couldn't help chuckling at that for a second before I caught myself. "Look," I said firmly. "The Nobles are *my* family—the only family I've got. I'll protect them no matter what, with everything I have. If there's any chance you're a threat..."

The paper crinkled in Mercy's fingers. She gazed down at it for a long moment. "I get that. At least, I think I do. I've never had anyone I could trust enough to be that loyal to them... No one other than myself. Colt betrayed *me*, and I'm never going to forgive him for that, just like you wouldn't forgive anyone who betrayed your people that horribly."

The softness of her voice wound around my heart. Fucking hell, this woman knew exactly how to get to me. Why did I want to believe her so badly?

Before I could say anything else, she tossed the paper to me. I caught it instinctively and opened my hand to find she'd transformed it into an origami dove. A peace offering?

My heart yanked in opposite directions. Anger was

the easier route, the one I had more experience with. I knew from experience that even the people who had the most reason to look out for you wouldn't, so why the hell would she care about me when she barely knew me?

"You can go now," I said without looking at her, forcing an edge into my voice.

Mercy frowned. "What?"

I raised my head. "You want to prove you're loyal to the Nobles? Do what Wylder asked and go deal with the groupies for the night. Otherwise none of this means shit."

21

Mercy

As I climbed in through the window from the fire escape, I had trouble deciding whether to take Kaige's abrupt dismissal as a loss or the fact that he hadn't gutted me where I stood as a win. At least I'd gotten in some kitty cuddle time, no matter how standoffish the guy had been.

What awaited me in the house was more likely to be a cat fight than anything cuddly. Meandering toward the area where I'd gathered the groupies had their designated room, I spotted a set of fireplace tools by a hearth. I went over and hefted the wrought-iron poker. It might not be a standard weapon, but it could do a hell of a lot more damage than a knife if wielded well.

As I returned to the hall, Anthea appeared, her heels clacking on the hardwood floor. She looked so infuriatingly perfect with not a strand of hair out of its place. One of the Nobles' guards had barred me from entering the wing with my guest room, so I hadn't even managed to change out of my sweaty clothes from this afternoon.

Anthea stopped before she reached me. "There you are. I've been looking for you." Her eye fell to the poker on my hand, and her lips thinned. "What's that for?"

I shrugged. "Protection?" I had no idea what exactly Wylder expected to happen to me in the groupies' room, but if Gia was anything to go by, the experience wouldn't be pleasant.

Anthea gave me an odd look and then shook her head. "I think it's time you turn in for the night—if you're insisting on staying?" When I raised my chin defiantly, she sighed. "Follow me."

We headed around a bend in the hall to reach a part of the mansion that I'd never explored before. The moldings and wallpaper were equally posh, but the hall was empty of the paintings and fancy side-tables that were scattered through the other areas I'd seen.

Anthea led me to a doorway at the end of the hall. She swept her arm toward a large room. I took it in from the threshold.

Mattresses and cots were shoved against the walls, covered with tangles of blankets and discarded clothes. Dance music thumped in a staccato beat from one girl's earphones as she bobbed her head. The air stunk of cheap alcohol and pot. I guessed Gideon never ventured into this area of the house for a smoking ban to be necessary.

Seven women in total perched on various beds—

including Gia. At the sight of me, her eyes widened and then narrowed into vicious slits.

"What are you doing here?" she snarled, as if this place belonged to her and not the Nobles, who could have kicked her out at any second if they'd wanted to. A few of the other groupies studied me and Anthea with interest, while the others didn't seem to care, or maybe they just hadn't registered our presence yet with their red-rimmed eyes.

"Mercy is going to stay the night," Anthea said smugly. She was enjoying my fall from grace way too much. I wouldn't be surprised if she went back and popped open a bottle of champagne to celebrate.

My grip on the poker tightened. If she thought a night in this zoo was going to scare me off, I was about to prove her wrong.

Gia smirked at me. "I guess the boys finally realized their mistake and showed you your proper place."

"Is this where mistakes end up?" I retorted. "I guess that explains why you're here."

Gia let out a hiss, but Anthea rolled her eyes at our bickering. "Make sure Mercy feels *very* welcome. Let's show her how we treat those who are caught fraternizing with the enemy."

I froze. Oh, fuck, she'd just had to rub that point in.

Gia flicked her tongue over her lips. "That's right. Poor baby went running home to her traitor fiancé, like the men here aren't good enough."

"I wasn't the one running away," I snapped. "Unlike you. Did you sprain your ass taking off so fast with your tail between your legs?"

Gia's face reddened. "What the fuck did you just say?"

I smirked in satisfaction. "It wouldn't bother you if it wasn't the truth, would it?"

Gia looked ready to strangle me, and behind her the other groupies were slowly rising, their jerky motions reminding me of zombies. No matter what they thought about Gia and her snark, they must have known that Anthea was a Noble. They'd take her word as gospel, and now they were out for my blood.

Anthea gave them a thin smile. "I know I can count on you to convince her to atone for her sins." As she turned, she practically shoved me with her shoulder. I glared at her retreating back and then turned to face the other women, who were watching me with pure hatred. If looks could kill, I'd be already dead and buried.

Drawing on the inner armor that'd gotten me through twenty-one years under my father's rule, I sauntered farther into the room, pretending I hadn't noticed the rising animosity. "So, what do you guys do for fun around here?"

Gia's gaze tracked me, but she kept her mouth shut for once. One of the other girls frowned. "What are you talking about?"

I noted a corner that held a crumpled blanket and nothing else—a good defensive position—and strolled toward it. "This is my first introduction to a cult. It's all very strange to me, but I keep an open mind. Where's the altar?"

"Are you mental?" another groupie demanded.

I shrugged. "I'm just wondering where you worship

the Nobles like the loyal fanatics you are. Or am I not privy to those mysteries yet?"

One of the girls lunged at me without warning, managing to snag my ponytail. As I whipped around, she yanked at it painfully, but a swing of my poker sent her dodging farther away, her fingers slipping from my hair. A shudder ran through her skinny frame. As high as she appeared to be, she recognized me as a threat.

I aimed the poker at her and then the others. "Take one step toward me, and you'll regret it." Best to establish boundaries immediately. I had an entire night to spend with them, and if Wylder had anything to say about it, maybe even more.

Sinking into the empty corner, I braced my back against the wall and set the poker over my drawn-up knees. I could already tell it was going to be a long, sleepless night.

The women paced around me. For a little while, they took turns hurling insults like "bitch" and "cunt" at me. Gia, who'd clearly established herself as the ringleader, murmured in one girl's ear. A few minutes later, the groupie came at me by leaping onto the nearest cot and slashing her fingernails at me. I managed to smack her arm away a split-second before she dug them into my face. Gia watched with a vindictive grin.

Someone hurled an open can of soda at me, the contents splashing over my already sticky clothes. I grimaced and kicked it away. Next I got a shoe to the forehead—it would have been my eyes if I hadn't ducked quickly enough. Gia let out an approving whoop, and the other girls giggled, their eyes sharpening with a predatory gleam.

After that, they took turns spitting at me, most of them missing but a few droplets speckling my face and hair. I grimaced, swiping at myself with my sleeve as well as I could without loosening my hold on my weapon. More curses and insults battered my ears; any hard object they could lay their hands on was fair game to be chucked in my direction. A beer bottle clipped my chin so hard I was pretty sure it'd leave a bruise. I refused to wince.

They got tired eventually, of course. Someone turned out the light, and most of them got into their beds. But every time my eyelids started to droop, someone would slip off their cot with a squeak of its legs or dart toward me through the shadows. I had to snatch up the poker again and wave it at them to show I was still awake and prepared to defend myself.

My head started to swim. The stuffy smell of the room was turning suffocating, and my eyelids were heavy as lead, but I kept shifting and twitching to hold myself awake. If I drifted off, I'd be an open target.

After what felt like an eternity, sunlight finally appeared in the window. Most of the groupies were curled up on their beds, but a couple had woken up to take over the watch. As I stretched my arms, their accusing eyes followed my movements. My ass and back ached with a stiffness that had seeped into my bones.

Gia yawned and stood up. She had the bed at the front of the room, a slightly wider cot with a few neat piles of belongings stuffed under it that all of the other women seemed careful not to touch.

She sashayed over. "Poor little princess. Is Daddy coming to save you? Oh, that's right, he can't because he's dead."

I gave her a weary glower. "If that's your best shot, you need to collect better ammunition."

She sniffed. "That guy who caught you in the Bend is the one who killed him, isn't he? I'm surprised he didn't do the same to you like you deserve, the way he had you surrounded like that."

My glower turned into a glare. "So you know it wasn't a friendly chat. Why the hell did you tell Wylder I *wanted* to talk to Colt?"

As if I had to ask. She gave an innocent shrug, but her eyes gleamed with malice. "I didn't want them to go easy on you. You might have been a snitch and that whole thing was a show."

"A show I set up for who? It wasn't as if I knew I'd run into you."

"I don't know," she said. "I look out for the Nobles over some bitch who thinks she's so much better than the rest of us."

In that moment, I believed her—that however horrible she'd been to me, it was out of some misguided attempt to protect Wylder and the others. In my sleep-deprived state, a twinge of curiosity caught me. "What is it like to want someone so badly who doesn't want you at all? Don't you ever get tired of it?"

Her jaw twitched. "You have no idea what you're talking about."

Just then the sound of footsteps carried from down the hall. Gia posed herself back on her mattress just in time for Wylder to stride through the door. He was followed by Axel and another man I didn't recognize.

"Just get someone on it," Wylder was saying over his shoulder to Axel. "The engine shouldn't be overheating like that—there's probably a problem with the radiator."

Gia leapt to her feet, her face brightening. "Do you need help with your car? I could take a look—I know a few things from helping my dad."

She reached for his arm, but Wylder batted her away. "That's not what you're here for."

He turned all his attention on me instead. At Gia's pout, Axel lifted his eyes heavenward and sighed. "I'll make sure it's handled." I couldn't tell whether he was more annoyed by Gia's antics or by having to follow Wylder's orders.

As I stood up, Wylder ambled over. "Good, you survived."

"Is that good?" I asked. "I thought you were hoping they'd beat me to a pulp."

He chuckled and stepped so close that it was either let his chest brush mine or end up pinned against the wall. I held my ground. His leather-and-brandy scent washed over me with a jolt of heat that shocked me out of my exhausted daze.

"Oh, no, Kitty Cat," he said under his breath. "I'd very much like to find out that you're up to everything I have in store. I just can't give you a pass if you skip the tests."

A weird tingle shot through me at the promise in his words, but a flicker of dread followed it. "What are you up to now?"

"Come along, and you'll find out."

I hated the sense of Gia's and Axel's eyes fixed on me as I had to decide between giving up and giving in. I huffed out a breath, but when Wylder swiveled and headed out, I followed him.

"Where are we going?" I demanded as I hurried to catch up with him.

"It's time for a very important lesson," he said in a sing-song voice that told me he was deeply enjoying this. "You're going to see just what happens when you double-cross a Noble."

22

Mercy

"The deal's still on, right?" I said, picking up my pace as Wylder walked faster.

He flicked his gaze toward me for just an instant. "Deal?"

A chill unfurled in my chest. "I figure out who really killed Titus, and you help me take down Colt. You swore on your fucking blood. Don't act like you forgot." Was he going to claim my supposed betrayal had voided his promise somehow?

Half a smile curled Wylder's lips. "Oh, that deal. Yes, if you can survive the next few days and you end up clearing Kaige's name, I think even he'll leap to your aid, yesterday's performance aside. But for now I think you should focus on the surviving part, Princess."

I didn't like the sound of that at all. But I couldn't imagine how he could put me through anything worse than the hell my father had. Wylder Noble had no idea just how much steel I'd built up beneath my skin.

I expected him to take me back to his section of the mansion, but instead he led me to an unmarked door and down a flight of stairs into what must have been the basement. The light dimmed as we descended. I pressed my hand against the wall for balance, willing back the spurts of panic provoked by the vague impression of the darkness crowding in on me. Basements and I did not have a friendly relationship.

Dank air met us at the bottom of the stairs. I crinkled my nose. We took a turn into a wide room where Kaige, Rowan and Gideon were clustered just inside. Kaige was talking to Rowan while Gideon scanned something on his ever-present tablet. All three looked up simultaneously.

"Is she ready?" Gideon asked.

A shiver ran down my spine. "Ready for what?"

The set of Rowan's mouth made my stomach ball even tighter. Then the three of them stepped to the side. The sight of what lay behind them made me glad I hadn't eaten since the small dinner I'd managed to scrounge up last night before my chat with Kaige.

A huge metal table stood in the middle of the room, looking as if its legs were melded to the concrete floor. The yellowy artificial light glanced off it—and off the sallow skin of the man sprawled at one end, naked except for a pair of blood-stained briefs.

I knew at a glance that he was dead. A bluish tint was already seeping over his chest. His hairy arms lay limp at his sides, his jaw hanging slackly open. That was all I could make out of his facial features. The rest had been battered violently: eyes gouged out, nose and cheekbones caved in so shards of bone showed through the torn flesh. I had no idea what he would have looked like alive.

No doubt that was the point—no way for any cop or other person happening on the body to easily identify him.

Even empty, my stomach lurched. The cloying scent of raw meat and drying blood assaulted me, and I covered my nose with my palm. Bile rose up my throat.

I forced myself to step closer, keeping my mouth firmly shut. I'd seen dead bodies before, but none quite so destroyed. Along with his mangled face, deep lacerations marked his arms, neck, and chest. He was missing a couple of fingers. His left ankle jutted at an odd angle that suggested it'd been fractured. Even as another wave of nausea rolled through me, I recognized the signs.

He'd been tortured. Not in here—there wasn't any blood on the floor. They probably had some other room for that. Someone had sliced and diced him to see if he'd squeal.

I took a few slow breaths against my hand, gathering myself, and glanced at the guys. None of them showed a hint of sympathy for the dead man or my reaction to him. Was there a trace of contempt in Wylder's eyes? He must have been waiting for me to burst into tears and flee from the room.

I drew my spine straighter. It was about time he figured out that I *definitely* wasn't that kind of girl.

"Who is he?" I asked.

Wylder gazed steadily back at me. It occurred to me that the destruction of the man's face might have also been to prevent *me* from IDing him to anyone if I tried to pin the murder on the Nobles. They were still that suspicious of me.

The Noble heir raised his eyebrows meaningfully. "A prick who double-crossed the Nobles and got what was coming to him. He was selling information to a competitor, enough to screw us over in a deal and get someone killed."

"And that wasn't enough," Kaige added in a rough voice. "He broke into one of our guys' houses to try to steal Noble property, and the guy's daughter came home early. That fucker, he— She was only thirteen, for God's sake."

His implication was clear. Any twinge of horror I'd felt at the man's brutal death was swept away by rage. Raping a *child?* This bastard deserved every bit of violence they'd rained down on him and worse.

"How's the girl?" I had to ask.

"As well as can be expected," Wylder said. "We'll see that she gets any treatment she needs to recover." He tipped his head toward the dead man. "Her father conducted the torture to find out just how deep his betrayal ran. It was the best justice we could give him."

My hands shook at my sides. "Someone should have cut off this asshole's dick and shoved it down his throat."

Wylder blinked as if startled by my vehemence.

"Well, if that's where you want to start carving, have at it."

I jerked my gaze back to him. "What?"

Kaige lifted a cleaver from a side table and offered it to me. "Here you go."

My fingers brushed his as I grasped the handle, and he pulled his hand away quickly. I balanced the heavy weight of the rectangular knife in my hand. A menacing glint reflected off its sharp edge. "You... brought me here to cut off his dick?"

Kaige muffled a snort of amusement. Gideon sighed and handed me a thin, crinkling garment that unfolded into something like a hospital gown. He made an impatient gesture toward the corpse and a large plastic sack lying on the floor by the end of the table. "Your assignment is to dismember the body for easier disposal."

"Get to work," Wylder said. "Chop, chop." He aimed a languid smile at me.

Ah. They didn't just want to show me what happened to traitors but to get me up close and personal with the corpse. My gut twisted queasily, but I tightened my fingers around the cleaver's handle.

I'd never carved up a human being before, but I'd heard Dad's men talk about it. No need to get too fancy. Lop off the legs at the knees and hips, the arms at the elbows and shoulders, and then the head... No one wanted to split an abdomen open and deal with the mess in there.

Nine cuts, that was all. Easy peasy.

I pulled the plastic gown over my clothes and picked

up the cleaver again. The guy's elbow seemed like the easiest place to start.

Bracing myself and fighting a cringe at the deathly chill of the stiffening limb I held in place, I dug the cleaver into the skin just below the joint. The blade severed the muscle, sluggish blood oozing out across the metal edge, but jarred to a stop against the bone. I dug in harder, my jaw starting to ache with how tightly I was gritting my teeth.

"Your technique needs work," Gideon observed unhelpfully. The guys were all watching me with total detachment, even Rowan's face hard.

"I'm trying," I snapped. "It's not like I've done this before."

Kaige walked up beside me and made a sweeping motion with his hand. "You really have to *chop*—lift the knife and slam it down. That'll get you through the bone."

He was speaking from experience, clearly. I swallowed thickly, hesitating just for a second, and Wylder's sardonic voice rang out. "If you can stomach it, Princess. Or are you ready to give up so soon?"

"Maybe if you're so impatient to have it done, you shouldn't have used it for your stupid games." I hefted the cleaver, its weight straining my arm, and whipped it down as hard as I could at the spot where I'd already cut.

With a sickening crunch, the bone shattered. I hadn't quite struck the same spot as my first gash, and bits of vein and tendon speckled the table-top. My gut lurched again. I closed my eyes, breathing as shallowly as I could, and then gave the arm another vicious *thwack*.

The forearm split off completely. I stared at it for a moment, this horror movie scene I was bringing to life in front of me, and couldn't restrain a shudder. As quickly as I could, I snatched the wrist and tossed the forearm into the open sack.

One down, eight more to go.

"Poor Kitty Cat," Wylder taunted. "Hissing and baring your claws isn't enough to win a place with the big boys."

"You think so highly of yourself," I retorted, approaching the shoulder with trepidation.

Now that I was getting the technique down, I hacked through the rest of the arm with just two strikes of the cleaver. A little more blood sputtered over my fingers, and I outright gagged as I dragged the upper arm to the sack, but I just swiped at my mouth with a clean section of my plastic sleeve and walked around the table to deal with the other arm.

This was the grossest thing I'd ever done, but it *had* to be done. I let my mind drift apart from the details of the job, going through the motions automatically, focusing on the horrors the man I was dismembering had carried out.

He wasn't the victim. I was an angel of vengeance, packing up the trash.

"Don't get careless," Wylder said, but when I looked up at him, something in my face flattened his smirk. The others had fallen completely silent.

I glared at him. "I think I can manage." Then I got back to work.

As I finished with the corpse's other arm and moved to his knee, I kept my attention just on that limb, barely seeing the form in front of me as a person at all. The bubble of disconnection thickened around me, numbness dissolving into something harsher. All my pent-up rage from the last few days came bubbling to the surface, fueling each smack of the cleaver.

It could have been Colt I was cutting up. Strapped down and screaming while I hacked him to pieces bit by bit. Pleading as I drew out the torture, when he hadn't given any of the Claws a chance to beg. I'd just smile and slice off one more piece of him until there was nothing left but chunks of meat packed into neat little Ziploc bags that could be tossed away and lost to oblivion.

An unsettling sense of savage satisfaction gripped me. I heaved the cleaver at the corpse's throat, picturing a gurgle cutting off Colt's last pathetic words. He could choke on his own blood before I chopped his head right off. He should get to experience the slow, painful agony he'd put my grandmother through.

I wrenched the detached head up by its greasy hair and chucked it into the sack. Then I turned back to the lump of a torso. The urge shot through me to stab the knife right into this monster's heart.

A hand snatched my wrist. I lashed out with my other arm for a second before the real world around me came back into focus.

That wasn't Colt in front of me. I wasn't getting my

revenge just yet. I was in Wylder's basement, and I'd just diced up a stranger's corpse. The smell of death wrapped all around me.

It was Rowan who'd caught my arm. "Enough," he said quietly. He pried the heavy weapon out of my hand and tossed it in an industrial-sized sink fixed to the wall. "You're done."

Wylder watched me with a hooded expression, but the fact that he wasn't heckling me was proof enough that I'd exceeded his expectations. Kaige's jaw had gone a bit slack, and Gideon's gaze was penetratingly avid.

I looked down at my blood-splattered hands and felt a shiver run through me.

Kaige let out a hoarse chuckle. "You've got a strong stomach."

Had he expected me to back down too?

Wylder's smirk came back. "And one hell of an appetite."

What the hell was that supposed to mean? I frowned at him and pushed myself to the sink to wash my hands. Gideon reached past me to grab a rag and a spray bottle, but he held a distance that felt weirdly respectful.

Kaige went over to heave the torso into a separate sack, and Gideon started wiping down the table. "Kitten is more blood-thirsty than any of us thought," Kaige said. His stance was softer now. Apparently seeing me cut up a man somehow put him more at ease.

I watched the congealing blood swirl away from my hands with the water gurgling down the drain. A bar of soap sat in a dish at the back of the sink—I grabbed it and rubbed it all over my skin from fingertips to wrists, digging in my fingernails, working the lather into the creases of my palms. It felt like forever until every trace of red was gone.

When I turned off the faucet and stepped back, adrenaline kept thrumming through me, leaving me dizzy. I swiped my hands across my cheeks and neck, haunted by the sense that I might have gotten the dead man's flesh on me somewhere else, although the gown I'd been wearing over my clothes looked pretty clean. Corpses didn't bleed much.

I wrenched the gown off and threw it into one of the sacks, longing for a shower. Longing to crawl out of my very skin.

This was what my father had wanted. When I was growing up, he'd never missed a chance to remind me that it was a son he longed for, an heir to carry on his legacy. Someone who'd be as strong and ruthless as he was. He'd trained me in combat while reminding me that I would never live up to *his* expectations, punishing me whenever I hesitated or fell short of the mark.

Would he have been impressed by the bloodlust I'd shown today? I wanted revenge on Colt, but the thought of reshaping myself in my father's image sent an uneasy quiver through the adrenaline dwindling inside me.

Rowan came up to me again. I didn't look over, but he spoke anyway. "You okay?"

"What do you care?"

"Rowan, Kaige," Wylder said, "prep the car for

transport. Quickly. I don't want this bastard stinking up my home any longer."

Rowan looked at me for a second before he followed Kaige out. Gideon stood off to the side, typing something on his tablet. "No missing persons reports yet."

"Won't anybody trace the murder back to you?" I asked.

Gideon smiled humorlessly. "I'd like to see them try." He glanced at Wylder. "I've got to tie up a few loose ends upstairs. The signal down here is pathetic. You don't need me for anything else right now?"

Wylder shook his head.

After Gideon was gone, I tried not to look in the general direction of the table. The smell of the disinfectant he'd rubbed over the metal surface had drowned out most of the fleshy stink already. When my gaze settled on the bags for a moment, no regret hit me, only a surge of triumph.

I'd done it. That was the important thing. I'd proved what I was made of—that I wasn't going to shy from a challenge. That anything they could face, I could too.

"You've got mettle," Wylder said as if he could read my thoughts.

I made a face at him. "Does that mean we're done with the punishments now?"

A sly smile curved his lips. "It didn't look like a punishment for you. You almost seemed to be... enjoying it."

He'd struck closer to the truth than I liked. "Maybe you're just projecting," I suggested.

He sauntered up to me and tucked his finger under my chin so I'd meet his gaze. "You're not quite how I had you figured."

"Really? And how's that?"

He teased his fingertip over the sensitive skin so delicately I couldn't ignore the tingle that shot through me. "I think under that righteous facade of yours lies something even more brutal than you let on."

I scowled at him. "You don't have the first idea about me."

"I beg to differ. I may have been wrong in my first assumptions, but that's only because I hadn't had the chance to see you for what you really are." He paused, his bright green eyes drinking in my features. "I think you liked cutting this asshole to pieces. I might even have caught a glimpse of a smile."

I shoved him away from me and tried to walk off, but Wylder caught me by my waist. With a swift heft, he settled me on the far end of the table. Not where the cadaver had been lying, thank God, but a flash of revulsion flickered through me for a second before Wylder nudged his body closer between my legs.

Abruptly, all I was aware of was how close he stood, his face less than a foot from mine, my thighs splayed around his.

"Did I say something you didn't like?" he asked. "Always stings when somebody puts up a mirror to you, doesn't it?"

"Fuck you," I spat at him, as much pissed off by the heat that had kindled in me with his closeness as by his words.

He got right in my face, his fingers tugging at my hair and loosening my ponytail so that strands of my hair fell loose against my neck. A sharper yank sent pain mixed with an undeniable spark of pleasure racing over my scalp. Leaning even closer, he brought his lips to mine, not quite closing the gap to a kiss. "Maybe you belong with us after all."

My heartbeat thundered. A distant part of my brain was urging me to recoil, but the lingering adrenaline had shifted into a wild flare of desire I couldn't fully explain.

The heat of Wylder's body and his tantalizing scent washed over me. Some crazy part of me wanted to melt right into him. I didn't let that happen, but I couldn't convince myself to pull away either.

Two of his fingers trailed along the seam of my jeans that ran up my thigh. I tracked their progress with bated breath, torn between pushing him off me and the voice in me that was screaming for him to hurry up and reach his destination.

When he paused just before the apex of my thighs, to my embarrassment, I couldn't help squirming as if to bring him the last short distance. He ducked his head next to mine, his breath vibrating over my neck with his laugh. "Steady there, Kitty Cat," he whispered in the hottest voice I'd ever heard. "I've seen you tough. Now I want to watch you come apart for me."

It felt as if every second of our interactions before now had been building to this moment, and those words in that husky tone nearly tipped me over the edge just like that. A growl escaped my throat—and turned into a stuttered gasp as he finally cupped my sex.

He trailed his hand over my scorching core, humming with satisfaction as if he could feel the wetness forming in my panties. His fingers swirled in torturous circles against my jeans over my clit before pushing harder. My lips parted with a panted breath, my own hands braced against the table for balance. He didn't sweep in to steal a kiss, just let his nose graze my temple in an almost-caress as his focus remained on my pussy.

My thighs tightened around his wrist. Fuck my best intentions. If this was what I wanted, then it didn't matter if he wanted it too, did it? And right now I wanted more of him, more of the exquisite feeling that he was making me chase. I reached for his shirt, clinging on, rocking into his touch.

With a grin I felt more than saw, he upped the tempo, rubbing two fingers up and down from clit to slit. With every stroke, he sent me careening higher, climbing to a place I wouldn't mind falling from.

"That's right, Princess of the Claws," he murmured, and just this once I didn't hate the nickname. "Let yourself explode."

He fondled me harder, faster, and I couldn't hold back a whimper at the pleasure bubbling up inside me. It swept over me in a searing wave. Another cry broke from me as I came.

My body bucked before I got a hold of myself, stiffening my spine. Wylder was already stepping away as if he was done with me, even though the throbbing between my thighs cried out for more. He gave me one of those cocky smirks, and I couldn't tell whether I'd rather fuck him senseless or chop *his* head off.

I had just orgasmed less than ten feet from a corpse I'd almost gleefully dismembered. This entire situation was messed up on so many levels. So how could it also feel so fucking right?

Mercy

Wylder looked so smug as he observed me that the flush of my climax cooled. Refusing to look at the bastard, I shoved myself off the table, hoping he didn't notice how my legs wobbled slightly when my feet hit the floor. The aftershock of that orgasm hadn't faded completely.

Was I fucking insane?

"You were already turned on," Wylder said, apparently reading my recovered defiance. "I just took you over the edge, exactly the way you needed it."

Before I could reply, footsteps sounded in the hall. I looked up to see Rowan and Kaige returning with purposeful expressions.

"The car's ready," Kaige said, his gaze falling on the bags of corpse pieces and a grimace twisting his lips. "This is the easy part now, right?"

Wylder laughed. "That depends on whether you

prefer chopping or digging. And this room needs a thorough cleaning too."

Kaige's grimace grew. "Who's on cleaning duty? Because I call dibs on doing absolutely nothing."

"I'll get someone down here to do that," Wylder said. "Who's been on the naughty list this week?"

All three pairs of eyes settled on me. It figured. I crossed my arms in front of my chest. "If you want me to do it, you can just come out and say that."

Wylder made a show of considering. "No, I think you've handled enough housework this week."

Relief coursed through me. I just wanted to get out of here and take a good long shower and ideally scrub myself raw. Even though I had gotten used to the smell, the room still stank of death and I was sure it had settled on me. I needed to wipe away all memory of this prick's touch, too. "Can I leave?"

"Oh, no, your work here isn't *done*, Princess. Finish what you started. You need to dispose of the body."

I blinked at him. "Excuse me?"

"You heard me," Wylder said. "Our rat friend is conveniently hacked into pieces and bagged. The car is prepped. All you need to do is find a nice quiet spot in the woods to give him a final resting place. Preferably deep and dark."

That did actually sound less unnerving than doing the hacking, but— "You're sending me off in one of your cars alone with the body of a man you murdered?"

Kaige's eyes flicked to me, his expression turning dubious. "Forget that." I'd thought I'd seen a flicker of trust in his eyes before, but I'd obviously imagined it.

Rowan stepped up, looking at Wylder rather than me. "Of course not. I'll go with her. You guys have had your fun—isn't it my turn?"

Disgust roiled through me. Had Rowan really just been waiting around for his chance to add to my torment? "No fucking way," I said. "I'm not going anywhere with him."

"Who said you get a choice?" Wylder clapped his hands with a definite sound. "I don't know what kind of issues you two have with each other, but if you want anything from me, you have to learn to deal with my men. That includes Rowan." He tipped his head to Rowan, who nodded back.

What had happened between them in the five years since I'd last seen my ex to cement their bond of loyalty so deeply? The Rowan I'd known up until he was sixteen had cringed whenever I'd talked about the violence of my family life. He'd looked most natural with a pencil or a piece of sketching charcoal in his hand, not a gun. How did anyone change that quickly?

No, I reminded myself. He hadn't changed that much. He'd been an asshole when he'd strung me along and then left me in the lurch, hadn't he? I just hadn't seen it.

Wylder gave us a dismissive wave. "So, it's decided then. Off you go. Be careful of her claws, Rowan."

"I know." Without looking at me, Rowan closed one of the sacks and hefted it as if its contents hadn't been a man less than an hour ago. As if he hauled around chopped-up corpses all the time. Another twinge of confusion rippled through me.

He stood there, and I realized I was supposed to pick up the other bag. Tying it off carefully to cover its contents, I heaved it off the floor. Kaige's expression flickered. "I can—"

"I'm fine," I interrupted. "Let's get on with this."

Rowan led the way up the stairs and down a couple of isolated halls that led to a discrete back door. By the time we reached it, my arms were straining from carrying—well, mostly dragging—even half of a grown man's weight in body parts. This kind of work would keep you in shape, I'd give it that.

A dark green Ford was parked right outside. No one wanted to use a fancy ride for this job. The trunk was already open and lined with plastic sheeting. We dumped the bags in next to a shovel—just one. It looked like I was doing all the digging. Hurrah.

"Can I drive?" I asked, because it was worth a shot.

Rowan looked at me as if I were insane before getting in on the driver's side. Maybe that was for the best, because now that the weird rush of the corpse carving had tapered off, my exhaustion from my sleepless night was creeping back in. As Rowan pulled away from the mansion, I rolled down the window to let the fresh air waft over me, perking me up just a little and washing away some of the lingering smells from the basement.

I definitely wasn't going to think about the fact that Wylder had made me come with nothing but his fingers over my freaking jeans, and then had the audacity to assume that I was horny because I had cut up some dude.

"So what's your idea of torturing me?" I prodded when it was evident that Rowan wasn't going to say anything. "I guess you feel ignored that the others got their turn and you didn't?"

Rowan sighed without taking his eyes off the road. "I don't want to fight, Mer. Let's just get this over with." He said my old nickname as if it still came easily to him.

"Don't call me that," I snapped. "You've absolutely no right to call me that anymore."

He paused and then swallowed audibly. "I know."

It was only two words, but they surprised me. This was the first time that he had so much as hinted that he realized he'd messed up.

I sank into the seat. "Where are we headed?"

"That's up to you. Wylder wants you taking responsibility for this burial. Do you know any place that could work?"

The moment I started thinking about it, the image came back to me of the trees looming in the night's shadows and the rasp of a shovel through soil. The shiver that had wracked my childhood self shot through me again. "Yeah, actually I do. Get on the freeway heading north. I'll tell you when we reach the right exit."

If I remembered right, it'd be nearly an hour's drive. Given a choice, I wouldn't have wanted to spend that much time with Rowan, but the place I'd picked was discreet. I'd be even worse off if I screwed up this mission.

Rowan glanced over at me. "You sound pretty sure of yourself."

I shrugged. "Dad took me there a few times as a kid. My tenth birthday, the first time. He figured I was old enough to learn about the darker sides of our business, including the discarding of bodies."

It felt strangely freeing to admit that without hesitation. Rowan already knew just how bad my father had been; I didn't have to pussyfoot around the subject. His hands tightened on the steering wheel for a second as if hearing it bothered him. Somehow that small gesture set off another flare of annoyance.

I wasn't here to chat, definitely not with him of all people. "I need to catch up on my sleep," I announced. "It'll be a while—wake me up when you start seeing woods."

He didn't argue, just turned on the radio, finding a folksy rock station that was exactly the sort of thing he'd have listened to back in high school. Closing my eyes and tipping my head to the side against the seat, I tuned it out, letting the rumble and the vibration of the engine soothe me into a sleep not even the horrors of this morning could stave off any longer.

I woke up with a start to a hand tugging on my shoulder. Rowan released me the second my eyes popped open. "Sorry," he said. "You were really out. You didn't respond when I said your name."

I rubbed my eyes, not sure I felt any less groggy than when I'd drifted off. I stared blearily out the window, noting the thickening trees on the right side of the highway. The place where Dad liked to turn off was just a little after the forest sprang up on the other side too: an overgrown lane that ended at a long-abandoned picnic spot the forest had reclaimed.

When I looked back at Rowan, he was studying me between glances at the road. Something in his expression brought my hackles up before he even spoke. He looked... sad. Maybe even *pitying*.

As if I needed his pity.

"You shouldn't be here," he said abruptly.

I scowled and pulled my legs up in front of me on the seat. "I know, I know, I'm cramping your new gangster style. Sorry not sorry."

"That's not what I mean. Why did you even come to the Nobles? They're worse than anyone in the Bend in some ways."

I glowered at him. "At least they're loyal and they protect what's theirs rather than abandoning people."

Rowan winced. He knew exactly what I was talking about. "The past is just—it's over. You had a chance at a fresh start, a chance to leave this life behind."

"You mean with my entire family getting brutally murdered? That's your idea of a fresh start?"

"How is getting revenge going to make things any better? You're in more danger than you ever were from your father *or* Colt."

Was that true? It didn't feel that way, regardless of the tests Wylder had put me through. As much of a prick as he could be, he'd treated me with more kindness than my father, even though he owed me a hell of a lot less. Somehow I thought Rowan was letting his own feelings skew his opinion—his feelings that having me around made *his* life more difficult.

"So what should I have done?" I demanded. "Run away like a coward and hidden for the rest of my life, never knowing when Colt might track me down as the sole witness to all those murders? Well, I have some news for you. I learned the hard way that there's no point in trying to run. So I decided to stay and fight."

"And you really think you'll be better off that way?" Rowan asked.

"Please enlighten me how living in fear until the end of my days would make me happier, since you seem to know so much about me already."

His voice softened in a way that was much too familiar. "I do know you, Mercy. I know you'll deny it, but it's the truth. I probably know you better than anyone else in this world. You told me you never trusted anyone else, and I think that's true."

His tone stirred up too many memories, drawing my gaze to the curve of the lips that had kissed me so tenderly, reminding me of how he'd sigh when I'd run my fingers through the thick fall of his hair and down his body.

My shoulders tensed. "And you broke that trust when you abandoned me without any explanation. Do you have any idea how long I waited for you that night? How awful it felt when I realized you'd completely *vanished*? I—"

I cut myself off before my voice could break with the emotions swelling inside me. I'd told myself I was over it, but it was easier not to care when the perpetrator of that pain wasn't sitting right here beside me.

Rowan was silent for a moment. "I didn't have much of a choice."

I narrowed my eyes at him. "What's that even supposed to mean? You'd already made your choice. We talked about it a million times, planned every step of how we'd get out of town and make sure Dad didn't find us. I had all my stuff packed, all the money I could quickly get my hands on—I went out to the park—and all I got from you was a fucking *text message* five hours too late, just saying you couldn't do it. And that was the last I ever heard from you."

I could still remember clear as day the way he'd hugged me before we parted ways at school that Friday, his kiss branding my mouth before he'd whispered, *I'll see you at midnight. I love you, Mer. You'll never have to be scared of him again.*

We could have made it. I'd had plenty of street smarts, and Rowan had some savings from his summer job and things like that. Maybe we'd have been living in a dumpy apartment somewhere, but it would have been the two of us together, living the way we wanted, having each other's backs like I'd thought he wanted just as much as I did...

"Where did you even go?" I demanded into Rowan's silence. "I never saw you at school again. You transferred just so you didn't have to face me?"

His phone had gone out of service. I hadn't known his address, since it'd never been safe for me to visit his house anyway. Any time we'd gotten together outside of school, it'd had to be stealthy, always so careful not to draw the notice of Dad or any of his associates.

Every connection I'd had to the boy I'd loved with all my heart for years had disintegrated in the span of a few days.

Rowan's expression had tensed. "It's complicated," he said. "I think we're better off leaving it at that. I had to go, and the rest doesn't matter. It's all in the past now anyway."

The rest didn't matter to *him*. How convenient when it included any explanation of why he'd turned his back on me so suddenly. I jerked my gaze away, wrapping my arms around my legs. "Fine, then I guess there's no point in talking at all."

We drove on in uncomfortable silence until I spotted the lane, looking pretty much the way I remembered it. Rowan turned down it, slowing as he navigated the overhanging branches, and parked when that rough track came to an end.

"Now we walk until we can't see the car and find a clear spot to dig," I said brusquely. "You can carry the shovel."

The breeze wove through the leaves overhead with an eerie rustling. The forest wasn't as creepy by mid-day as during the night, but it wasn't exactly cozy either. We tramped around for about fifteen minutes before I settled on a spot I was satisfied with. Rowan hefted the shovel as if to start digging, and I held my hand out for it. "This is my job, remember? I'll happily let you haul the bags over."

He headed back to get them without protest, and I dug the shovel into the dirt. It was dry and pliant, not too difficult to shift, although the summer heat was already making me sweat. By the time Rowan returned with the second bag, I'd scooped out a shallow grave.

It needed to be deeper. We didn't want any random animals scenting the flesh through the plastic and digging the bags up.

I stepped into the hole to get better leverage, and a chill crept over me despite the warmth in the air. Images rose up of the light snapping away overhead, the ominous click of the lock, the damp scents invading my nose...

Rowan's voice broke through the vision. "Mercy, are you okay?"

I realized I'd stopped with the shovel clenched in my hands, staring at the overturned earth. Shaking myself, I shoved the tool deeper into the dirt. "Perfectly fucking fine."

By the time I'd dug two holes I judged deep enough, blisters were forming on my hands and my head was spinning with exhaustion, but I'd refused to relinquish the shovel. At least Rowan hadn't acted as if he didn't think I could handle a little physical labor. He dumped each bag into a hole and stepped back while I filled them in again. As I patted the earth down, he scattered pine needles and twigs he'd scooped up from elsewhere in the forest in the meantime to hide the evidence of what we'd been doing here.

"Thanks," I said grudgingly.

He nodded. We didn't speak again until we'd reached the car. I tossed the shovel into the trunk, turned, and Rowan caught me by the elbow, spinning me to face him.

The feel of his bare skin against mine with him standing so close, after so many reminders of the past, made a familiar heat coil beneath my skin. This boy who was now a man—a stunning man, if I allowed myself to be honest—had been my first... everything. Those hands, that mouth, had explored every part of my body.

I shoved the sensations rising through me away and pulled away from his grasp. I'd just buried a man—and I'd gotten off with a different guy just hours ago. How could I even be thinking anything along those lines?

Maybe there *was* something wrong with me, something sick woven into my nature. But if that was the case, all I knew was I'd been brought up that way, with violence seeping right into my soul.

"Wylder isn't done testing you yet." Rowan said. "I just thought you should know."

I glared at him. "I'm not an idiot. You want to give me any tips on what he might have in store?"

His lips pursed. Of course he wouldn't betray his captain. His gaze slid away from me and then back again. "I'm not sure. All I know is that it can get even worse than this."

I shrugged. "Let him bring it on. Maybe eventually you'll *both* realize I don't break that easily."

But as I got back into the car, the chill that'd come over me while I'd been digging the grave returned to wind around my heart.

Mercy

WHEN WE RETURNED TO THE MANSION, MOST OF THE day had passed. I felt ready to collapse on my feet, but I dragged myself inside and headed to the nearest shower as fast as my weary legs would take me, leaving Rowan far behind.

I ran into Kaige on my way down the second-floor hallway. His eyes lit up for an instant at the sight of me, a glimpse of the old him showing in his expression before it was replaced by cold aloofness. "I see you're back."

"Yep," I said. Awkwardness hung around us. Well, even after our brief heart-to-heart conversation—and the intense physical intimacy we'd shared before that—I didn't really know him.

And apparently we were both going to pretend that we hadn't had hot sex on the hood of his car.

He let out a gruff sound and tipped his head toward

me. "You might want to burn that shirt. Just saying." With that, he put his hands in his pockets and headed down the staircase.

I inspected the shirt carefully, but I didn't see any blood on it, only dirt which presumably a good wash could take care of. But I *was* going to need something to change into after my shower. Groaning inwardly, I took a detour toward my old guest room, which it appeared Wylder was allowing me access to again.

I pushed open the door and halted in my tracks, my jaw dropping.

The entire room had been vandalized—there was no other word for it. A bunch of my new clothes scattered the floor, drenched in some dark, viscous liquid. I picked up a shirt, pinching it between my fingers, and recognized from the smell that it had to be kitchen grease.

The same stuff was splashed all over my bed. And the origami creatures I'd been making and placing around the room were now nothing but shreds of paper scattered across the mess.

"Good, you're here," somebody said behind me. I whirled around to find Anthea standing at the door. She was barely hiding a smirk. Annoyance flared through me.

"Did you do this?" I asked. The mess was going to be hell to clean up. I wasn't even sure all the clothes would be salvageable. Grease didn't come out easily, and who knew how long it'd had to set.

Anthea looked at me with mock horror. "What are you talking about? I would never—"

My jaw twitched. I knew she had something to do with this.

"Before you go around blaming me, I'll just tell you. A few of the groupie girls took it upon themselves to redecorate."

I gazed back at her narrowly. "How convenient that no one bothered to stop them."

"Well, this is the guest bedroom, not exactly a place of interest."

Her words were clear. The room and its contents were of no consequence. Maybe she even meant me.

"If this is meant to be a threat, it's not going to work," I said. "I'm not scared of a few girls who decided to ruin my room for fun—or anyone who might have been standing on the sidelines egging them on." I touched the bracelet in my pocket that was always with me no matter where I went. At least they hadn't been able to get to it.

"Oh, but you should be scared." Anthea walked into the room, forcing me to back up. She might have been half a foot shorter than me, but she was no less intimidating for it, maybe because of the hate that radiated off her. "There are seven of them, and one of you. And as you can see they're extremely protective."

I snorted, keeping my head high. "They're junkies who want some clout. Even if you're helping them—"

Her eyes flashed. "I already told you I didn't."

"And I'm finding that very hard to believe for some reason."

Anthea raised a hand and tapped my shoulder with calm precision. "I can tell you this. If you don't take the message to heart and finally run off to wherever you belong, what I *am* going to do to you will be so much worse than this."

More threats. How passé. I mock-shivered, pretending to hug myself. "Oooh, look, I'm shaking in my boots."

"This is not a joke, Mercy Katz. The guys listen to me. And I will personally make your life a living hell, I guarantee you that."

I raised my chin. "Do it then. What's worse you can throw at me? Kill my family? Oh, that's right, they're already dead. Colt Bryant got there before you. So go ahead, take your shot."

Anthea turned on her heel, tossing her last words over her shoulder. "This is your last chance. If you don't take the hint, whatever happens is all on you."

"Pretty sure you'd blame me for it anyway," I muttered at her retreating back.

As I looked around the wreck of the room, the satisfaction of her departure fell away under a wave of dread. I'd seen enough to know Anthea was capable of making good on her promise.

But nothing she could do would drive me out of here. Giving up on getting the Nobles on my side would mean giving up on justice for my family, on getting back the only home I'd ever known... on everything.

I sighed and turned to my bed, yanking the sheets off to take them to the wash. Thankfully, a few days ago one of the cleaning women had shown me the linen closet that held the spares as well as things like towels.

But, damn, all I wanted to do was flop down on that mattress and let sleep take me over.

While I was staring at it, contemplating doing just that and cleaning properly in the morning, a knock sounded on the door, which Anthea hadn't bothered to close. Gideon leaned against the frame. His eyebrows arched when he took in the state of the room. "Christ, what happened in here?"

"Ask Anthea Noble," I said. "I'm sure she'll have a great story about it. What do *you* want?"

"I'm simply informing you that based on the GPS information we got from the car and Rowan's report, you can consider today's work done."

"Halle-fucking-lujah." Seeing him, hearing him speak so matter-of-factly about the job they'd sent me on, sparked a renewed fury in me. It burned through my exhaustion enough for me to start snatching up my soiled clothes, heaping them on top of the stripped sheets. I pummeled them into a tighter ball for good measure, imagining it was one of the guys' heads I was punching. Wylder, Kaige, Rowan, the jerk in front of me—really, any of them would do at this point.

When I hefted the heap of fabric in my arms and turned to the door again, Gideon was gone. Would Wylder be stopping by next to make some of his ever-so-insightful commentary?

I didn't know who I was angrier at—them or myself. No, make it neither. It was Colt's fault I was going through all this shit, Colt's fault I had nowhere else to turn. Which only made it that much more important that I rammed his head on a pike ASAP.

The fresh wave of anger gave me the energy to march to the laundry room, rub detergent furiously into the grease stains in the hopes they'd come out, and toss everything into the massive machines that serviced the mansion. Then I stomped back to the bathroom with my one clean change of clothes that remained and let scalding water beat down on me until every particle of dirt and blood was gone.

After I'd pulled my clothes on and gone to collect clean sheets, my lack of sleep was catching up with me again. I trudged back to my room to discover a mouthwatering scent drifting out.

Someone had left a dinner plate on the bedside table. It was heaped with thick slices of pork roast and mashed potatoes, both slathered in gravy, and a pile of buttered green beans on the side.

Any sense of hunger in me had been swallowed up in my fatigue. Now it came roaring to the surface. I grabbed the fork next to the plate and started shoveling food into my mouth.

I polished off the entire meal in a matter of minutes and sat back with satisfaction warming my stomach. Okay, there might be a few minor benefits to staying under the Nobles' roof.

Ignoring the groaning of the rest of my body, I forced myself to stay on my feet long enough to tuck the sheets properly onto the bed. Then I tumbled onto it, lost to the world almost as soon as my head hit the pillow.

Wavering dreams chased me through the night, but I didn't wake up until bright sunlight was glaring through my bedroom window. I blinked, rubbing my eyes, wondering just how late I'd slept after going without the night before. My mouth tasted like ash and my head felt stuffed full of wool.

At least the room around me looked back to normal. Someone had even brought by the clothes I'd chucked in the washer, neatly folded in a pile beside the door. I'd have to figure out which of the staff was feeling friendly toward me and pass them a little of my remaining cash in thank you.

There was an odd shadow streaked across the floor, a blotch in the middle of the mid-day brightness. I looked up at the window, frowning. The glare was harsh enough that I couldn't make out more than a blurred shape pasted against the glass.

I got up, stepped toward it, and the bottom of my stomach dropped out.

It was a tail. A severed, bloody-ended cat's tail, black fur jutting all along its dangling length. Who the fuck—Why would anyone—?

My mind shot to the stray cat Kaige had talked about so fondly the other night. *Her name's Mittens.* Acid seared up my throat.

I stumbled backward, still trying to process the horrific image, and the door burst open behind me. Kaige barged inside. "Slack-off time is over," he declared, wrenching me off my feet before I could so much as take a breath and whipping me around to face my doom.

25

Rowan

I SMOOTHED OUT THE FOLDS IN MY SUIT AS I LOOKED at my reflection in the mirrored window. I had patiently ironed it myself, but I couldn't help noticing a couple of tiny wrinkles that'd slipped through. Maybe no one else would have spotted them, but I chided myself silently anyway.

A lot depended on this meeting going right, and even though I knew that my clothes didn't have much to do with it, every detail counted. I made an effort to always look pulled together, to project strength and competence in every possible way.

"Mr. Finlay," a voice called.

I turned around, flashing my most charming smile. I'd perfected it over the last five years when it'd become difficult to offer a genuine one. People rarely looked beyond what you wanted to show them.

"Mr. Takashi and Mr. Gordon," I said, nodding to

the two men in front of me. They were flanked by two beefy men wearing sunglasses, who I assumed were their bodyguards. I shook their hands and then led them into the establishment. "The Nobles send their regards. I'm pleased to speak to you today on their behalf."

I'd chosen this hotel because I'd learned from hearsay that these men absolutely adored Italian food. The hostess came around and seated us at a table in the brunch area. Gordon's eyes lingered on her butt, and I glanced away. There were a lot of things I didn't enjoy about most of the company I kept these days, but you couldn't get the good without the bad.

All that mattered this morning was the deal. It was still in its early stages of development, and I'd been handpicked by Ezra Noble to handle this meeting after smoothing the way for a few other agreements Wylder had initiated. The old man himself was taking notice of my skills now. Maybe if I could swing a few crucial negotiations in his favor, my position within the Nobles would stop feeling so precarious.

"So, Mr. Finlay," Mr. Takashi said. "Let's get down to business."

"Why don't we have some appetizers and drinks first?" I said, flashing them another manufactured smile. "Easier to do business on a full stomach."

Sometimes when I looked at myself in the mirror, I didn't recognize myself. I felt like a puppet being pulled by strings I wasn't sure I fully controlled. But there was nobody else to blame for the life I was living. I'd chosen it all on my own.

I'd gotten here early to speak with the staff and emphasize how important it was that they give this table their very best service. Ezra had a stake in the hotel, and it'd been clear everyone was aware of how great the rewards—or punishments—for their performance could be. Soon we all had heaping plates and glasses of wine in front of us. As the other men exclaimed over the food, a satisfied warmth filled my chest.

I might still be a relative newcomer among the Nobles, and this might not have been the life I'd envisioned for myself, but I was damn good at what I did. I'd worked my ass off to ensure my value.

I swirled my wine in my glass but only took sips. As my company gorged themselves, ties loosened and their own smiles came easier. I smiled to myself. Businessmen were so fucking predictable.

I leaned forward in my chair, taking on a conversational tone. "So, about the riverfront project. Mr. Noble has taken a keen interest in real estate in that neighborhood. He's willing to invest a lot if he can take the reins."

Gordon nodded. "We've seen the bid. But I'm not aware that Ezra Noble has all that much experience with this type of development...?"

Of course the money wasn't enough to persuade them. That was where I came in.

"Mr. Noble keeps many of his pursuits discreet, as I'm sure you can understand," I said. "He's in the business of making money—for himself and everyone on board with him—not bragging about it. Did you know he's the majority owner in this chain of hotels? He handpicked the chef who cooked your brunch personally when the restaurant opened three years ago."

Takashi's eyes widened. They wouldn't have known —even *I* hadn't known until I'd done some digging to prepare for this meeting.

Gordon took in the restaurant again with renewed respect. "He has done a good job with the place."

And it made one of many excellent fronts for the Nobles' true, not-entirely-legal interests, not that I was going to mention that. These men were undoubtedly aware of Ezra's reputation. They just needed enough of an excuse to look past it. Seeing a clean-cut, sharp-looking young man with no tattoos or piercings in sight speaking up for him should set a lot of those doubts to rest all on its own.

"Everything Ezra Noble puts his mind to, he gives his all," I said. "And to show you how serious he is about this offer, he's graciously seeing to the updated landscaping in the vicinity of the project with no commitment required."

I pulled open my briefcase and extended papers to the other men, who read through the proposal. Takashi's eyes widened when he noticed the amount printed. "Are you sure your boss is fine throwing this kind of money away?"

I chuckled lightly. "He doesn't consider it throwing away. Improvements to Paradise City benefit all of us. He'd simply like you to consider this as a proof of our interest. As you can see, by giving us this project, you'll ensure a long and meaningful partnership that will be beneficial to both parties. And I'm certain your firm will thank you for it."

Takashi and Gordon conferred over the details. Then Gordon stepped aside to place a call. Hope swelled in my chest as he returned with a smile, but I kept my expression mild. Eagerness was easily read as desperation.

"I believe Mr. Noble has a deal, Mr. Finlay," he said, holding out his hand for me to shake it. "And I hope that means we get to enjoy more of his—and your—hospitality in the future. Please pass on our compliments."

I gave his hand a solid shake, holding back the sense of triumph racing through me. "I'll be sure to do that."

The joy of the victory stayed with me through the rest of the brunch and the walk out to my car. As I got in, checking my phone and confirming I had no missed messages, the urge hit me to call my dad and tell him how well the meeting had gone.

Not that he'd known I even had a meeting or had any clue what I did for work these days. Chances were he was either already three sheets to the wind or still sleeping off whatever cheap alcohol he'd drowned himself in last night.

I tossed my phone onto the passenger seat, some of my elation fading.

By the time I returned to the mansion, it was nearly noon. Ezra wouldn't be back from his business trip until tomorrow, so I couldn't inform him of the good news just yet. It was better to do that in person, to establish the personal connection of the success face-to-face.

I headed inside, fighting down the compulsion to check on Mercy again. I'd let myself peek in on her before I'd left, and she'd still been sound asleep.

Wylder had been pushing her hard, and the exhaustion must have caught up with her. Why couldn't she have just left? When I thought of her expression as she'd cut apart the corpse yesterday, first so sickened and then with growing determination, my own stomach turned.

But Mercy had never been one to back down. I'd used to think that was one of her best qualities. Now I wasn't so sure. Playing chicken with Wylder wasn't a game that tended to end well for the other person.

It turned out I didn't get much choice in finding out what state Mercy was in. As I stepped into the foyer, her voice rang out from above. My head jerked up.

Kaige had her slung over his shoulder, carrying her down the hall from her room as she thrashed in his arms. Wylder and Gideon followed close behind.

"I didn't do it!" she protested. "It wasn't me. I woke up, and it was just *there*."

What was she talking about? I hustled up the stairs and noticed the confused furrow forming on Kaige's brow. He craned his neck around, stopping in his tracks. "What are you talking about? You didn't do what?"

Mercy went still. "Isn't this about Mittens? Her tail... There was a bloody cat tail stuck to the outside of my bedroom window. I assumed she..."

"Mittens?" Gideon repeated in a puzzled tone, but Kaige's expression had shifted. He swung around without putting Mercy down and stormed back to her room. Halting in the doorway, he let out a breath of relief.

"I don't know what the hell is going on there, but that's not Mittens' tail. She's a tabby—hers is striped."

"What the hell is going on?" Wylder demanded. "We didn't come up here to talk about tabbies."

"It's a long story," Kaige told him. "I'll get back to the job." He started marching to the stairs again.

Mercy squirmed against Kaige's grasp. "What the hell are you *doing* if you're not pissed off about that?"

Wylder answered for him. "You've been asleep way too long. Lucky you, Anthea suggested the perfect way to wake you up nice and fresh."

"What?" Mercy struggled harder, beating her fists against Kaige's back, but he strode on down the stairs as if he felt nothing. Sometimes I wondered if any feeling really did penetrate that muscle-bound body.

I wanted to ask what they had planned for her now, but Wylder looked pissed about the earlier interruption and Gideon was flicking through a chart on his tablet. It seemed wiser to follow along and see for myself.

They headed down to the basement. "Remind me, Gideon," Wylder said. "How many men have managed to pass the test?"

Gideon recited the data he must have already been looking at. "Just under fifty percent of prospective recruits make it out before they faint from lack of oxygen. Of course, making it out isn't enough. The record for quickest release is three point five minutes. If they take more than ten, that's a fail no matter how you slice it."

A chill settled over me with the suspicion of where this was headed.

"Make it out of *what?*" Mercy demanded, nearly managing to elbow Kaige in the back of the head.

"Don't worry, Kitty Cat, you'll survive it." Wylder pushed open the door to the last room I'd ever have wanted to see Mercy dragged into. Oh, no.

"I'm tired of your games," Mercy snapped at him.

"This isn't a game, Princess," Wylder said. "This is the real thing—one of the trials we put any man who wants to become one of the Nobles through. We've all done it. You want to run with the big boys, you have to walk the walk. Or faint the faint, if you're going to take the route of our least impressive candidates. Kaige, get her ankles."

He strode into the dimly lit room, pulling a rope from his back pocket. As he caught Mercy's wrists and bound them together, Kaige tied her legs. Mercy cursed and jabbed at them, but she didn't get in a strong enough blow to make a difference.

She hadn't seen what was waiting for her yet. The room was bare except for a deep freezer the size of a coffin set against the opposite wall. It wasn't plugged in, but that was a small comfort.

Even though I hadn't been down here in three and a half years, I remembered it like yesterday. Being shoved into that cramped space with my wrists and ankles tied, the lid slamming shut over me, taking the light with it. The unnerving choked silence, the sense that every breath was draining away far too much of my remaining air.

The trick was kicking the lid hard enough despite your bindings to force it open again—and keeping your cool well enough to figure that out. I'd managed it in seven minutes, sweating and dizzy by the end. Mercy could have handled the physical side of it no problem—I was sure she was stronger than I'd been back then. It was her head that'd be the problem.

The guys had no idea what even a few seconds inside that thing would do to her. "Wait," I said before I could think better of it, catching up with Wylder. "We've given her plenty of tests already. We don't have to—"

Wylder gave me a shrewd look. "What's the matter, Finlay? Have you developed a soft spot for our guest? Was her pussy really that good once upon a time?"

I flinched inwardly, but the sight of Kaige carrying Mercy the last few steps to the freezer seared away all my previous hesitation. All I could think of was the moment nearly a decade ago when I'd found her in that cabinet at the museum, shaking and babbling as if her very soul was being wrenched apart.

I couldn't watch her go through that again.

"No, stop!" I shouted, lunging at Kaige, but Wylder caught my shoulder.

"Tick, tick, tick, Princess," he called to Mercy. "Every second counts, so make sure you get out fast!"

I wrenched myself from his grasp, but in the same instant, Kaige dumped Mercy into the freezer and shoved down the lid with a resounding thud.

26

Mercy

STUPID, STUPID, STUPID.

As I struggled against Kaige's hold, anger rose inside me like a cresting wave. I'd been so distracted by the cat tail I'd let Kaige capture me, let these assholes drag me into yet another ridiculous situation. His bone-crushing grip offered no give.

I couldn't even squirm away from the rope he wrapped around my ankles, and Wylder managed to trap my wrists at the same time. Shit. What the hell were they up to now?

"Wait," Rowan said, his face weirdly pale. "We've given her plenty of tests already. We don't have to—"

Wylder cut him off with another snarky remark that I barely processed. Why was Rowan arguing about *this* after everything else he'd seen his friends put me through? Was he just feeling guilty about the past after our conversation yesterday?

Kaige hefted me, striding forward again, and Rowan sprang after us. "No, stop!"

His frantic tone made my pulse hitch. Wylder simply smirked as he blocked him.

"Tick, tick, tick, Princess," the Noble heir said. "Every second counts, so make sure you get out fast!"

Then Kaige dropped me—into a huge, thick-walled box some part of me recognized as a freezer. My shoulder jarred against the smooth surface inside before my back hit the bottom.

My lungs seized. I opened my mouth to spit out a protest, but the lid was already banging shut overtop of me.

A scream caught in my throat. Total darkness enveloped me, smothering me. I flailed my bound limbs, futilely banging at the walls.

Get out. Wylder expected me to get out.

But the old panic was already rolling over me. In the darkness, this didn't feel like a freezer at all. My mind fell back through the years to the concrete pit in the basement back home.

Dad used to stuff people he had a beef with in there to torture them. He'd leave them in there for hours until they'd pissed and shit themselves, until they'd do or say anything just to end the horrible impression of being buried alive, the sense that any breath might be their last.

I knew because he'd tossed *me* in there whenever he got particularly frustrated with my failures. As the heavy cover had thudded into place, air thick with the scents of stale vomit, urine, and blood would clog my nose. The utter darkness would suffocate me. I'd scream until my throat was hoarse, scratch at the slab of cement that sealed the pit until my fingertips were scraped raw, but he'd never come. Not until *he* was ready.

The first time I'd been five. I hadn't stopped shaking for the rest of the day afterward. The nightmares had haunted me for weeks.

And each time after, it'd only gotten worse. Just the feeling of the walls around me and the closing darkness would trigger all the worst sensations of every time before.

Those sensations rolled over me now, dragging me down deeper into the pit of my mind. Another scream tore from my lungs. I flailed and gasped, sobs choking me and setting off a fresh flare of panic. I couldn't breathe.

The stench clogged my nose, the darkness squeezed tight, and my whole body turned cold. Shivers wracked my body. I was down there again, down there in that void of nothingness, and maybe this would be the time he never came at all, not until I was dead.

I couldn't manage even a shriek now. A whimper spilled out of me with a hitch of breath. Then the door above me flew open.

Light flooded in on me with a wash of gloriously fresh air. Arms descended and hauled me out of my coffin. Rowan—Rowan was holding me.

He tried to set me on my feet, but my legs gave. I slumped to the floor. Four figures stood over my quaking body, their features blurry to my tear-hazed eyes.

I had to get a hold of myself. Had to pull myself together. But no matter how much air I sucked into my lungs, I still felt as if I were drowning.

"What's wrong with her?" someone said.

Rowan knelt and started untying my limbs. The release of the pressure around my wrists soothed my nerves just a little. "She's having a panic attack. She just needs to— No, don't do *that*."

Cold water splashed across my face. I flinched, and some dribbled into my mouth. A shudder ran through me with the vague sense that it was seeping from the coffin I'd just been dragged out of.

No, not a coffin. A freezer. I wasn't back in my family home in that awful pit. I was in the basement of the Nobles' mansion.

Rowan wrenched the rope off my ankles and gripped my shoulder. "You're okay now. Can you sit up? What do you need, Mer?"

I needed him to get away from me with his false concern. I needed to regain control and break out of this meltdown. Fuck, fuck, fuck.

Grudgingly accepting his help, I managed to push myself into a sitting position. The shaking was subsiding, but my chest still trembled with every ragged breath. Gideon knelt down in front of me and flashed a light on my eye. My hand jerked up instinctively to shield my face.

"Hey," Rowan protested.

"I was just checking to see if she had a concussion," Gideon said. "She doesn't."

"No, she's just a pathetic little girl." Wylder loomed over me. "After all your boasting, you're just a spoiled brat who can't handle a minute in the freezer without freaking out."

Now that my panic was fading, the familiar rage surged back to the surface, giving me a burst of strength. "You don't know what you're talking about."

Wylder scoffed. "Oh, I think I do. When it came down to the wire, you couldn't hide how weak you are. How the hell could we ever stand with someone who'd fall apart so easily?" He shook his head. "What happened to the girl who swore that she was going to avenge her family? Was it all for show then, huh?"

He sounded oddly angry, as if my panic attack had been an even bigger betrayal than when he'd thought I'd run off to conspire with Colt. I caught a trace of frustration under the vicious edge in his voice as if he were taking my incompetence personally. You'd think he'd be happy that he'd finally found a way to knock me down.

I met his gaze in fury, refusing to look away. I wanted to lash out at him in return, but I was afraid my voice would quaver if I tried to speak more now, and that would only make me seem weaker. Instead, I focused on taking slower breaths to regain my composure.

"There you are." Anthea walked into the room with a clack of her heels. I shifted my glare to her. Gideon had mentioned something about her being the one who'd come up with the idea, hadn't he?

She'd made those comments on the fire escape the other day, almost as if she'd recognized my fear. Had she realized the kind of trauma she might be triggering?

She barely glanced at me. "How did it go? I'm assuming not well."

"She couldn't do it," Wylder said with scorn. "In five seconds flat, she was screaming worse than an animal about to be murdered."

I winced at his description. Did this man not have a bone of sympathy in him?

Silly question. He was heir to the Noble legacy—of course he didn't. That was why I'd come to him, wasn't it? Why I'd stayed, despite all the warnings from the first to Rowan's yesterday. I'd needed a brutal ally to take on Colt.

But that brutality could be turned on me just as easily.

Anthea's lips curled in a sneer. "Well, what do you expect from the Katz princess? I'd imagine she's spent her whole life playing with dollies. I told you she wasn't worth your time."

Rowan was watching me, the intensity in his gaze making it hard for me to look at him. He was the only one who knew just how far from the truth her assessment was, and suddenly I was angry at my younger self for opening up to him. It didn't feel right that the boy who had betrayed me was the only person left in the world who really knew me.

"That's not—" I started, but Anthea cut me off.

"How did she get out?"

"You can thank Rowan for that," Wylder said. "He was feeling awfully generous toward her today."

Rowan scowled at him. "It isn't her fault. She—"

Oh, God, I couldn't sit here and listen to him defend me now, laying out the worst scraps of my history for them to mock.

"I'm not weak," I broke in, raising my voice and relieved to find it held steady. The guys thought I was a liability now, and I didn't know if I could do anything to change their minds, but I knew I had to try. I motioned to the death trap beside me. "I can take anything you throw at me as long as it doesn't involve burying me alive. Is that a scenario that comes up so often?"

Gideon snorted. "I'd hardly consider that a burial. And it isn't as if we were setting you up for a fail. Many people have managed to get free, restraints and all, including every person currently in the Nobles."

"Well, I was at a disadvantage," I said, gritting my teeth.

"What disadvantage?" Kaige asked, as if I was going to share my dark memories with him. I had decided a long time ago that I wasn't letting anybody else that far inside to give them a chance to hurt me.

"I just don't like closed spaces, okay? Ever heard of claustrophobia?"

"Those are excuses for why you failed," Wylder said. "I've already told you, we can't stand with someone we can't count on."

I raised my chin, my heart thudding. "So what are you going to do about it?"

This was it, the moment of truth. Were they going to drag me right out of the house?

My stomach bunched up as I waited for him to answer. He glowered at me. "Get out of my sight. We're done here."

"I'm not going anywhere," I said. "You saw one bad moment after I've proven myself in every other possible way. We still have a deal. You swore on your blood; you promised me you weren't going back on it. I'm not leaving until I see my side through. You don't trust me to stand with you when you come down on Colt? Fine. I'll stand back and watch. But it's going to happen." And we'd see whether he could hold me back when the chips were actually down.

Kaige and Gideon stared at me in disbelief. Even Anthea looked surprised by my refusal.

"Your stubbornness isn't going to work when you don't have the actions to match your words," Wylder said.

"I already told you, this may be my weakness but it isn't a failure, and I'm sure as hell not weak." I managed to stand up, wiping my hands on my jeans, and met each of their gazes one by one.

I saw grudging respect in Gideon's eyes, and Rowan was looking at me in a way that I didn't want to delve into further, even if he'd protected me in the end. I expected Wylder to order Kaige to knock me out and then kick me down the front steps, or worse just put a bullet in my brain and get it all over with. Well, they could try.

Wylder spun on his heel, not even bothering to look

at me. "If you insist on hanging around, you can go back to the groupie room. That's the level of company you clearly fit in with. I'm sure you'll be incredibly welcome there."

Gia's face flashed through my mind and then the mess some of the women had made of my room. My teeth gritted.

"Sure," I forced myself to say. At least I was still here. I hadn't failed completely, no matter what the guys said.

"Go," Kaige said with a jerk of his chin.

I stalked out of the room, not waiting for them to change their mind. My anger was building steadily inside me, and I needed to find a way to put it to good use.

27

Mercy

I STORMED INTO THE GROUPIE ROOM IN A TEMPER. Most of the beds were unoccupied at this time of day, just a couple of girls in tight crop-tops and cut-off shorts giggling over some magazine.

I stopped in the middle of the room with my hands on my hips. "Did either of you pour grease all over my room last night?"

Their heads snapped up. They stared at me like deer trapped in headlights. Hell, every one of the groupies might have joined together to trash my stuff. I'd bet they'd all laughed about it afterward. Maybe Anthea had stopped by to join in the party too.

"Maybe we did, maybe we didn't," one of them said in a nasal voice. "What are you going to do about it?"

"Oh, there's lots I can do." I stepped toward them with fists raised, and both of them flinched. "Get the hell out of here, or I'll be happy to demonstrate."

They weren't the ones I should have been the angriest at, but they were the only people in front of me, and I needed a quiet space to think. Unfortunately, I only got that for about five seconds after they scrambled out, because Gia came sauntering in right after.

"So that's how the princess gets things done?" she said, adding a heavy sneer to the word *princess*. "Going around beating up people who talk back to you?"

I scowled at her, my hands clenching. I had no patience for her snark right now. "However you want to put it. They destroyed most of my clothes and belongings, and I'm sure you had fun watching them do it."

She chuckled. "It *was* fun to watch."

"Right, because what would you know about caring about your own things? You expect men to fuck you and then pay you for it with nice clothes and a place to stay and whatever else you need."

She narrowed her eyes. "You don't know shit about me, you bitch."

"It's not nice to call other people names, didn't your mama tell you?" I shot back. "Besides, isn't that the reason you all hang around? Hoping you'll catch some gang prince's eyes long enough that he'll invite you to warm his bed?"

Gia drew her skinny frame up taller, as if she thought she'd intimidate me that way. "*Nobody* paid for my clothes. I'm here because I want to be and because I genuinely care about what happens to—" She shook her head, and I assumed she'd been going to say Wylder.

"These jeans are mine. Every piece of clothing I own I bought with my own money, and I'll have you know that I can more than afford to pay it."

My eyes drifted to her jeans. They did look expensive—almost designer. "How do you manage that?"

She tossed her hair haughtily. "You have no fucking right to my business. I'm sure I can take care of myself better than *you* can now that you can't go running to your daddy."

The jab stung more than I should have let it— probably because I *didn't* have much means to pay my way through life at this particular moment. My tongue flew without consulting my brain. "Maybe you're right. But since you're so concerned about Wylder and his crew, you might want to consider just how close I've gotten to them now." I took a step toward her so I was right in her face. "So close."

She took my bait easily. "What is that supposed to mean?"

I batted my eyelashes. "Kaige likes me. Very much." Maybe not anymore, but she didn't have to know that.

She snorted. "No, he doesn't. Kaige doesn't like anyone."

"He liked me enough to fuck me," I said.

She stared at me, her jaw clenching. "You're fucking lying."

"We did it on the hood of his car in the garage. Rough and hard. He loved every second of it and was practically begging for another round. Which I didn't give him, but even then, he never gave *you* the slightest time of day, did—"

Gia lunged at me, shoving me so hard I staggered backward a few steps before toppling to the floor on my ass. My shoulders throbbed where she'd smacked her hands into them.

Holy shit, the girl had some guns on her, and not the kind that took bullets. I'd never have guessed she could hold her own in a real fight.

I sprang back to my feet, ready to have a proper go at this, but Gia's stance had gone rigid. Worry flashed across her face, and she pushed herself backward, holding up her hands.

"Forget it. You're not worth the energy."

She stalked out of the room, leaving me staring after her. She'd looked almost *scared* for a second there. Because she'd been afraid of how I'd retaliate for her shove? But she hadn't hesitated to goad me every chance she'd gotten before. I'd never gotten the impression she was worried about what I'd do to her.

So what was she nervous about now?

I rubbed my shoulder, which twinged at my touch. Damn, I was pretty sure I'd have bruises in the morning. How had Gia turned out to be such a powerhouse?

That was the one thing different about this altercation compared to all the other ones. Before, she'd only thrown words at me. Which was kind of strange if she had that kind of fighting power up her sleeves. Why had she been hiding it?

A quiver of uneasiness wove through my thoughts. Something about the situation just felt *wrong*.

Thankfully, Gia had given me the solitude I'd been searching for—but I had other things on my mind now. I scanned the room, my gaze coming to rest on Gia's bed, her possessions neatly stacked beneath it like the wall of a fortress. Driven by an itch of curiosity, I walked over and crouched by the bed.

The stacks at the front of the space were all carefully folded clothes, some of them as nice as the jeans she'd been wearing. I sifted through them, not finding anything particularly interest-worthy until my hands paused on another pair of jeans at the bottom of one stack.

The dark blue material was flecked with little white dots. Not like purposeful styling—it was only in one spot around the knee, not even on the other side. And they were so tiny I doubted anyone would see them unless they were peering this closely anyway. It looked as if she'd been doing something with bleach and gotten some stray flecks on her clothes.

Anthea's voice came back to me from our chat on the fire escape. The mixture for making rust appear— vinegar, salt... and hydrogen peroxide. That was practically the same as bleach, wasn't it?

I shook my head at myself. That line of thinking was insane. There was *no* fucking way...

But ten minutes ago, I'd have said there was no way Gia could shove me to the ground, wouldn't I?

Gnawing at my lower lip, I peered farther under the bed. There were a few more pieces of clothes she mustn't have bothered with anymore lying crumpled here and there... and something rectangular showing faintly through the slats of the cot.

Glancing around to make sure I wasn't about to be interrupted, I hefted up the mattress and reached underneath. Gia had a few magazines of her own stashed under there, right toward the back—rumpled looking as if she'd paged through them a lot.

I picked them up and eyed the glossy covers with their cover models in the latest fashions of several months ago. Why was she hanging on to these? Why go to such lengths to hide them?

I rifled through one, and the pages naturally opened to a spot near the middle. A napkin was wedged in there, with a smear of ketchup—not blood, I determined by sniffing—at one corner. Oh-kay. Why the hell would she save something like that?

In the second magazine, I found a flyer for a gym in the Bend, which maybe wasn't so odd—if her family lived down there, it could have something to do with them. Farther in, a single shoelace was lodged between the pages.

With rising trepidation, I fanned open the third magazine. The pages rippled apart, revealing a tuft of hair that looked like it'd been gathered together from a hairbrush.

Black hair, not Wylder's bright auburn. The only guy I'd seen Gia hanging around who had *black* hair was Kaige.

I rocked back on my heels. I'd noticed glimmers of jealousy in her before when Kaige was paying attention to me, but I'd figured she was just generally possessive of everyone in Wylder's vicinity. She'd certainly hung off the heir himself plenty.

But this looked like Kaige's hair. And it'd been Kaige I'd been taunting her about when she'd lunged at me with that never-before-seen show of aggression.

He obviously hadn't given her this stuff on purpose. Who offered up used napkins and stray shoelaces as gestures of affection? I'd never seen him give her even the scraps of attention Wylder sometimes did.

But she was totally hung up on him anyway. Creepily obsessed with him, even. I glanced at the tufts of hair and cringed.

Had she left that freaky drawing in my room too? Pasted that lopped-off cat tail to my window? My stomach flipped over.

The pieces were starting to pull together in my head, but the picture they were creating still didn't make sense. I rubbed the bridge of my nose, and a memory rose up.

When I'd run into her in the Steel Knights territory the other day, she'd been carrying a duffel bag. Where was that? She hadn't been carrying it when she'd left just now.

I peered under the bed again, but there was no sign of it. So she'd gone into the Bend with a bag she wasn't comfortable stashing with the rest of her things here.

I flipped to the gym flyer again, studying the name and the address. I hadn't paid that much attention to Colt's business with the MMA fights, but this place was in his domain. His voice came back to me from the rehearsal dinner, one of the last friendly remarks I'd heard him make.

We've got a new fighter who's become a real talking point —a woman who's been taking on the men, and she's good enough to topple them.

I was insane to even be considering this, right? Gia was... Gia. Cringing, mewling Gia, who spent more time clinging to the guys than fighting her own battles.

But...

I shook my head and stood up. Sitting here speculating wasn't getting me anywhere. There was one person who could at least confirm that I didn't have the most important part totally wrong.

Leaving the magazines in their hiding place so Gia wouldn't know I'd discovered them, I slipped out of the room and made my way through the house, checking what I figured were the most likely places. The kitchen and the room with the pool table let me down, but coming out into the hall, I ran into just the man I was looking for anyway.

Kaige stopped at the sight of me with a frown, folding his massive arms over his chest. "What are you doing wandering around here? Wylder told you to stick to the groupie room."

I shrugged. "He told me to act like a groupie. Last time I checked, they have free run of this part of the house."

"Back to snark, are we?" Kaige kept his voice easy, but I could detect the tautness at the back of it.

"I got tired of sitting there," I said, watching him carefully. "Your girlfriend doesn't like me."

Kaige looked at me strangely for a second. As far as I could tell, his confusion was genuine. "Who are you talking about?"

Somehow my heart managed to lift and sink at the same time. I was ridiculously glad he wasn't serious about any of those girls, but that also meant I'd pegged Gia's obsession right.

"Gia, of course."

He snorted. "It's Wylder she has a crush on, not me. But then most of the women usually go for him, so that's no surprise. Comes with the territory of being an actual Noble in name as well as loyalty."

I gave him a wry smile. "Nope, you're definitely the one she wants. You never indulged her flirtations? She throws herself at you all the time."

He furrowed his brow as if this was news to him. "That's because of Wylder. Anyway, I don't fuck the groupies—any of them. I want nothing to do with that."

I raised my eyebrows, legitimately surprised. "Don't tell me you haven't taken the occasional interest in one or two of them? They're easy targets."

Kaige looked me up and down, his gaze leaving a trail of goosebumps. "I don't need easy targets," he said, his intention clear in his voice. Then he shook himself and stepped back.

My gaze dropped to his sneakers, the same midnight blue ones I'd seen him in most days. I'd never noticed before that the laces didn't quite match. The ones on the right shoe were a little thinner and more of a pale gray than white like the ones on the right. Thin and pale gray like the lace in Gia's magazine.

"Your shoelaces don't match," I said in a distant sort of way, the enormity of what I was slowly becoming convinced of nearly overwhelming me.

Kaige glanced down. "Yeah. Some jerk around here thought it was funny to steal the laces out of one of them. Like that was going to stop me from wearing my favorite pair." He let out a huff and then fixed his dark eyes on me again. "You don't want Wylder catching you lurking around here, kitten. Scurry on back to your room, or he'll give you much bigger things to worry about than Gia or my shoes."

As he marched off, I rubbed the tingle of attraction from my arms as well as I could. I already had bigger things to worry about than the fact that he could somehow still turn me on with just a glance.

And Gia was right in the middle of it. Her little psycho mementos must all tie back to Kaige.

I couldn't dismiss the suspicions that were crowding my head more by the minute, but I couldn't do anything else to investigate them right now. But soon... I'd do a little digging and find out whether this crazy idea of mine was actually so crazy after all.

28

Gideon

Anthea's sharp voice crackled out of the phone at my ear. "Are you sure you sent me all the files?"

I bit back a sigh, pausing in the hall. When was I *ever* less than thorough? But Wylder's aunt didn't often work alongside her nephew and the rest of us, so I supposed it was understandable that she might not be fully aware of my meticulousness.

"That's everything our contact sent to me."

She made a frustrated sound. "He's holding out on us. My brother wanted this situation settled before he got back. I'll have to take a look at the set-up with my own eyes to make the right call. Where can I find that prick?"

I could pull that information out of my head without even consulting my tablet, since I'd been delving into the matter just an hour ago. "He'll be at work now—store manager, a place with a lot of foot traffic, not good for public confrontations. But he'll be off when it closes at eleven. You could catch him then."

"Perfect," she said with an edge of malicious satisfaction that I had to admit made even me a little nervous. Anthea was definitely not someone whose bad side I'd ever like to be on.

A lesson someone else had recently learned. I slid the phone into my pocket and strode the rest of the way to the groupie room, my stance tensing the closer I got even though it'd been my idea to check on the Claws heir.

The women who hung around the mansion came on to me just as much as they did with anyone else they knew had a solid position in the gang, but it was rare that they stirred anything other than uneasiness in me. They were too desperate, too clingy. My physical needs rarely became so intense that I had any need to indulge them with a sexual encounter anyway.

But the urge to confirm that Mercy was following Wylder's orders had driven me here anyway. The girl already caused more disruption than I liked in our close-knit unit. It was my job to protect the Nobles and Wylder in particular, and my list of potential threats to our security now included her.

If there was a small, deeper impulse in me to see her just for the sake of setting my eyes on her again, I didn't have to pay attention to that.

She wasn't in the room with its rows of cots and its weed stink, though. The smell reminded me of the other reason I didn't normally come around this part of the house. Even though the few girls currently lounging on their beds weren't smoking at the moment, the traces in the air prickled into my lungs in an instant.

I drew back, frowning. Where had the girl gotten to now?

Missing information irritated me at the best of times. In this particular circumstance, it dug into me like a thorn. I marched through the house, checking every room I passed. Finally, as I approached the exercise room around back where the guys did some of their physical training, a feminine-sounding grunt reached my ears. Ah ha.

I shoved the door open, ready to tell her off for using the equipment that *definitely* wasn't for the groupies' purposes, and stopped on the threshold at the sight in front of me.

It was Mercy, all right—in the middle of a round of tumbling that had her flipping and spinning across the rubbery mats so swiftly and nimbly she barely seemed to touch them. In that first instant, I could almost have believed she was flying. Her ponytail whipped around her, she jackknifed at the waist, and her feet hit the ground, planting with only the slightest wobble.

An instant later, she launched herself forward again, somersaulting in the air and bouncing off the floor on her hands, whirling across the room as if she were made of nothing but muscular power and grace. She rebounded off the far wall, grabbing the bars mounted there to heave herself even higher, and soared a good eight feet off the ground, so high she might have touched the ceiling if she'd tried.

Even from that height, she landed with a thump but

not a stumble. I mentally revised the odds I'd given to her having told the truth about her encounter with Colt Bryant. She'd said she knew parkour. Watching her now, it wasn't hard at all to believe she could have tumbled her way down three stories without breaking a bone, even with a still-healing wound. I'd seen only the slightest hint of her favoring that arm as she'd grasped the bars.

She swiveled, catching her breath, and froze when her gaze snagged on me. The mask of steady concentration that'd come over her face stuttered for a second before her expression tensed. I almost regretted seeing that focused calm leave her.

A twinge of self-consciousness traveled down my spine. If I'd tried to so much as jog across the room a few times, my lungs would have started to tighten. Even if I'd practiced my ass off, I'd never have been able to train hard enough to accomplish the moves this girl had just made appear so effortless. Anywhere near that much exertion, and my chest would seize up completely.

But even as that brief pang of mourning flitted through me, it came with a flicker of desire. I wanted to touch the strong, flexible limbs I'd just seen on exhilarating display, discover how they could move against mine—

I clenched my jaw, reining in the errant desire. I couldn't get distracted.

"What are you doing in here?" I asked, folding my arms over my chest.

She shrugged. "I got tired of hanging around the

groupies and went exploring. No one was using this space. I didn't figure it'd hurt if I did. Working out helps me focus."

Her gaze dared me to complain. "You're not a guest in this house anymore," I had to remind her. "You're lucky Wylder hasn't kicked you out already."

"Lucky," she repeated with a snort, and sat down on the mat to stretch. I couldn't help studying the curve of her back, the flex of her calves and thighs... the way her breasts rose beneath the sweat-damp fabric of her tank top when she lifted her arms over her head. My hands itched with the urge to trace over those slopes.

She was curves and softness, but her body was toned enough to give her the leanness and definition of an athlete. How could that combination be so fucking alluring?

The hunger gripping me only annoyed me further. She should have been *more* than even this. Wylder had expected more. After Anthea's suggestion this morning, he'd been so energized in anticipation of putting Mercy through the freezer trial. He hadn't said it out loud, but it'd been obvious to me that he'd been sure she could conquer it like she had everything else we'd thrown at her. That he'd been looking forward to watching her crush the challenge.

I doubted he'd ever have admitted it, but he'd *wanted* her to conquer it. Maybe to have a clear point of evidence to say she'd passed every test she needed to, that we could lay off her and let her see what she could make of her place here.

And instead, somehow she'd let us down—let him

down. The power I'd just seen in her had left her the moment the freezer lid had closed. She'd been as helpless as I was in the grips of an asthma attack. I might not have fully understood why that had infuriated my best friend quite so forcefully, but remembering it, I bristled on his behalf.

And possibly my own as well. I had to admit that after seeing her brave the piranhas in my tank, becoming more radiantly defiant with every passing minute, some part of me had started to bet on her success. A sinking sensation of disappointment had passed through my gut as Rowan had hauled her quaking body out of the freezer.

My next question came out harsher than I'd intended. "Why are you even here?" She'd failed; she'd faltered. She should be able to see she didn't have any real place after all. She obviously didn't enjoy the groupie life. I honestly didn't understand what she hoped to gain at this point. It made no logical sense.

She looked up to glower at me over her shoulder. "I told you, the exercise clears my head."

"No," I said. "Why are you still here at all? Things have only gotten worse for you. You should just leave."

She snorted. "So I've heard. Rowan has already given me several variations of that suggestion. Oh, and Anthea too. Guess what—it hasn't worked."

"I think it should be pretty clear by now that you don't belong with us."

She pushed back to her feet with an ease of movement I couldn't help envying. "Why, because I freaked out this morning? Are you going to tell me that you've let one moment of weakness define *you*?"

A prickle ran down my spine. How much had the other guys told her about my situation when I wasn't there? "It was more than a moment," I insisted, ignoring the discomfort that rose up at her question.

"And I've had tons more moments when I did more than any of you ever expected. I don't see why one flaw should cancel everything else out. Why do you?"

"Like Wylder said—"

"Stop with Wylder's bullshit," she snapped. "He's trying to scare me off, but it's not going to happen. That night when I was surrounded by the men who were slaughtering my family one by one, I decided that I was going to survive it and I was going to make Colt pay for what he'd done. I'm not stopping until he's dead. And the Nobles are still by far my best chance of accomplishing that. Unless Wylder has me escorted out at gunpoint, I'm not going anywhere."

Passionate determination rang through her voice. I couldn't detect any lies in her tone. Nothing mattered to her but seeing Colt destroyed—and something in that bloodthirstiness woke up a thrum of understanding in my own blood.

"You people don't trust me, and that's fine, because frankly I don't trust you either," she continued. "We don't need to be *friends*. We just need to agree to crush a common enemy. I know I can be an invaluable resource to you when it comes to the Bend. Whatever it takes, I'm going to prove I'm all in, to the point that none of you can deny it. You'll see."

The heartfelt declaration unnerved me more than I liked. I stepped back to the doorway. "Fine. You can stay."

"I don't think that's your permission to give or take away anyway," she retorted.

That was true. Her words made my lips twitch, but I wasn't going to lie. I just turned my back on her and stalked away.

Neither of us had chosen our weaknesses, but they were still weaknesses. And if I hated myself for mine, why should I forgive her for hers?

29

Mercy

I'D OVERHEARD COLT TALKING ABOUT THE MMA fights often enough to know they usually started pretty late, when the gym he held them in had closed for the night. After prowling through the mansion restlessly, avoiding the Nobles men and nabbing some leftovers from the kitchen when no one was around, I was relieved when the sky beyond the windows darkened. I pulled on my hoodie, tapped the outline of my childhood bracelet in my pocket for good luck, and headed for the door.

Unfortunately, no one had left any unattended weapons around for me to nab, so I had to make do with a paring knife from the kitchen. Luck willing, I wouldn't need anything tonight except my eyes anyway.

I was halfway across the foyer when a voice carried from behind me. "Going somewhere?"

I whirled around to find Rowan emerging from the

hall. I hadn't crossed paths with him since this morning, and the sight of him made my stomach twist.

"Is that a problem?" I asked. "Haven't you been telling me to get out of here since the start?"

His gaze, far too knowing, swept over me. "You don't look like you're beaten. You look like you're on some kind of mission."

"What's it to you if I am? I promise it won't make anything more difficult for *you*."

A shadow crossed his face. "Are you okay? This morning—if I'd known what they were going to do—I was out at a meeting when they decided."

Irritation jabbed at me. I could do without yet another reminder of how I'd fallen apart during the freezer test. And when was he going to see that I wasn't some fragile girl on the verge of shattering? I hadn't been when we'd first met; I hadn't been at sixteen when he'd left me in the lurch either.

"What's it to you?" I snapped.

"I'm trying to say I'm sorry," he said, the words tumbling out roughly. "I should have stepped in sooner. You didn't deserve—"

I cut him off with a swipe of my hand. "I haven't deserved anything I've had to deal with, but that's just life. In case there's been some misunderstanding, I don't need your sympathy. The last time I needed anything from you was five years ago, and I learned my lesson then. Just let me do what I need to do."

We locked eyes for a long moment. Was he going to go running to Wylder to tattle on me? Would Wylder even care that I was going out?

But something softened in Rowan's eyes, and I saw an echo of the boy I'd loved. A quiver of electricity ran through the air between us. For just a second, a shred of that old sadness returned. I swallowed it back down.

He broke the silence first. "Wherever you're going, do you want my car?"

I frowned. "Why would you lend me it? Kaige didn't seem so happy about how that worked out for him."

Rowan lowered his gaze for a moment before meeting my eyes again. "I'd rather know you have an easy way to get back if you run into trouble again."

It felt like a peace offering—an apology I could actually use. But was it even that? Kaige had told me that Gideon had trackers in all their cars. Maybe Rowan just wanted to know he could check where I'd gone.

I didn't think any of the guys would be keen on finding out I was heading back into Steel Knights territory. I couldn't let them interrupt me until I had the proof I needed—for myself and for them.

"Thanks, but no thanks," I said, more evenly this time. "I think it's better if I get around by my own steam until you *and* your boss see me as an equal. Maybe when I get back, we can settle that for good."

Concern crossed his face. "Where *are* you going?"

I shot him a tight smile. "To find the Titan's killer. Don't wait up."

I strode out of the house, and Rowan didn't chase after me. But just in case, I sped up to a lope on my way down the hill to the busier streets where I could hail a cab.

By the time the taxi reached the area around the

gym from Gia's flyer, night had fully descended over the Bend. The only lights still blazing were the streetlamps not knocked out, the windows of a few bars... and the back door of the gym, standing open as a bouncer ushered a stream of boisterous figures inside.

It didn't appear he was turning anyone away, at least. Pulling my hood up and ducking my head low, I joined the line. The guys in front of me were debating the odds for a fight and how much they should put on their favorite to win. Clearly I'd come to the right place.

The real question was whether I'd find Titus's murderer here too.

When I reached the door, the man briefly scanned my shadowed face before he waved me in. But as I passed him, he said. "You there!"

I froze where I stood, torn between the urge to run or to play innocent. A man shoved past me from behind. "Keep moving, bitch."

Glancing over my shoulder, I saw the bouncer had stepped aside to talk with some bearded biker-looking dude. He hadn't been talking to me at all. I exhaled slowly and hustled the rest of the way inside. Getting jumpy wasn't going to do me any good.

Tarp had been taped over the gym's windows to hide the light from anyone driving by. Most of the equipment must have been pushed aside to make room for the temporary aluminum bleachers set up around the boxing ring. The space was dim except the floodlights glaring off the red floor of the platform and the metal bars surrounding it. No one was likely to pick me out of the crowd now that I was in.

The smells of booze and old sweat made me grimace. I squeezed past a guy selling bottles of beer and nabbed a spot at the end of one of the upper tiers where I could see the whole platform and also jump for the floor to jet out of here if need be.

The rest of the audience was mostly men, getting rowdier as the minutes ticked by. Hip-hop music thumped from the speakers placed all over the room, heightening the sense of anticipation.

A few guys I recognized from Colt's crew walked by the edge of the ring, and my pulse stuttered. But they didn't even glance my way, circling the platform to take seats in the shadows on the other side.

I pulled my hoodie closer around me as if it could shield me. There'd been no sign of my ex-fiancé himself, but I doubted he oversaw most of the fights personally.

The music cut out. "Ladies and gentlemen," a man's voice boomed from the speakers. "I hope you have placed your bets because we're ready to begin."

Two bulky guys who looked as if they had about one brain cell between them lumbered into the ring, their hands taped and tattoos dappling their bare chests. I shifted on the hard bench, nervousness turning my saliva sour in my mouth. What if the famous female fighter wasn't going on tonight at all?

I held myself as still as I could through the first two fights, watching both pairs of men pummel each other until they were dripping sweat, spit, and blood. Just as impatience wound from my stomach up to my chest, the announcer's voice called out the third set of names.

"And now, the face-off you've all been waiting for: Lady Diamond vs. The Hammerhead!"

I sat up a little straighter. The man next to me elbowed his friend. "Diamond'll take it again."

"I don't know. Hammerhead is pretty good too."

"Pfft, good my ass. Diamond's going to knock him out in seconds. The bets are mostly on how long he's going to last in there."

This was it. Two figures entered from opposite sides. The first was a man almost as broad-shouldered and tall as Kaige. I focused my attention on his opponent.

The slim woman had her long blond hair pulled up in a high ponytail. Under the glaring lights, I couldn't tell if it was the exact same straw-pale shade I was looking for. A white mask covered the upper half of her face. The rest of her was clothed in a matching white leotard with a belt of glittering stones around her waist.

The announcer gave the call for the fight to start, and the crowd went into a frenzy, screaming and shouting for them to draw first blood. The girl—Lady Diamond—was nowhere near the size of her opponent, but that didn't seem to faze her at all.

The man barreled towards her, making the first move. She ducked easily and landed an uppercut to his jaw. Spit burst from his mouth, and the crowd groaned right alongside as if feeling his pain.

I tracked Lady Diamond's movements as she circled the guy, weaving and dodging and lunging in with strikes when he gave her an opening. She was fast on her feet in a slippery way that felt increasingly familiar. Something bounced against her collarbone as she evaded her opponent again and again. I squinted, and an uneasy certainty solidified in my gut.

Those were dog tags, weren't they? Kaige had told me he'd used to carry his father's dog tags everywhere... until he'd lost them. Or they'd been stolen. After seeing the contents of Gia's magazines, I wouldn't have put it past her.

At the same moment, the woman spun toward me, her mouth twisting into a sneer I'd have known anywhere. I stiffened in my seat.

It was her. I had no doubt left. That was Gia bounding around the boxing ring. Gia the crowd was cheering on after all the duels she'd won before.

She dodged the big guy yet again, but this time instead of continuing to move away, she swung around and careened right into him. Hammerhead lost his balance and stumbled.

Gia flung herself at the bars and leapt off them to snap her legs around his neck. She heaved upward, digging her fingers into his jaw as her thighs squeezed tight.

The guy staggered, trying to buck her off. Gia smirked out at the crowd. Her stage name rang out from every side. "Diamond! Diamond! Diamond!" The entire room was rooting for her.

Hammerhead struggled to shake her off, but no matter how he twisted and snatched at her, he couldn't break her hold. His face was turning progressively blue. With just one wrench of her hips and hands, I had no doubt she could have broken his neck if she'd had killing rather than winning in mind.

Hammerhead sank to the floor, and Gia bashed his slumping head into the mat with all her strength. As he lolled there, gasping, she climbed off him and raised her hands in the air. Cheers rained down on her.

She only stayed for long enough for the announcer to acknowledge her win. As she ducked out of the ring, I slipped over the edge of the bleachers and squeezed through the latecomers who'd been left with only standing room in the aisles. I'd lost sight of her, but there was only one door people were using right now. I made a beeline for it.

I'd been closer and got there first. I ambled out into the darkness past the bouncer casually, and he didn't say a word. When I'd made it partway to the street, I heard him call out, "Great match!" to someone behind me. I darted into the shadows next to the building.

"Thanks!" Gia said, picking up her pace as she came around the side of the building. She'd left her mask on for the moment, and she had the duffel bag I'd been searching for slung over her shoulder.

I let her pass me and then slunk behind her. A short distance down the block, she tugged off the mask and shoved it into her bag. I took the moment to jog up beside her. "Hello, Gia."

Gia squeaked in shock, spinning around, clutching her bag as if she were going to use it as a weapon. When she caught sight of me, she froze in place. I readied myself to chase after her if she took off, but instead she drew herself up, the muscles in her arms flexing. Muscles I now knew could subdue a trained fighter.

Muscles that had killed a man twice my size.

I took a step back into the empty parking lot behind me, my hand going to my pocket with the paring knife. I needed answers, but I already had more than Gia might be willing to let me leave here with. So I'd just have to make sure she didn't get a chance to stop me.

Her lips curled as she watched my partial retreat. She dropped her bag on the ground to give her better mobility. "So you figured it out. You've got such a bad habit of snooping into other people's stuff."

"Is that really any worse than making up a whole secret identity?" I asked.

She barked out a laugh. "I do what I have to do to survive."

"But surviving isn't all you've done, is it?" She moved toward me, and I sidestepped. "I saw the move that you used on Hammerhead. Catching his neck like that... it reminds me of something."

An emotion closer to panic flickered in her eyes. She sprang at me, but I'd watched her moves carefully, and she was already tired from her brawl in the ring. No matter how many fights she'd won in the past several months, I'd been training to hold my own since I could walk.

I dodged and ducked, weaving back and forth as she followed me into the parking lot. I wasn't going to bring out the knife until I had to. As long as she didn't see me as too great a threat, I could hope to keep her dancing and talking a little longer. I still needed more answers.

"Is that the best you've got?" I said.

Fury flared on her face. She threw herself forward to

catch me by my knees, and I managed to kick her in the shoulder before twisting away.

We circled each other. As she lunged for me again, I spun around her and snatched at the back of her neck. My fingers closed around a leather strap that snapped at my swift tug.

I darted backward, the dog tags dangling from my hands.

Gia clapped her hand to her throat. "Give those back," she snarled.

I could barely make out the letters etched in the metal by the dim light of the streetlamps, but the last name *MADDEN* was unmistakable. I raised my head.

"These don't belong to you. You stole them from Kaige."

"Whatever belongs to him belongs to me," she said.

I resisted the urge to roll my eyes. Her obsession had made her delusional.

"We don't need to play this game anymore," I said. "I know you killed Titus."

To my surprise, instead of denying it, she started giggling. "Oh, did I? And how are you going to convince anyone else of that?"

I ignored the question, focusing on my own need for answers as I kept out of range of her swings and grabs. "Why'd you do it? Don't tell me it was for Kaige. He doesn't care one bit about you."

Hurt flashed across her face before it was replaced by rage. "What do you know about that, you heartless bitch? You fucked him and then gloated to me about it. I love Kaige. I've loved him for ages. Titus was going to have him killed, so I did whatever it took to protect him."

I raised my eyebrows. "You murdered a man over an empty threat fueled by too much testosterone?"

Gia scowled. "I know what I heard. I'm not a fucking idiot. He was talking about it after—he really meant to screw Kaige over any way he could, even setting him up to take a bullet that would seem like just the wrong place, wrong time."

I didn't know if I should believe her or if she'd justified the act to herself with more delusions. It didn't really matter. "You could have just warned him instead of going all murder-happy yourself."

A maniacal glint lit in her eyes. "But my way worked, didn't it? And Kaige never even needed to worry about it. I was his avenger in the night."

What, did she figure she was Batman now? More like batshit crazy.

"Did you leave that drawing in my room? And the severed cat's tail?" I demanded. "Was it a way to scare me off?"

The confused knitting of her brow looked genuine. "What are you talking about? I wasn't threatened by you. I knew you'd never get to the truth."

"And yet here we are," I said. "Looks like you underestimated me."

"Do you think any of that matters? Wake up, I've already gotten away with it. It's the perfect crime. Titus is buried six feet underground, and he sure isn't coming back from the grave to snitch on me. Nobody believes I could be capable of it. If you manage to get back to the house alive and tell them your story, they'll laugh you out of the place."

She was probably right. I had no hard evidence, only circumstantial proof, and repeating her confession was just hearsay. The story sounded so ridiculous I hadn't even believed it myself until I'd watched her fight.

Gia drove her point home. "It doesn't matter what you say. They don't trust you. They'll never believe you."

And it'd look like I was just grasping at straws to convince Wylder I'd met his end of the deal. Damn it.

"You see," Gia continued in a taunting voice. "You're hopeless. Really there's only one person in that house who might have figured it out eventually with all her nosing around, but I finally managed to take care of that problem too."

She had to mean Anthea. I stared at her. "What the fuck are you talking about?"

She offered a sharp little smile. "Let's just say the next drive Miss Prissy goes on will definitely be her last."

Dread climbed up my spine. She'd messed with the other woman's car somehow—and after what Gia had managed to do to Titus, I wasn't sure even Anthea could survive this insanity.

Mercy

As soon as the realization hit me, I spun away from Gia and took off across the parking lot. I couldn't waste precious time trying to reason with her or haul her back to Wylder. Any second I delayed could mean Anthea's death.

Maybe she'd been an ass to me, maybe there'd been times when I'd wanted to punch her face in, but I knew behind it all she'd only been looking out for the guys the best way she knew how. If I stood around and let Gia murder her, her blood would be on my hands too. Nothing about that possibility sat right with me.

Gia's voice rang out behind me, pitched to carry all the way down the block. "She's here! Mercy Katz is here!"

Fuck. I didn't risk looking back, but a sharp exclamation somewhere down the street told me that at least one of Colt's men had heard her announcement.

As I pushed myself faster, Gia let out another holler, sounding almost gleeful. "That's her! That's Mercy Katz. Don't let her get away!"

I gritted my teeth and ran faster for both my sake and Anthea's, pumping my arms to keep my momentum. I couldn't let Colt haul my ass in again. Lord only knew what he'd do to me now that I'd defied him to his face.

I bolted down an alley and across the street on the other side. Veering left to mix up my path, I sprinted on. Kaige's dog tags bit into my palm where I was still clutching them. I didn't dare stop even long enough to safely stuff them in my hoodie's pocket.

Tires screeched around a corner way too close for comfort. I swerved down another narrow alley and burst out by a street that still had a decent amount of traffic at this hour. Jogging against the flow, I spotted a cab heading my way. I waved my arm, bouncing on my feet to catch the driver's attention as I hustled to meet it.

The cab had barely rolled to a halt when I yanked the door open and dove into the back seat. The driver stared back at me.

"Paradise City, top of the hill," I said, panting. "Please. Just step on it."

The engine revved as the cabbie hit the gas. Requests that tested the speed limit probably weren't unusual in this part of town. I jolted back in the seat and scrambled for my phone.

Even driving fast through the dwindling night traffic, it would take at least half an hour to make it back to the mansion. I skimmed through the profiles I'd saved in my Contacts. The Nobles kept a handy list of all the important numbers on the fridge, since I supposed they changed burners regularly and it was easier to spread the word that way. I'd entered all four of the guys on a whim I now thanked God for.

After a moment's hesitation as I debated who I'd hate speaking to the least, I tapped Rowan's name. He'd offered me some kind of help—he was the most likely to listen to me, right?

The call went through to voicemail. With a groan, I dialed Gideon, but he didn't pick up either. No way in hell was I counting on anything from Wylder after the way he'd laid into me this morning, so I jabbed the entry for Kaige instead.

Relief flooded me at the click of him answering. "Hello?"

"Kaige, it's me. Mercy." I dragged in a breath to steady my voice, but Kaige broke in before I could go on.

"Mercy? Where the fuck are you?" The angry growl in his voice chilled me.

"It doesn't matter," I said. "You just need to—"

He interrupted me again, his tone even harsher. "I think it matters. Gia just called Wylder—she's saying you followed her into the Bend and *attacked* her? She was sobbing her heart out on the phone. Is this why you were asking all those questions about her?"

Fucking hell. I wanted to wring that bitch's neck. "Of course not," I snapped. "She's lying again, just like she was about Colt. You have to listen. I—"

"I don't want to hear a word out of your mouth until you're back here and you can explain to all of us where the hell you ran off to. And you'd better get here fast, because Wylder's getting more pissed off by the second."

"Kaige!"

He'd already hung up. Dead air filled my ear. Swearing, I bit the bullet and tried calling Wylder, then each of the other guys again, but if they were seeing the calls, they were ignoring me.

They had no idea this was anything other than a spat between two supposed groupies—and who knew what other lies Gia had spun to antagonize them against me.

"Can you go any faster?" I said to the cabbie as I frantically tapped out a text message. *Anthea's in danger. Don't let her get in her car.*

I sent it and stared at the screen. The message remained unread. Why did they have to be such blockheads?

I pushed both the phone and the dog tags into my pockets and spent the rest of the drive tipped forward in my seat as if I could urge the car faster that way. Buildings whipped by outside the window. Every time we had to stop for a light, my pulse thudded at the base of my throat.

I was probably worrying over nothing, right? Why would Anthea be driving anywhere in the middle of the night? She might already be in bed, for fuck's sake.

But was Gia unstable enough to have revealed her

plan to me if she hadn't been pretty sure it'd be in motion before I could get back to the mansion?

It was absurd. Wylder's aunt had been a thorn in my side from the moment she'd spoken her first words to me, but I couldn't relax until I knew I'd done everything I could to stop Gia's awful plan. Maybe I hadn't become as ruthless as my father would have wanted after all.

And actually... I was okay with that.

Finally, the taxi careened up the steep hill. The second the mansion came into sight, I spotted a car pulling out of its driveway. Not one I recognized as belonging to any of the guys, either.

"Stop!" I shouted at the cabbie, and smacked into the back of the seat when he slammed on the brakes. I tossed a handful of bills that should cover the ride at him and hurtled out of the taxi. The driver muttered some comment, but he drove off a moment later.

The car from the mansion cruised toward me, already picking up speed to take the turn and head down the hill. The light from the streetlamps reflected off the windshield, and then I caught a glimpse of Anthea's red hair and startled face behind the glass. My pulse hiccupped.

There was only one way my panicked brain could come up with to stop her. I dashed forward and threw myself into her path, my arms spread. "Stop! There's something wrong with the car!"

I couldn't tell whether she'd heard me. She honked the horn, but I didn't budge. Her eyes narrowed, and for a second I thought she was going to speed up instead and run me over.

Then the engine's growl eased. The car started to slow. I let out my breath—and all at once Anthea's expression froze.

Her body jerked as if she was stomping on the brake, but the car kept traveling forward, slower than before but fast enough that it'd still break bones if it hit me. It was gaining speed as it reached the first gradual incline before the turn. I wavered, caught in the crazy sense that if I jumped out of the way, I'd have let her down, even though I could hardly have stopped the vehicle with my bare hands.

Anthea jerked the wheel, and the car whipped to the side. It lurched up over the sidewalk and smashed straight into a telephone pole.

The hood crumpled around the pole about a foot deep, the engine sputtering. I raced over and yanked open the driver's side door.

Anthea was rubbing her chest where the seat belt must have jarred against it, her breath coming roughly. It didn't look as if she'd injured herself in any major way, but appearances could be deceiving.

"Are you okay?" I asked, every nerve in my body jittering.

She stared at me so blankly that I couldn't help worrying she'd sustained some kind of brain damage after all. Then the haze started to clear from her eyes, but she didn't look all that much less confused. With her scowl missing, she seemed much younger than her twenty-eight years.

"The brakes failed," she said. "And then the airbag failed too. You were trying to stop me. You... knew?"

"I heard that something was wrong from the person who screwed up your car," I said. "I've been *trying* to let the guys know..."

I trailed off, a shudder running through me at the thought of how Anthea would have ended up if I'd gotten here even a minute later. All the momentum from going down the hill—the car would have been flying by the time she reached the bottom, and she'd have had no way to stop it. What were the chances she'd have survived *that* crash?

Anthea was still staring. "You *saved* me. You threw yourself in front of the car..." She trailed off.

A shaky grin crossed my face. "We might not get along all that well, but you haven't *quite* pissed me off to the point of wishing you dead yet."

She didn't smile in return. Swiping her hand across her mouth, she frowned at the steering wheel and then at me again. "*Who* did this?"

Here was the hard part. "Gia," I said. "I know it sounds insane, but I wouldn't have known if she hadn't bragged about how she messed with your car. That's the whole reason I rushed back here. I guess she knows about auto mechanics from her dad."

Anthea blinked, thinking that over, but she didn't argue with me. "Why would a *groupie* want me dead?" she asked instead, shifting to pull herself out of the car.

I swallowed hard. "Because she killed Titus, and she was getting worried that you'd figure that out."

Anthea jerked to a halt. "*What?* That skinny little thing?" She looked as if she was going to make some caustic remark about my judgment, but to my surprise, she paused, and her tone came out almost respectfully. "What makes you say that?"

"I—it's a long story. We can get into it in the house. Let's just say it all started with an obsession with Kaige." I dug out the dog tags and handed them to her. "Did you hear he was missing these?"

She glanced down at them in her hand, and her lips twitched into a dazed smile. "He asked if I could keep an eye out for them while I searched for evidence. That big dolt."

Her tone was more affectionate than I'd ever heard it, in a maternal sort of way. If I hadn't realized it before, I'd have known now just how much she cared about Wylder and his crew.

"Come on," I said, stepping back to give her room. Down the street, the mansion's door banged, and I glanced over to see several figures marching toward us, with Wylder, Kaige, and Rowan in the lead. "It looks like I have a *lot* of explaining to—"

Another car came screeching around the corner. Before I could process what was happening, it'd lurched to a stop beside us, and Gia was launching herself out, straight at me.

"You little bitch!" she snapped, wrenching me toward her and nearly pulling my arm out of its socket. "You just had to screw everything up."

I tried to dodge, but she had my arm clamped too tightly in those hands that were more powerful than they looked. With an eerie chill in her eyes, she rammed her knee into my stomach hard enough that I buckled. Pain seared through my abdomen.

I regained my balance just enough to shield my face from her next blow, but my elbow throbbed from the impact, which radiated up my arm to wake up my bullet wound too. Gia swung both her fists at my side and knocked me right to the ground, my hip and shoulder smacking into the asphalt.

Scrambling to focus, I rolled away from her. I had to get distance, had to get into a position where I had room to dodge—

She came after me with the force of a Mac truck, her fists flailing. One glanced off my throat, making me choke and sputter. I snatched the paring knife out of my pocket, but an instant later she was smacking it away.

"You couldn't just let her die?" she screamed. "You didn't even like her! You just had to act like you're so much better than me."

I lashed out at her and managed to land one good kick to her calf, but then she snatched at my hair and yanked me up, my scalp crying out in pain. She clocked me in the temple and the ribs before I managed to twist around, punching her in the jaw as I did.

Gia only recoiled for a second. She whipped her leg around as I tried to retreat and toppled me onto my hands and knees this time.

Springing at me, she shoved me onto my back and slammed her forearm against my throat. My airway constricted, cutting off my breath. Her other hand grasped my jaw, her muscles flexing, ready to snap my neck. "I didn't get to kill her, so you'll have to do. Any last words, bitch?"

I couldn't speak, couldn't even gasp. One thought swam up through my desperate mind, the first tenet of parkour that the videos I'd watched had drilled into my brain: Make use of your environment to pursue your goal every way you can.

I couldn't reach anything in my environment except Gia, but why couldn't I use her?

Instead of resisting her clutching hand, I jerked my head to the side in the direction she'd been braced to twist. Her hand flew aside at the unexpected motion, and I jabbed my elbow at just the right angle to fling her arm back into her own face.

Her grip on my throat loosened for an instant, but that was all I needed. I heaved up, and we tumbled over, rolling several feet while we grappled with each other. I spotted the curb and braced my foot against it to flip myself onto her solidly enough to pin her in place.

She was already squirming with enough strength to break my hold, but as her wrist slipped from my grasp, another figure leapt in beside us. Wylder stared down at Gia, crouching with his gun pointed straight at her head.

"That's enough," he said in a cold, fathomless voice.

Gia froze for only an instant. Then she let out a shriek more animal than human. With a renewed surge of strength, she yanked her other arm free, one hand clawing at Wylder, the other closing around a chunk of concrete that'd crumbled off the sidewalk. She thrust it toward my head.

In that instant, I could already feel how my skull would crack with the impact. I recoiled, not sure yet if my reflexes would be fast enough, and in the same moment a *bang* rattled my eardrums.

The side of Gia's head burst open with a splatter of blood and brains that flecked my body from head to torso. The life went out of her eyes like a flame doused with water. Her body sagged, the concrete chunk only glancing off my shoulder instead of reaching my skull.

I shoved myself off her, my stomach flipping over. The smell of her blood clogged my nose, my shirt sticking to my skin with its dampness.

I'd been around violence and death all of my life, but I'd never seen it come for someone just inches away from me like that. A shiver ran through me from head to toe.

Wylder lowered his gun. I turned to him, lost for words. He nodded as if to say, *It's done*.

He might have just saved my life. A few minutes ago, I'd have assumed he didn't give a shit whether I made it through the day. But then, Anthea would have said the same about me and her, wouldn't she?

I stared down at Gia's ruined body, blood pooling under her and staining her pale hair, and a twisted sense of relief washed over me.

It *was* done. It was over. Titus had been avenged. Kaige's name was cleared.

Where exactly did that leave us now?

Wylder

MERCY LOOKED LIKE A GODDESS OF WAR, BATHED IN her enemy's blood. Taking her in, I had to catch my breath despite the gore. The way she'd fought back, kept grasping at every hope of survival no matter how fiercely Gia had attacked her, was nothing short of spectacular.

How could I have thought this woman couldn't stand strong alongside us?

She drew herself up straight, and I had the urge to offer a supporting hand, but I could already tell from the tensing of her jaw that she'd refuse it. She wiped her fingers across her cheek, and I was jolted back to the full reality of the situation. *I* might be admiring her in her blood-drenched state, but it was doubtful she was enjoying the experience all that much.

"I can explain all of this," she said, her voice rasping. It'd looked like Gia had nearly crushed her throat.

I reined in my emotions. Some of my father's men had come out at the commotion. They were watching me now, evaluating how I handled the situation.

"I'm looking forward to hearing that explanation," I said. "But why don't we get you cleaned up first. I'd rather talk without you dripping blood all over the furniture this time."

The corner of her lips curled with what might have been the start of a smile. The sight made my cock twitch in response. Fucking hell, just like that I wanted to kiss her, blood and all.

To my surprise, Anthea stepped up beside her, nudging Mercy toward the house. "Come on. I'll walk you in."

"I'm fine," Mercy muttered, but she let herself be ushered.

"Sure you are," I heard my aunt say as they walked away. "But you'll be fine-*er* if you stop being so stubborn about letting people give you a hand now and then."

What the hell was going on there? I guessed I'd find that out when Mercy was ready to talk.

My gaze fell to the woman sprawled on the road. It was hard to see Gia as a person anymore, as anything more than a hollow shell.

There'd been a time when I'd felt a pang of guilt when I had to kill someone. Now, I could recognize it as inevitable. It'd been Gia or Mercy, and I'd seen and heard enough even without Mercy's full explanation to know I'd made the right choice.

"Let's go," I said to the guys, jerking my head toward the house. "Call the clean-up crew and have this taken care of. I need a drink before storytime starts."

———

By the next morning, I was beginning to think that an entire bottle of brandy wouldn't be enough to numb the ache in my head from untangling the bizarre scenario I'd been faced with. I swirled the liquid in my snifter and leaned back in my armchair as Rowan, Kaige, and Anthea trooped into my study at my summons. Gideon was already seated next to me, his fingers flicking over his tablet's screen.

Kaige looked from me to him and back again. He seemed to read my expression. "It's *true*? All of it? You're fucking kidding me."

My mouth twisted into a crooked smile. "I'm as serious as Mercy looked splattered in Gia's blood last night."

"Fuck," Rowan murmured. He hadn't raised any arguments against Mercy's convoluted tale last night, but I suspected we'd all found it difficult to accept at face value.

Anthea propped herself against my desk. "Well, we know that psychotic bitch definitely tried to kill *me*. I talked to a guy who saw her tinkering with my car yesterday afternoon—she told him I'd asked her to give it a tune-up." She rolled her eyes. "Naturally, just like the rest of us, it never occurred to him that 'some groupie chick' would have murder on the mind. What else did you manage to dig up?"

She was taking this whole situation pretty calmly considering her first point. I guessed it ran in the family.

"I excavated Gia's cot in the groupie room after the others were up this morning," I said, and motioned to the evidence on the side table by the arm of my chair. "Everything Mercy mentioned was there —the jeans with the bleach stains that could be hydrogen peroxide, the magazines with the flyer and various... tokens that appear to have come from Kaige."

Kaige's mouth pulled into a grimace. He touched the dog tags hanging around his neck where he'd kept them during every waking hour for as long as I'd known him, until they'd disappeared one night a few months ago. "Just like she stole these. Why the fuck— I barely *talked* to her."

I shrugged. "Who knows? She was clearly unhinged. I mean, anyone would have to be to fall in love with *you*, right?"

Kaige glowered at me, but the teasing remark lifted the gloom that had settled over the meeting just a bit.

Anthea picked up the jeans and studied the marked fabric. She leaned closer and sniffed. "She washed them, but there's still a trace of vinegar scent too. She must have been wearing these when she doctored the fire escape railing."

"And then she managed to ambush Titus—to overpower him?" Rowan said, not exactly disbelieving.

I nodded. "We all saw she was a lot stronger than we'd have suspected from the way she went at Mercy last night. And Gideon tracked down some footage from the fights that'd been uploaded online..."

On cue, my right-hand man turned his tablet around so we could all see the screen. It showed a man and a woman inside a boxing ring, the woman slim and blond, decked out in a shiny white bodysuit and mask.

As the video played, the two circled each other, exchanging blows, until the woman managed to get a chokehold on the guy. When she stepped forward in her victory stance, Gideon paused and zoomed in on her face. Even slightly blurred, I could see Gia beneath the mask now that I knew to look for her.

"One of our men also found the duffel bag Mercy mentioned tossed behind a dumpster at the edge of the parking lot where they initially argued," I said. "Gia mustn't have had time to stash it properly in her hurry to get back here and make sure Mercy didn't reveal too much. It had her mask in it and tape for binding her knuckles, a bunch of cash, and some flyers she must have been going to put up in town for her father's auto shop."

"Jesus Christ." Kaige raked a hand through his dark hair. "I'm just—this is all so crazy. Titus was the strongest guy here. I still don't see—getting the jump on *him*..."

"Well, we all assumed she was weak and stupid until about twelve hours ago, didn't we?" I said dryly.

Anthea nodded. "She must have tucked herself against the wall on the fire escape so he wouldn't see her as he climbed out, and then jumped on him from behind. Once she'd caught him in the right position, there wouldn't be much he could do. And she'd already set him up to fall by messing with the railing beforehand."

"Huh. I guess we should start keeping a closer eye on the groupies." Kaige let out a rough chuckle.

Rowan watched me carefully. He might have had some tie to Mercy I didn't think he'd fully shared, but he'd proven over and over that he'd do whatever it took to support and defend the Nobles. I wouldn't have welcomed him into my inner circle if I hadn't been sure of his loyalty.

As expected, his next words were an offer to be of service. "Is there anything else you need done to tie this all up?"

I shook my head. "Most of it was contained right here. We'll share the evidence with my father, and he'll ensure his people know who the real killer was. Some Steel Knights lackeys might miss their cash-cow fighter, but that's their problem, not ours."

At my gesture of dismissal, the guys, including Gideon, headed out. Anthea lingered, pushing herself off the desk. "Wylder, a word?"

I spread my hands. "Say whatever you want." Anthea could sometimes be very stubborn about particular ideas, but she had our family's best interests at heart no matter what. And from the moment I'd been designated as heir, she'd treated me as if she couldn't imagine anyone better for the position, unlike... more people than I'd prefer to consider right now.

She sank into the chair Gideon had vacated. "I want to talk about Mercy."

I raised an eyebrow. "What about her? If you're going to suggest we kick her out after all this—"

"No," she said with much more vehemence than I was prepared for. "Don't be ridiculous. I'm telling you that you'd better lay off the games and give her the respect she deserves."

I blinked at her and pretended to examine her head. "I'm not sure I heard you right. Are you sure you don't have a concussion after that accident?"

She swatted me. "I'm serious. She saved my life yesterday even though she had no reason to. She could have let it happen—I'm sure Gideon could tell you the chances of my dying if my brakes failed going down that hill are incredibly high—and after the way I've come down on her, I wouldn't have blamed her. But she threw herself in harm's way to protect me. You can't buy that kind of integrity." A hint of a smile touched her lips. "I might even call it 'nobility.'"

"It's not as if we Nobles are exactly known for living up to the name," I muttered, and threw back another gulp of brandy. As it burned down my throat, I considered her point. "I told her I'd crack down on the Steel Knights if she cleared Kaige's name. She's done that, and I'm at least noble enough to be good to my word. But it sounds like you're suggesting we don't just take up her cause until we've crushed those pricks but actually make her one of our own."

"It sounds like that because that *is* what I'm suggesting."

I studied my aunt for a long moment. She wasn't won over easily. Neither was I, and part of me had been picturing what it'd be like to have Mercy by my side for good ever since I'd seen her in all her bloody glory last night. But that didn't mean it was a wise idea. There were other considerations.

"It might be difficult for her to fit in, in the long run," I hedged.

"She doesn't have to fit perfectly," Anthea said. "She'll make her own place, just like I made mine. She's been a formidable enemy, as much as it was my fault for making her one, and I suspect she'll become an even better ally."

Mercy really had done a number on her. I'd never seen Anthea support anyone quite so emphatically— especially after being on a tear to get the same person removed from our lives just a day before.

I groped for another argument and couldn't come up with any I wanted to say out loud. Annoyingly enough, Anthea read my silence. Her voice softened. "I know why you're hesitant. But she's not Laurel."

I stiffened. "I have no idea what you're talking about. Of course she's not. Why would I be comparing them?"

"Loss changes a fundamental part of us," Anthea said, her eyes crinkling at the corners. "I don't blame you for being wary at all."

"My concerns about Mercy have nothing to do with that," I said, but even to my own ears, it sounded like feeble defense.

Maybe it didn't matter why I was hesitating but only that I could see I didn't need to. Mercy had managed to hold her own against Gia, who was a seasoned MMA fighter with brutal strength. She hadn't backed down when I'd asked her to chop up a man, not shying away once despite her obvious disgust.

I'd pushed her and pushed her again, determined to find a weak point, to bring it out into the open while I could still get her out of here in one piece. But she'd always pushed right back.

Until the freezer. I worked my jaw, remembering how Mercy had shuddered and gasped on the floor afterward. Like she was already dying. I closed my eyes.

All I'd been able to see in that moment was a frail thing I'd almost thrown into the line of fire. But it really had been just a moment, with so much strength on either side of it. How could I call her weak over that? *I* sure as hell wasn't totally invincible. Gideon could be done in by a puff of smoke.

How often would a phobia of being buried alive actually get in the way of doing what she'd need to? No one knew about it except us, and I could ensure it stayed that way.

As long as I kept a little distance, I wouldn't draw attention to her the way I had Laurel anyway.

"Fine," I said. "I'll have a chat with her."

Anthea beamed at me and ruffled my hair like I was a kid again, laughing at my scowl. She headed off to take care of whatever business she had on her plate, and I walked down the hall toward the guest bedroom that'd become Mercy's. After yesterday's horrors, I hadn't been about to toss her back into the groupie room.

I knocked on the door. "Anyone home, Kitty Cat?"

She opened the door with a jerk and eyed me as if

she wasn't sure she'd actually wanted to find me on the other side. Ignoring her expression, I nudged past her to stroll into the room over to the window where the bloody present she'd been left had thankfully been cleaned up. "Huh. I didn't realize this room had such a beautiful view."

Mercy sighed in resignation. "What do you want? I was about to scrounge up some breakfast."

"Oh, nothing much. I just thought I should thank you for saving my aunt's life."

"Am I hallucinating, or did you just say thank you to me?"

I turned to face her. "Don't be so surprised. Anthea is important to me. She's family, and you saved her by putting your life on the line. That couldn't have made it clearer how far you'll go for the Nobles, so it's only fair if we extend a hand in return."

"What's that supposed to mean?" she asked cautiously.

"I already promised you that you'd have my support against the Steel Knights if you found Titus's real murderer. That's a done deal. But if you want to go at him right alongside us—and if you want to stick around after and see what other trouble we can get up to— there's a place for you here."

Her lips parted—those plump, succulent lips I'd imagined wrapping around my dick far too many times. I couldn't help taking a step closer to her, feeling the mood between us shift into something tinged with anticipation.

Mercy folded her arms in front of her, her elbows

grazing my chest. From the glint in her eyes, I got the impression she was trying to provoke me on purpose. "This isn't yet another test? I've finally convinced the great Wylder Noble of my incredible prowess?"

I chuckled and let my voice drop low. "Keep calling me great, and I could be convinced of a whole lot more."

I let my hands rise to her waist, and she swayed toward me just slightly. If I leaned in to kiss her now, I was pretty sure she'd kiss me right back. Instead I held myself still, watching her.

"So you're a man of your word after all," she said, the playful lilt to her voice going straight to my cock.

"I bled for you," I reminded her, wanting nothing more than to throw her down on the bed and fuck her until she scored my skin with her claws and screamed my name in ecstasy. Only a tiny thread of self-control and the name Anthea had invoked held me back.

Mercy tilted her head to the side. "And what happens next?"

I grinned. "Now it's time to make Colt Bryant and all the assholes propping him up bleed way more than I ever did."

She matched my smile with a smirk of her own. "I'm looking forward to it."

I left Mercy's room feeling far more satisfied than any man should with a raging hard-on straining his pants. As I willed it down, the slam of a car door filtered up through the foyer. I walked toward the staircase, peering down through the windows over the front door.

A familiar gold Porsche was parked outside. A man in an impeccable slate-gray suit stood beside it, the sun catching on the silver strands that were starting to overtake the auburn in his hair.

Dad was home.

Axel had already come over to greet him. As the other man spoke, Dad's hawkish eyes roved over the mansion, darkening at whatever Axel had told him. My spine stiffened.

I needed to talk to him about Mercy before he heard too much from anyone else. The subject was going to require a certain amount of care.

Even with Anthea on her side, even with the self-control I'd managed to demonstrate so far, having the Claws princess here at all was still walking a line that was awfully dangerous—and not in a way I liked.

Mercy

STEPPING OUT INTO THE MANSION'S YARD, I COULDN'T help tipping my face to the sun and simply basking in it for a moment. Its warmth seeped right through my skin to mingle with the triumphant glow already lighting me up from the inside.

I'd been through hell and back over the past few weeks, but this was a new beginning. This morning, Wylder had all but pledged his allegiance to my crusade. It wouldn't be much longer before we had Colt on his knees and I'd see justice done for the way he'd torn apart my life and so many others.

Footsteps rustled through the grass behind me. Kaige came to a stop at my side, glancing up at the sun for a second before looking at me, his smile more relaxed than I'd seen in the past couple of days. I'd tensed up at the sight of him, but his easygoing attitude reassured me.

"I hear you've officially joined the team," he said.

"That's one way of putting it. I have the Wylder Noble stamp of approval, anyway."

"If you've got his approval, you have all of ours too."

Would Gideon and Rowan have said the same? I guessed they kind of had to. What Wylder said was the law for them, regardless of their personal feelings.

Kaige cracked his knuckles. "So, when do we get started delivering our brand of justice to that jackass ex of yours?"

I couldn't hold back a laugh. "As soon as possible, if I have anything to say about it. I noticed the man in charge got in this morning—I assume Wylder needs to run the basics by him first."

Mentioning Ezra Noble created a brief but awkward silence. Kaige seemed to struggle to figure out what to say, which was a little ominous. "I'm sure once the old man hears the whole story, he'll be on board." He rolled his shoulders and switched quickly to a different subject. "I was actually wondering if you were up for a workout. I don't know about you, but I have a lot of built-up tension after all the craziness we've dealt with lately."

I cocked my head at him, unable to stop the images of him leaning over me on the hood of his car, plunging inside me, from crowding my head. To my annoyance, my voice came out slightly breathy. "What kind of workout did you have in mind?"

Kaige's gaze seemed to linger on my lips. Then he yanked it up to meet my eyes. His tone came out sly. "Oh, just a power jog around the block. There's a path that winds around the backs of the yards up here, so we don't have to bother going up and down the hill or through downtown. Want to join me? I mean, unless you'd rather something more—"

"No, that sounds perfect," I cut in. The bastard, getting me riled up for fun. Two could play that game. "But why don't we make it competitive."

He arched an eyebrow. "How so?"

I tapped my lips, letting the movement draw his attention back to my mouth. "First one to make it three rounds wins."

"You think you can take me on, huh? And what does the winner get?"

I shrugged. "Whatever they want. Winner's choice. Wherever their... urges take them."

Heat flared in Kaige's eyes. "In that case, I'm *definitely* going to win."

"We'll see about that." I glanced down at my jeans, which were comfy but not made for running. "Give me a second to change into something more appropriate."

"But I like it when you're inappropriate," Kaige called after me as I jogged back toward the house.

I held up my hand with my middle finger raised, and his laughter brought a smile to my own lips. I already felt better, looser, than I had in days, even with the lingering twinges from the bruises I'd gotten during last night's fight.

Once I'd swapped my jeans for more flexible sweatpants, I found Kaige waiting for me in front of the house, stretching his legs. My gaze might have roved over the muscular planes of his thighs for a bit longer than was totally polite before I met his eyes again.

"Ready?" he asked with a grin.

I tossed back my ponytail. "Of course I'm ready. First one to tag in at the front steps three times wins. But you'd better prepare to lose."

"You'll have to catch me first." He took off without another word.

Cursing half-heartedly at his back, I took off after him. Kaige was strong, but a little top-heavy. His legs weren't *that* much longer than mine, and my parkour practice had given me a lot of training in speed. I followed close at his heels, trailing right behind him as he swerved at the end of the street onto the packed dirt path he'd mentioned. It looped around past the fences of the grand properties along the top of the hill, just like he'd said.

Perfect.

We tapped the front steps the first time just seconds apart, but on the second loop, Kaige started to pull farther ahead. Flat-out endurance wasn't my forte, and he'd obviously jogged this route thousands of times in the past. I loped along behind him at a steady pace, my heart thumping in an enjoyable rhythm, sweat trickling down my back. My brain shut down and let my body take over completely.

Kaige tapped in a second time several paces ahead of me and turned around with a wave and a cocky grin. Oh, I'd wipe that off his face soon enough. He'd forgotten that not all of us needed to stick to the paths.

I let him take even more of a lead, pacing myself as

we started the final circuit. When I came up on the back of the Nobles' property, Kaige was already charging past the estate beyond it. I swung around and threw myself at the brick wall that surrounded the massive mansion's yard.

It only took a quick scramble and a twist of my hips to fling myself over. I landed on the grass and took off across the lawn to meet Kaige out front, tapping my toes against the front step for good measure.

When I reached the sidewalk in front of the mansion, he hadn't come around the corner yet. After bobbing on my feet impatiently, I jogged several paces back and forth. Stopping in the shade of a tree at the edge of the neighbor's lawn, I pulled out my phone, thinking I'd text a few taunts to get his ass into gear.

My thumb was just reaching for the screen when a van roared down the street and jolted to a halt right next to me. As I spun around, three guys dressed in black from their pants to their ski masks leapt out and tackled me.

My phone slipped from my fingers, but I was too busy fighting to snatch after it. I rammed my elbow onto one guy's gut, getting a grunt out of him, but when I opened my mouth to shout, another clapped his hand over my lips, snuffing out the sound. I struggled harder.

The heel of my hand smacked into a masked nose with a satisfying crunch, but three against one were shitty odds at the best of times, and they'd caught me by surprise. One wrenched my arms behind my back, another scooped up my legs, and they hauled me into the van.

I hit the thinly carpeted floor, the blood seeping from a scrape on my lip leaving a metallic flavor in my mouth. With a lurch and a rumble, the van peeled away from the curb. Before I could strike out again, someone lashed a rope around my wrists behind me. A bandana was tied across my mouth, half-choking me.

As I squirmed onto my side, glaring at the figures around me, a face loomed over me that turned my blood to ice.

Colt gazed down at me and let out a cold chuckle. "Hello there, Mercy. You didn't really think the Nobles would ever respect a cunt like you, did you? We've struck a very generous deal, and they've called me in to take out the trash."

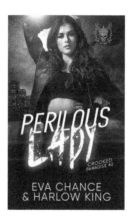

Perilous Lady (Crooked Paradise #2)

Keep your enemies closer...

I've proven I can stand with the fiercest gang in Paradise Bend. Now it's time to crush my traitor ex-fiancé and his stooges into smithereens.

They've already butchered my family. I can't let them destroy the streets I called home.

Wylder Noble and his inner circle are ready to rain down their own brand of justice. Too bad they can't seem to decide whether they'd rather kiss me or kill me.

To be fair, I'm having the same problem when it comes to these four infuriatingly hot and dangerous men.

Whichever we pick, we'd better decide fast. Because my ex isn't pulling any punches... and the greatest threat may come from right within the Nobles' ranks.

Get it at https://smarturl.it/PerilousLady

ABOUT THE AUTHORS

Eva Chance is a pen name for contemporary romance written by Amazon top 100 bestselling author Eva Chase. If you love gritty romance, dominant men, and fierce women who never have to choose, look no further.

Eva lives in Canada with her family. She loves stories both swoony and supernatural, and strong women and the men who appreciate them.

Connect with Eva online:
www.evachase.com
eva@evachase.com

Harlow King is a long-time fan of all things dark, edgy, and steamy. She can't wait to share her contemporary reverse harem stories.

Made in the USA
Monee, IL
08 April 2022

94400008R00197